To Hillary:
my writing buddy, puppy cuddle supplier,
and emotional support human

A Love Connections Sweet Romcom

THE FEAR OF FALLING

DANA LECHEMINANT

CHAPTER I
Avery

"It's for the best," I whisper to myself and type out a cutesy caption that perfectly opposes my mood. "You both knew it was a bad idea."

A bad idea to disrupt the status quo of our six-year courtship and try to turn it into something more permanent. A bad idea to mix business with pleasure. A bad idea to think I could experience my own love story instead of only reading about it.

I let out a heavy sigh.

It's hard to think about anything to do with love when yesterday should have been my wedding day. Instead of leaving for my honeymoon, I'm looking up synonyms for romance. *Courtship, affair, liaison, passion.* None of them fit right, but I think the root cause of my poor mood is the fact that Eric, my fiancé—my *ex*-fiancé—went into a panic this morning about the social media account for our shared publishing company not being trendy enough. He's not wrong, especially as we start gearing up to announce my sister's second book.

But that doesn't mean I want to be fixing it right now.

I'm still planning on going on the trip we booked for our honeymoon, but my flight time is creeping closer by the minute, and I'm still at the office because Eric doesn't think we need to hire a social media manager. While I work, my mind won't stop thinking about how we wouldn't have had this disagreement if we hadn't broken up. He always listened to me when we were a couple.

Not so much lately.

My phone dings for the eighth time in the last ten minutes, and I don't need to look at the screen to know it's Dani. My little sister is...persistent when she wants to be. It's a trait we share, though I'm not usually on the receiving end, but I guess this is what I get for hiding from her yesterday.

If she'd known where I was, Dani would have kidnapped me and done her best to distract me from the fact that I am still very much unmarried. She means well, but I doubt any of her plans would have been beneficial to anyone. So I worked at the library instead of here at the office or at home, leaving my phone on silent so I could focus on work and get everything done before today. Dani had the right idea when she ran away to Oregon last month to get her book finished.

While I thought I'd set myself up for success, Eric apparently thought otherwise. So here I am. Making cutesy posts about our lineup of romance books while trying not to think about how my own love story failed.

"I'm fine," I say out loud and rearrange the text on the graphic. "I'm fine today, and I was fine yesterday, and I'm totally fine."

"Fine people don't talk to themselves," a cheery voice says in the doorway.

I groan without looking up from my computer. Maybe I *should* have looked at my phone. It probably would have warned me that Dani was coming into the office. She might be my best-selling author, but I regret giving her a key.

Even if I hadn't, Lynda, our office manager and receptionist—and, of course, Eric's mom—would have let her in anyway.

"Avery," Dani says, her tone full of warning. "Your flight leaves in like two hours."

I glance at the clock, wincing when I realize I've spent more time on these graphics than I thought. But I need to get the whole week done so it's not all on Eric. "Two and a half," I hedge. "I have time."

"Security has gotten faster," a male voice says, "but not that fast."

I look up, my stomach twisting at the sight of Dani's brand-new boyfriend, Mason, embracing her from behind. They look so...happy. I shouldn't hate that they look happy, given I helped get them together, but I do.

"I still have time," I whisper right as a message pops up on my computer.

It's from Eric, which is funny because his office is right across the hall from mine. Literally within speaking distance. But over the last couple of months, since the breakup, we've both done a pretty good job of avoiding face-to-face interaction whenever we can.

It's really fun working with your ex...

Eric:

> Do you have those quotes from Feinman Printing? I can't find the email.

I open my email and find the message he needs, forwarding it to Eric though I can feel my sister glaring at me. If we want to switch to this other printer, we need to do it sooner than later so we can get on their schedule, so getting the info to my partner quickly is crucial.

"Avery," Dani says again.

Another message pops up.

Eric:

> I'm going to send you the projections spreadsheet so we can get that nailed down before Sonny gets here next week. Let me know if you see any issues.

My jaw clenches when I read that one. While I'm glad Eric hired a consultant to help us figure out how to scale our company, I'm not sure why he thought the week after what would have been our honeymoon was a good time to bring him in.

Dani twists in Mason's arms, looking behind her—toward Eric's office—before meeting my eyes again. "Give us a second," she tells her boyfriend. In a flash, she slips out of Mason's hold and shuts herself in my office, leaving her man in the hallway. "Is *he* the reason you haven't left yet?"

As Eric sends another message, I try not to let my stomach tie itself in a knot. "Who?"

"Ave, you have to go!"

"On my honeymoon? By *myself*?" My words come out harsh—too harsh—and Dani flinches, flooding me with guilt. She was planning to come with me to Italy and take Eric's spot, but then she met Mason. He's been good for her and is the only reason I got a first draft of Dani's next book, but thanks to him, Dani isn't spending the week with me in Florence. Sighing, I get to my feet and wrap an arm around her. "I'm sorry. I'm not mad at you. It's not your fault you tamed a handsome womanizer while you were supposed to be writing me a bestseller."

She smirks—apparently I've been forgiven. "I *did* write you a bestseller."

"We'll see." I'm joking, but also not. I want her second book to do as well or better than the first, both for her sake and for Rose & Quill. The little publishing company Eric and I started a few years ago has suddenly made a name for itself thanks to Dani, and I would hate for us to be a one-hit wonder.

Are books called hits, or is that just songs? Where did that phrase come from, anyway?

Dani nudges her elbow into my ribs, hitting me right in my ticklish spot. I squeak and duck away, and she narrows her eyes at me. "You're not scared to go alone, are you? You used to travel by yourself all the time."

"That's not technically true." Most of the time, I ended up making friends whenever I went somewhere, so I was never *alone*. Technically. "I'm not scared, I'm just...busy. And no, Eric isn't the reason I'm still here." That part's a lie. He *is* the reason I haven't left the office yet, though I haven't figured out if it's intentional or not. Our breakup was mutual, and he's known about my plans to go to Italy anyway. Eric isn't the type of guy to be petty, but I'm also leaving him for a week when we're barely keeping our heads above water as it is. I can hardly blame him for not wanting to handle the company on his own. But it's only a week...

"Avery!" Dani snaps, opening the door to reveal Mason still standing there, patiently waiting for her. She smiles like it hasn't been mere minutes since she saw him. "You need to stop working or you're going to miss your flight. All of this can wait until you get back, or your *colleague* can handle it."

Eric coughs from his office. Dani has refused to speak his name since the breakup, and it drives him nuts. Now I know he's been listening to all of this, which makes his messages feel deliberate.

He's trying to stop me from going.

As I glance at the clock again, sudden panic hits me, fueled by my independent streak that I've gotten used to burying since partnering up with Eric. He's not my boyfriend anymore, so he can't decide what I do or don't do.

"I'm going to miss my flight!" I growl the words almost angrily as my mind kicks into gear. I don't bother shutting down my computer. I just grab my purse and usher Mason and Dani out the door. "I'll be back next week!" I shout at Eric, ignoring whatever he says in response because I'm too busy listing out loud the things I still need to do as I hurry down the stairwell to the parking garage. "I have to go pick up my suitcases. Water the plants. Check the fridge for leftov—"

"Whoa!" Dani grabs my arm before I can start running toward my car. "Relax! We have your suitcases."

I frown and search for Dani's CRV. "Why?"

"And we both know you've already watered the plants and emptied your fridge," she continues. "I even grabbed the dinner you made for the plane even though they give you food on the flight."

As she leads me to her car, I can't help but wonder how she knows me this well. Yeah, she's my little sister, but lately I've hardly recognized myself when my life is nothing but work and convincing people I'm perfectly fine. "Have you ever eaten airline food?" I mumble.

Mason opens the back door for me, and I'm halfway into the seat before I see the giant schnauzer taking up most of the space. "Sorry," he says as I squish myself into the little available room left. "I was against taking Herc to Oregon, but I was outvoted."

"Oregon?"

"Yep!" Once she's in the passenger seat, Dani twists around to grin at me and scratch the dog's ears. "That's why we have your suitcases. We're heading to Cascade Harbor for a bit, and since I couldn't leave Hercules with you, he's coming with us!"

I scowl at her, only sort of annoyed. "You're heading to the airport," I guess. "And you planned your flight to be close to mine so you could make sure I go."

With a triumphant smirk, she faces forward again and slips her hand into Mason's. I watch Mason play with the bold-colored bracelet on Dani's wrist in between holding her hand for the next twenty-five minutes as we drive to the Salt Lake airport, hating the jealousy that bubbles up.

I'm happy for her. I really am. But three of our cousins also started dating guys this summer—heck, Chloe went and got *married*—and when they're all younger than me, it's hard not to feel bitter. I was so close to my happily ever after, only for it to just...fizzle out. It wasn't some epic tragedy or heartbreak, and there are moments when I'm relieved that Eric and I didn't go through with the wedding. But that doesn't make the envy hurt any less.

When we hit the airport, Mason drops me off at the terminal. Their flight is an hour after mine, so they have some time to park and check Hercules onto the plane. I, on the other hand, do not have time, so my goodbye to Dani is rushed.

We hug each other tight, like we always do, but there's more to Dani's embrace this time. "Please try to have some fun," she tells me with a squeeze. "Don't think about work or my book or Sir Lost Cause. Just enjoy Italy, okay?"

Enjoy Italy. Those words are on repeat all through security, where I forget to take a hair tie out of my pocket and am rewarded with a pat down. The words repeat when I stop at the first bathroom I find, and then the next because I have a nervous bladder.

And they're still on repeat when I pass the shop called The Wandering Reader and barely register my name being called before I'm practically tackled. Thank goodness for my neck pillow protecting me from being strangled. "Avery!"

Struggling to stay upright, I force a smile. "Poppy."

Somehow I managed to forget my youngest cousin would have made sure she was working during my flight. I should have prepared myself better, or maybe avoided her entirely. At twenty-one, Poppy is unerringly sweet, but with nine years between us, I've never been able to fully figure out what her deal is.

"Avery!" Poppy says again, way too loud for a crowded airport as it pulls a dozen glances our way. She presses her hands to my cheeks and seems to stare into my soul for a moment. Her eyes squint and her lip trembles, like she might burst into tears. "Oh, Avery. You're hurting so much!"

"I'm fine," I say, and I'm sure she would have believed me if my voice didn't crack. I try to salvage my credibility by adding, "Really."

She clucks her tongue and grabs hold of my hand, dragging me to the store where she works. "You're not fine, but you will be."

"That sounds...ominous."

Laughing, she reaches for her display of handmade jewelry and grabs a necklace with a transparent, yellowish crystal swinging at the base, holding it out in front of my face like she might start trying to hypnotize me. I don't know if hypnotism is something she's into, but I wouldn't be surprised. She's the sort of person who reads the horoscopes every day and thinks a rock can heal your aura. "Avery, your luck is about to change. I can feel it!"

As long as that change of fortune doesn't affect Rose & Quill, unless it's for the better, I'm okay with that. "Great," I mutter. "I have a flight to catch, so—"

"I also made you this!" Poppy holds out a bracelet to match the necklace, only the rock on this one is a light pink encased in a braided leather band. Compared to the bold colors on the bracelet she gave Dani last month, this one is quite tame. It's pretty. At least, I think it's pretty until she says, "This one will help you find love."

"I don't want it." The words are out of my mouth before I can stop them, but they're true. "That's the last thing I need right now."

Poppy deflates, looking like she did when she was three and following me around anytime the family got together. I was too grown up—a whole twelve years old—to want to spend time with a little girl, but for some reason she would never leave me alone. I once got mad at her for bothering me and made her cry, and I'm getting sudden flashbacks of her nonstop tears that day.

Before her sad eyes can make me feel worse, I cave. "Okay! Fine. I'll take the love bracelet." I snatch it from her fingers and stuff it into my purse along with the necklace. She really is sweet to look out for all of us the way she does, but if she thinks love is going to be good for me, she clearly has no idea how stressful my life is right now.

That's not her fault. It's not like I've been big on sharing with my cousins lately.

By some miracle, a woman over the loudspeaker announces they're boarding my flight, giving me the perfect excuse to duck out of the store before I'm overrun by guilt and start telling Poppy all my woes.

"Thanks, Poppy," I mumble on my way out. "Have fun at work."

"Have fun in Italia! I'll see you when you get back!"

At the moment, she and I are the only ones still single unless she ends up with some guy she met here at the airport a few weeks ago. I didn't fully pay attention to that whole thing when she told us about it in our cousin chat, but apparently she practically tackled the guy and still managed to get a date out of it. And if that doesn't work out, she's got some rando texting her cute but questionable things.

It must be all these love bracelets she keeps around.

Since neither of those men sound like viable dating options, most likely she'll stay single along with me, and I don't like what that might mean for future cousin get-togethers. Am I about to become Poppy's favorite again? Maybe I need to find her a man she could actually end up with so she can be as distracted as Dani.

Then I can have some peace.

Right as I reach my gate, my phone starts ringing, and I reluctantly pull it from my pocket to find Eric's name on the screen. Well, technically it reads "Colonel Buzzkill" because Dani got her hands on my phone at some point after the breakup, and I haven't had the energy to change it back. It's not like he ever calls me anymore, so it hasn't mattered.

Given my mostly silent interactions with Eric lately, I figure if it's worth an awkward phone call, it must be important. Sighing, I swipe the answer button. "Hey, I'm about to board, so—"

"Don't go."

My heart in my chest turns to lead at the sound of his desperation. "What?" Is he really doing this? Now?

"I need you, Avie. Don't go to Italy."

He's really doing this. My chest grows tight, and I can't decide if I love this declaration or hate it. It's been almost two months since we officially decided to split, and I gave up hope on him showing any signs of regret. Do I want this change of heart? I don't know. No. Maybe?

"Eric," I say, pressing myself against a pillar so I'm out of the way of the people lining up to board. Why do they do that when they're not in the current boarding group?

"I need you," Eric says again, but then he adds a line that instantly turns my hope into irritation. "There's so much we need to get done on the marketing plan before Sonny gets here."

Rolling my eyes, I consider hanging up on him. But that feels petty, and I'll leave that part to him. "Sonny isn't coming to Utah until next week, and I thought the whole point of hiring him was so he can do all that work for us." Why else would we hire a consultant? I was skeptical about bringing in a guy from out of state, but Eric and Sonny were college buddies, and Eric thinks his friend can work some kind of miracle for Rose & Quill.

We *need* a miracle after Dani's book went viral and put our little company on the map. We're barely keeping up with demand, drowning in the giant ocean we were plunged into at the start of the year, and if we don't find a way to grow with Dani's fame, we're going to flounder.

"I want him to think we know what we're doing," Eric says.

"But we don't know what we're doing," I argue. "Neither of us expected Dani to hit the *New York Times* list like that."

"Even so, we have too much to do. Don't go to Italy, Avery. Please."

"I'm already eating the cost of your half." Plus, I splurged last night in a rare moment of impulsivity and upgraded my longest flight to business class. That would be a lot of money wasted if I stay home.

"I told you I can pay for it." He can't. He just finished paying off his MBA a few months ago, and he signed a two-year lease on a townhouse that was going to be ours. Not to mention the business loan we're both on the hook for. "Besides," he continues, "the only reason you paid for the trip was because your card had the better rewards."

I sigh, my eyes on the dwindling line to board. This flight is going to JFK, where I'll have a few hours before my connecting flight to Rome, and then to Florence. In less than twenty-four hours, I could be in the city I've dreamed of visiting ever since Sandra Bullock fell in love with Bill Pullman in *While You Were Sleeping*.

Or I could stay in Utah and pretend it isn't totally awkward working across the hall from a man I used to make out with on a regular basis and now barely talk to.

Enjoy Italy.

I stand up straight and pull my shoulders back. I plan to.

"If there are any emergencies," I tell Eric, "send me an email. Otherwise, I'll see you in a week."

I hang up before he can argue, and I hold my head high as I march to the gate. My breakup may have sucked, but I'm going to go to Italy and have the time of my life because I am totally, completely *fine*.

TICKET
PASSPORT
N
W
E
S
HOTEL
Time To
Travel

CHAPTER 2
Benson

EVEN IN BUSINESS CLASS, it's surprisingly hard to sleep when the person next to you is sobbing hysterically. I've done my best to ignore her, as a good seatmate should, but this is getting ridiculous. It's been *hours*. We still have five hours before we land in Rome, and I worked through the night and up to the wire today to ensure I'd be able to get on this flight. I just want to sleep.

The woman sniffles, hiding her face in her blanket while I pretend not to look at her. At least she's trying to stifle her noise, but this is clearly not the sort of cry she can hold in. I doubt it's stopping anytime soon.

Sighing, I shift in my seat and fully open my eyes. "Funeral?"

She startles and meets my gaze, only her red-rimmed eyes visible from behind the blanket. "What?"

"Is that why you're going to Italy?" If it's anything else, I'm going to question this level of crying. And maybe her sanity.

Sniffing, she stares at me for a long time before wiping her eyes with her sleeve and slowly lowering the blanket. She had her nose deep in a book when I boarded last-minute, so I didn't give her much attention before takeoff, but I kind of wish I had. Aside from the blotchy redness from her crying, she's cute. In an innocent, messy kind of way. "My..." She hiccups and drops her gaze to her lap. "My honeymoon, actually."

Message received. No attraction allowed. "Oh. Uh. Are you crying because I stole his seat or something?" I glance behind me, though I can't see much in the dark plane. Is there some guy back there snoring away while his new wife is in hysterics?

With a scoff, my seatmate bends down and unzips the enormous backpack she brought with her. She has to dig for a while, but she eventually pulls out a packet of tissues. "Of course not," she says, snippier than I expect. Suddenly she's less of a damsel in distress and more of a woman scorned, and I regret starting up a conversation. That type of woman is *not* my cup of tea, and I've encountered it far more often than I'd like. At least she's not crying anymore. Crying is almost worse. "He's not here. *That's* why I'm crying."

There are a few different ways this could go. I could ask where he is and satisfy my curiosity, or I could remember that her life is none of my business and try to go back to sleep now that she's quiet. Or she could not give me a choice at all and—

"We broke up a couple of months ago." She tugs a tissue from the plastic wrapper and loudly blows her nose, pulling a couple of disgruntled gazes our way.

Woman scorned. *Nailed it.*

"Why are *you* going to Italy?" she asks.

I'm not about to tell her that I'm going to a wedding. With my luck, that would set off the tears again. "Seeing some friends." While that could easily be the end of the conversation, my curiosity won't let me leave it alone. "So you're still going on your honeymoon without the man? Good for you."

She flashes a brief, joyless smile as she stuffs her used tissue into her pocket. "Non-refundable," she mumbles, bending to dig into her backpack again. "Rewards points. You know..."

"Great reasons to leave the guy behind for a while." I chuckle, adjusting myself to a slightly more comfortable position and closing my eyes. While I would rather be in first class, anything beats economy when a flight is more than two hours. If I'd known earlier that I would have the time to make it to this wedding, I would have booked a better seat, but I'm suffering the woes of last-minute plans. Maybe I *did* take this woman's fiancé's seat, and I send a silent *thank you* to the guy.

I don't care for weddings, but I would have hated to miss this one for a number of reasons. Plus, it's in Florence. I love that city.

Anyway, the woman next to me has stopped crying, which means I might get a few hours of sleep now.

"Have you been to Italy before?"

My jaw clenches. Debating the pros and cons of ignoring her, I think about spending the next five hours with her negative energy if I cut the conversation short. She'd probably spend the whole night glaring at me, and there's no way I'd be able to sleep with her looming over me. With a sigh, I lift my seat up. If I'm not going to sleep, I might as well talk to her.

She's still cute, especially now that I know she's single.

Newly single, yeah, but sometimes those are the best kind. They're not looking for commitment.

"A few times," I say with a shrug. "You?"

She shakes her head. "No." I could have guessed as much with the size of her backpack. She's not planning on carrying that thing around Rome, is she? She'll be a prime target for pickpockets, not to mention she'll get some serious back pain lugging that beast around. "I've always wanted to go, but I haven't..."

Studying her, I wonder if she's ever traveled before, but I'm thinking not. I would bet money that she brought more than one suitcase and will be that tourist who wears tennis shoes and hangs her wallet around her neck and tucked down her shirt. I wouldn't be surprised if she has a travel guide in that backpack of hers and a few months of Duolingo Italian lessons under her belt.

"Well, the city is great," I mutter instead of telling her that her mediocre Italian phrases aren't going to do her much good. No one needs to know that the horse is brown. "I'm sure you'll love it."

"I'm hoping it's like riding a bike."

I frown, rubbing my jaw as I try to figure out what she means. "What is?" I ask when I come up blank. I'm usually pretty good at interpreting people in conversation, but I'm too tired for this tonight.

She smiles again, only this time it's warm and lasts longer than half a second. "Traveling. I used to travel all the time, but it's been a few years."

Huh. Color me surprised. "What stopped you?"

She shrugs, settling a bit in her seat like she's relaxing for the first time since getting on the plane. "Life? I guess. My fiancé—my ex—he isn't much of a traveler, and then with work and stuff it wasn't..." Another shrug. "And I think I used to be braver than I am now, you know?"

Not really, but I nod anyway.

She keeps talking, which makes my side of the conversation exceptionally easy. Why can't all conversations with attractive women be like this? "Why does adulthood do that to us?" she asks, clearly not expecting an answer as she continues. "Like, it takes all the fun out of life and makes us responsible and anxious all at the same time."

I have to fight the urge to roll my eyes. She has fallen into the classic adult blunder of thinking there's only one way to live, one full of boring jobs and routines without deviation. It makes me sad but also incredibly grateful that I didn't fall into the trap like most people. My career takes me all over the country, constantly meeting new people and facing new challenges, and I would never call my life boring.

I was smart enough to take a more adventurous approach to life when I hit adulthood.

"Well," I say, feeling her eyes on me even though mine are locked on the seat in front of me, "it looks like you're heading in the right direction by taking this trip. I hope it reminds you of the good old days."

"Me too. I'll, uh, let you sleep. I'm Avery, by the way." She sticks her hand in front of me.

I'm surprised by her boldness and can't help but smile as I grasp her hand. Her fingers are warm and soft, and now that she's less blotchy I'm finding it harder to look away from her. She really is beautiful, and there's something inviting about her, like there's a lot more to her than what I can see in the dim cabin lights.

Do I really need sleep? Or do I spend the next few hours flirting with Avery before we part ways forever? That sounds more fun. I squeeze her hand, broadening my smile in a way that usually works to my advantage. "Benson."

"Benson," she repeats as a bit of color brightens her cheeks. "I like that."

That gets a chuckle out of me. I didn't always like my name, but I've grown into it. "Thanks. I like your name too."

"I'll really let you sleep now."

And she does. She pops in some headphones and starts an audiobook on her phone—romance, from the look of it—and though I'm wide awake the rest of the flight, she doesn't say a word.

I'm almost disappointed when we land in Rome and I know nothing about her but her name.

TICKET
PASSPORT
N
W E
S
HOTEL
Time To Travel

CHAPTER 3
Avery

I DIDN'T THINK GETTING a taxi would be this hard, but there's a whole line of people waiting to grab a cab, and there are no cars in sight. If I were still the Avery of a decade ago, I would start chatting with the group of people waiting in front of me, maybe start wandering the city on foot to find my hotel. But I am *not* that Avery, and there's no way I'm lugging two suitcases and my backpack down cobblestone streets when I have no idea where I'm going.

This is what I get for stress-packing.

It would help if my phone had better service, but I can't get enough bars to pull up the hotel's address on my maps app. According to someone a few groups ahead of me, the McDonald's across the street has Wi-Fi, but I don't want to lose my place in line to test that claim.

Clutching the straps of my backpack, I lean out to see if anyone has gotten a ride yet, but it looks like the same people are at the front of the line that were there when I got here. Are we all just going to stand here for the next hour?

I'm so tired. I want to collapse in my hotel room and sleep until morning, even though it's two in the afternoon here in Florence. Experience has taught me that I should stay up as late as I can tonight to acclimate to the time change, but I doubt I'll be as energetic as young Avery was. An afternoon nap will fix me right up, and I'll hopefully have energy to find a nice restaurant tonight and settle in.

If I ever get a cab.

Sighing, I try my phone again, begging it to get enough data to download the route to the hotel. If it isn't too far, maybe it will be worth the walk.

"Hey, Avery, right?"

I tense, but the male voice that says my name is mildly familiar. Looking up, I'm shocked to see Benson looking at me from a taxi window. Goodness, he's more handsome in the Florentine sunshine than he was on the plane, and heat floods my cheeks. Which is ridiculous. "Oh, hi. It was Benson, yeah?" As if I don't vividly remember his name after that humiliating conversation during the flight. There is nothing more mortifying than being caught mid-sob by a total stranger. Especially one with enough swagger to have walked out of an edition of *GQ*. I've never even seen that magazine before, but I'm pretty sure it's full of hot men.

Benson's eyes trail along the line of people, his eyebrows dipping low as if he's thinking about something. When he looks at me again, there's a soft hint of a smile on his lips that makes my stomach squirm. The man has a *smile*. One that has been haunting me in the back of my mind since disembarking in Rome a few hours ago. "Need a ride?"

A few of the people around me murmur varying degrees of disgust and envy.

I bite my lip. Part of me knows it's a bad idea to climb into a car with a strange man, particularly one who looks like he regularly charms women with his sharp, scruff-covered jawline and sky-blue eyes. But the other part of me knows it could be hours before I make it to my hotel at the rate this line is moving. "Um, I don't want to make you go out of your way."

Saying something to the driver, he slips from the car in a smooth motion, looking for all the world like he was made for Italy. His white button-down shirt may not be crisp—he wore it on the plane, after all—but the way he starts rolling up his cuffs as he approaches is completely movie-worthy. "I don't know if you've noticed," he says in a voice so low that I have to lean in to hear him, "but it's not going to be easy for you to get a car. Our plane came in at the same time as a train from Venice, and this is right at the edge of peak tourist season."

"Then where did you get yours?" I ask, forcing my eyes to focus on the taxi rather than Benson's muscled forearms. But he doesn't respond, so I look up at him—up because of course he's tall too—and meet his gaze.

My breath slides out of me the moment he smirks. "Trade secret," he says and winks.

I have never seen a guy wink and found it attractive, but Benson manages it. Is this guy real? Maybe he's a strange jet lag hallucination.

"Come on," he says, wrapping a hand around the handle of my bigger suitcase. "It's just sharing a taxi."

Praying I'm not about to be set upon by a charming scoundrel, I nod and follow Benson to the cab. He helps me get my luggage into the trunk and opens the door for me, and I'm more convinced than ever that this is all a dream and I'm really back in my office, passed out at my desk because I stayed at work too late again.

But when Benson climbs into the taxi after me and his fresh, masculine scent envelops me, I decide there's no way I could dream up a man this enticing. He's real, and we're really sharing a cab, and his shoulders really are that big.

What am I supposed to do with all of this information?

"Where to?" he asks, fixing me with those stunningly blue eyes again.

It takes three tries to unlock my phone so I can find the name of the hotel in my spreadsheet because my hand is shaking. "Um, Villa Fiorentina dei Fiori."

After looking at my phone, Benson repeats the name to the driver. Only, his version actually sounds Italian, unlike my butchered one. When we're on our way, he leans his head back and closes his eyes. "I thought maybe you were going to be in Rome," he mutters. "I was surprised to see you here in Florence."

"Oh, uh, no." I don't know what else to say because I *did* know Benson would be here. I passed his seat when boarding the small plane in Rome and felt a stupid thrill of excitement over the fact that we would be in the same city. I'm not here to have an Italian romance...with an American...who is way out of my league, so I shouldn't be allowing *any* attraction.

Besides, it's only been a couple of months since Eric and I called things off. I'm in no way ready for a relationship.

"Any fun plans while you're here? Whole itinerary?" He sounds either tired or bored. Or both. Something about the way he asks that second question rubs me the wrong way, though I can't figure out what it is. It's like he already knows the answer and disapproves.

"My fi—my ex and I made sure we wouldn't have any wasted time," I say, looking back down at the spreadsheet we made, complete with screenshots of our tickets for the museum and the walking tour. "I only get to be here for a week, so I don't want to miss—"

"You have it planned down to the minute?"

I look over, shocked to find Benson looking down at the schedule on my phone again, a furrow in his brow. "Huh?"

He scoffs. "I thought you said you used to travel all the time."

His condescending tone makes me feel itchy, and I lock my screen and tuck my phone between my legs as if that might erase the last few seconds. "What's wrong with a schedule?" I ask indignantly. "Unlike you, this might be my only trip to Florence."

"What a sad way to live."

"I didn't ask for your opinion on my life, Benson." My sharp retort catches me off guard, leaving me hot and dizzy. When did I get so rude?

To my surprise, Benson's lips curl up in a smile before he looks out the window to his right. "No, you didn't," he mutters. "But could I give you a little advice?"

I don't want his advice, but I'm too curious to say as much.

When I stay silent, he glances at me and smiles wider. "A city like Florence is better enjoyed as a discovery than an itinerary. Would you agree, Enzo?"

The driver glances back at us in the rear view mirror and nods vigorously. "*Sì, signore. Signora*, let Firenze tell you her secrets."

Before I can say anything, Benson points out his window, then takes my hand like it's a totally normal thing to do. "Case in point."

I'm about to tell him to let go of me when the most beautiful building I've ever seen comes into view, and all my stranger danger vanishes in an instant. Bathed in sunlight, the building appears out of nowhere, its patterned bricks of white, pink, and green giving it an ethereal feel beneath a massive dome of deep orange. Ignoring propriety and politeness, I lean over Benson's lap to get a better view as we drive past, marveling at the arches and details and *oh my gosh it has bells*. I didn't know it had bells!

With a chuckle, Benson rolls the window down, letting the sound of the bells fill the car. We're driving too fast, and I've only gotten a taste of the majesty before it's out of sight, the bells' music fading behind the buildings.

I've seen pictures of the Duomo—the Cathedral of Santa Maria del Fiore—but none of them came close to doing it justice.

"Don't worry," Benson murmurs, and his breath brushes my hair and sends a shiver through me. "It'll still be there tomorrow."

Oh, I am full-on lying on this man's lap. Mortified—again—I twist and look up at him. Logically, I should sit up, but that building hit me like the ton of bricks that it's made from, and I am overcome with awe. "That was…" I don't have words. It's been so long since I saw anything like that that I'm completely overwhelmed and apparently totally cool with staying where I am.

Maybe Benson wasn't judging me as much as I thought he was, because the smile he's giving me is enough to warm me to the bones. He's looking at me the same way Eric looked at me when we first met, and my stomach does a little flip as my imagination sparks to life.

One of Benson's fingers loops around a bit of my hair, pulling it from my face in the most romantic gesture I've experienced in I don't know how long, and he is not helping me cool down. "The whole city can be like that if you do it right," he murmurs. "A schedule won't give you that feeling you just had."

No, he's not wrong, though right now I'm more focused on the attraction burning through me than the lingering effects of seeing the Duomo in the afternoon sunlight. If ever I wanted a fling—not that I do—this would be the guy to do it with. With his handsome face and silky voice and rugged build, he's likely the man of many a woman's fantasies. He doesn't seem to mind that I'm lying here in his lap like it's perfectly normal after freaking out about a *building*.

"Those bells…" I whisper, trying to distract myself from imagining the whole of this trip with Benson at my side. That's not a fantasy I need to conjure right now. Or ever. "They were…" Again, words can't do the moment justice. "I've been to Notre Dame, and I didn't think it was possible for anything to top that."

Chuckling, Benson moves more hair from my face, tucking it behind my ear as he gazes down at me. Crap, maybe I *do* want a fling. He opens his mouth, but before he can say anything, the taxi pulls to a stop, and he looks out the window. "We're here."

"We?"

He helps me sit up. "Coincidentally, I am also staying at the Villa Fiorentina."

This has to be fate, right? Poppy would call it fate. Cosmic coincidence has pushed us together, putting us next to each other on the plane and making him notice me waiting for a taxi and setting us up in the same hotel.

Do I *want* it to be fate?

As Benson climbs out of the car and starts unloading luggage with the driver, Enzo, I take a moment to breathe and look down at the few texts I've gotten from Eric over the last day. Real life, with all its stress and awkwardness, will still be waiting for me when I get back. Indulging in a fantasy will likely only leave me even more brokenhearted when I have to let it go. I don't know anything about Benson—where he's from, what he does for work, whether he's even single—but he radiates adventure and passion and the energy of a person I used to be.

I miss that more than I realized.

Benson opens my door and holds out a hand to me with a dazzling smile brightening his features, and my stomach twists in a knot of apprehension and excitement. It's just a week. It's not like I'll fall in love in a week, so I'll be fine. I'll just have a little fun and make the most of this escape from reality, and then I'll be able to go back to work feeling refreshed and energized and ready to face this beast that is my company and failed relationship.

As I step out of the car, my foot catches on the edge and sends me tumbling straight into Benson's chest. He catches me, of course, looping an arm around my back to steady me. "You good?" he asks, and his voice rumbles in his chest, where I'm getting a noseful of his clean scent.

Oh boy. "Never better," I breathe.

I'm pretty sure I mean that.

TICKET
PASSPORT
HOTEL
Time To Travel

CHAPTER 4
Benson

"Bens! You made it!" The shout from my old client and longtime friend carries across the hotel lobby, full of energy I wish I had.

I fall into Riccardo's boisterous embrace with a laugh, though I am desperate to go up to my room and take a nap. Two days of no sleep? Not great. But I didn't tell Riccardo I was coming, so it's a good thing I ran into him here so he knows to include me in all the events of the week. "Hey, man."

"Dude, I was just telling Siena how much it sucked that you weren't going to be able to get away, but she said you would pull off some miracle like you always do and..."

I tune him out—the guy has always been a nonstop talker—and look for Avery out of the corner of my eye. She's at the front counter, deep in discussion with the woman behind the desk, and neither looks like they're having a good time. In fact, with her furrowed brow and pursed lips, Avery looks like she might burst into tears again, which is a far cry from the woman full of wonder I got to hold in my lap for a few minutes during the drive from the airport.

"Hey, hold on a sec, Ricky," I say, interrupting him mid-sentence. Though he nods, he doesn't stop talking, switching instead to talk to another guy in the lobby I don't recognize. Rolling my eyes at his ridiculousness, I cross the lobby to the desk and try to catch the gist of the conversation. The hotel receptionist doesn't have great English, and Avery clearly doesn't speak a lick of Italian, and neither seems to be getting anywhere.

"But I booked this months ago!" Avery says, holding her phone toward the receptionist. "Here's the confirmation number."

"Sì," the receptionist says. *Giulia*, according to her nametag. "You do not..." She waves her hand, searching for the word. "...say yes."

"But I *did* say yes! I put down a deposit. I very much said yes."

I step forward, and both women shift their attention to me so fully that I almost turn right back around to escape it. I'm blaming this uncharacteristic shyness on my lack of sleep and food that doesn't come out of a plastic container. Shaking my head clear of whatever intimidation just hit me, I offer a smile, then turn to Giulia.

"*Ciao*, Giulia," I say brightly, then ask her what the problem is in Italian. I can't claim fluency, but I know enough to get through a conversation.

Giulia sags with relief, throwing a nervous glance to Avery. "She didn't confirm her room and her deposit has been returned to her," she says in Italian. "We are fully booked, and I don't have anywhere to put her."

I wince but quickly shift my expression back to calm and carefree. "Nothing?"

"No. With the wedding, all of the rooms are taken."

"What's she saying?" Avery asks, leaning so close that I catch a whiff of...something. Her hair, maybe? It's an incredible smell. Sweet and subtle. Peaches, I think. I smelled it in the taxi too, and I had to roll down the window to get some fresh air before I did something impulsive. Though, it didn't stop me from playing with her hair, something I inexplicably want to do again.

"You didn't confirm the room," I tell her, hating that I get to be the bearer of bad news when I'd rather be the dashing hero again. Now that she's no longer tear-streaked and puffy—I suspect she spent a decent amount of time in the bathroom at the airport making herself look bright and chipper again—she's prettier than I thought on the plane. I nearly gave Enzo a heart attack when I shouted at him to stop the taxi the moment I caught sight of Avery in the line of tourists, but I couldn't help myself. Something about her...

Avery's eyes go wide, filling with tears at the same time. "Oh no," she whispers, looking down at her phone. "Is that a thing I was supposed to do? I thought for sure I did that!"

"If you booked it out far enough, it was probably a way to make sure you still wanted the room," I say with a shrug. Suddenly I worry I'm the one who took her room, since mine was a last-minute booking. As guilt pools in my belly, I try to come up with some solutions before she freaks out. I'm good at solutions. That's my whole job. "There are plenty of hotels in Florence, Avery. I'm sure you can..." My words trail off when I catch sight of Giulia's wide eyes and slight shake of her head.

I should have guessed from the line of people waiting for a taxi that this is a popular week to visit Florence. If it had been earlier in the month, the city would have been quieter with a lot of the locals off celebrating Ferragosto, the height of summer, but that doesn't help us now. "No open rooms?" I ask Giulia in Italian.

"Maybe on the outskirts of the city. But I do not recommend..."

"She's not saying anything good, is she?" Avery asks, leaning in so now her arm is pressed to mine. Given the first impression I got of her, I wouldn't have expected her to touch me, but this is the third time I've been in close contact with this woman and she is...compelling? That's not the right word, and *interesting* doesn't do her justice. *Intoxicating* is too much.

Intriguing. Avery is intriguing, and she might be a great addition to this wedding week.

But if I'm going to spend more time with her and see whether she's the woman who plans minute by minute or the one who climbs over a stranger to admire a cathedral, I can't have her in some sketchy hotel on the other side of the city.

"Give her my room," I tell Giulia, once again in Italian. Hopefully I can swing this in a way that doesn't clue Avery in to what I'm doing. "Benson West." Avery lifts an eyebrow when I say my name, but I ignore her, keeping my focus on Giulia as she looks up my reservation.

"You want to give up your room, signore?" she asks, clearly skeptical of my Italian abilities because she speaks so slowly that even Avery might catch a few words here and there. "But you are in the wedding party, no?"

"I can stay in someone else's room with them. There will be a spot somewhere." There had better be a spot. I don't know much about Riccardo's friends—we met through business avenues and haven't spent much time together over the last several years outside phone calls and video chats—but I can make this work. "It'll be fine."

"Are you certain?" Giulia asks again.

"She needs it more than I do," I say, gesturing to Avery with my head. I offer Giulia a broad smile that will hopefully help her believe that I fully mean what I'm telling her.

As a blush slides up her cheeks, Giulia makes a few clicks, her eyes darting from her computer to me multiple times. Maybe I overdid it with the smile. But hey, if it gets us what I need, then whatever. "Sì?" she asks once more, and when I nod, she slides a key across the counter to Avery.

Avery's eyes go wide. "Wait, is that mine?"

"Turns out it was a glitch in the computer system," I say, which is a total lie and I'm pretty sure Avery knows it. But she wraps her fingers around the key with a look that tells me I might be about to get a particularly nice thank you.

"Benson," she whispers. "Whatever you did, thank you."

"Computer glitch," I say again.

She throws her arms around my shoulders, her whole body pressing into me as she hugs me tightly. Though I expected something like this, her enthusiasm still catches me off guard enough that I barely manage to return the gesture before she's pulling away. "You are seriously my hero today. How can I repay you? Buy you dinner tonight?"

I glance across the lobby, where Riccardo and his fiancée are now watching me with unabashed interest. They're going to have questions, and I'm not sure I'll have the answers. I'm not usually the hero type, so this little act of selflessness is going to be hard to explain. "Uh, rain check?"

Her cheeks bloom with color, and she also looks over at Riccardo, likely realizing we have an audience. "Oh, yeah. Of course. I'm sure I'll see you around."

"Sure." Unless there are absolutely no beds in this hotel and I have to find out why Giulia was so worried about sending Avery somewhere else.

"Thanks again!" With a wave, Avery grabs her multitude of luggage and heads for the elevator, where she can barely fit with all her stuff.

"*Grazie*," I tell Giulia, sliding a twenty-Euro note across the counter. "You are an angel."

Though she hasn't lost her blush, Giulia's gaze is less heated than it was before. Avery's display must have dampened her interest, which is a good thing. Unless I need her to find me a place to sleep. "*Prego*," she says. "Good luck. If you need anything, Mr. West..." She leaves that open ended, and a bit of invitation enters her gaze.

I can't help but smile at her as I heft my bag onto my shoulder and head back to where Riccardo is eagerly waiting for me. Thankfully, Siena is talking to one of the hotel staff now, so I'll only have to endure one person's interrogation.

"Benson West," he says, clucking his tongue. "Really playing the field, aren't you? Who was that? Backup in case the receptionist doesn't go for your charm?"

"Everyone goes for my charm," I say with a chuckle. "She's just a woman I met on the plane and needed some help with something. And no, I'm not about to go after the receptionist at the hotel where I'm staying. Speaking of, I find myself without a room, and I'm hoping you can help me."

"You flew all the way to Italy and don't have a room? I knew you were crazy, but that's next level."

I debate telling him that I gave my room to Avery, but he would give me crap about it the rest of the week. It's out of character for me, and he would know it. "There was a mix-up with my room," I say, which is kind of the truth. "So please tell me one of your buddies has an extra couch or something." I don't want to sleep on a couch. I'm so tired that I unequivocally want a bed, but I don't want to sound needy.

Riccardo looks in the direction of the elevator, and though a part of me wonders if Avery has come back to the lobby or something, I don't let myself look. Yeah, she's intriguing, but that doesn't mean this will become a thing. "I'll ask around," Riccardo says. "Some of the boys are already sharing because they're cheapskates, but I'm sure there's an opening somewhere."

"Thanks, man."

His grin widens as we stand there, and he pulls me back in for another hug. "It's good to have you here, Bens. It's been way too long."

It has, which is part of the reason I worked so hard to make it here. Riccardo was one of the first guys I worked with when I started my business, and it's thanks to him that things took off as quickly as they did. But part of the problem with being in demand is how often I'm traveling, which makes it hard to keep up with people. It hasn't bothered me before, but the last few months have left me with a strange emptiness I don't like. It started around the same time I came home from a long job away to an invite to Riccardo's wedding, and it only seems to be getting worse.

I'm hoping this wedding fills some of that space, and then I'm planning on catching up with one of my old buddies as soon as I get back to the States. Try to figure out what I'm missing.

"Benson, you remember Siena, right?" Riccardo pulls me over to his gorgeous fiancée, who is Riccardo's exact opposite in personality except for her friendly nature. She is everything sweet and calm and practical.

"Of course I remember. More beautiful than ever," I say, lifting her hand to my lips as I give her my most charming smile.

Riccardo smacks me. "You have your own beautiful woman to fawn over. Stop flirting with mine."

I wink at Siena, who rolls her eyes good naturedly. "Why? Afraid she'll want to marry me instead of you?"

"Nah, but only because you're not the marrying type. But seriously, stop holding her hand."

"You know you're the only man for me, Ricky," Siena says, pulling Riccardo into a gentle kiss that he immediately intensifies, probably for my benefit.

I sigh. He really doesn't need to be staking his claim right now, for so many reasons. I'm not the sort to step on toes when it comes to romantic interest—been there, done that—and he's right. Marriage is about as far from my future goals as it can get.

"I'll start asking about a place to sleep." I leave them to it, making my way out onto the back terrace that doubles as a restaurant. Several of Riccardo's friends and associates, many of whom I've worked with in years past, are out here enjoying the afternoon sun and Tuscan wine. Luckily for me, charming people—especially tipsy people—is one of my specialties, and it shouldn't take me long to find someone with a bed to spare.

Movement catches my eye, and I look up right as Avery appears on one of the balconies looking onto the terrace. I don't like the way my heart stumbles in my chest at the sight of her basking in the golden light, but she really is beautiful, with her reddish brown hair and the dusting of freckles on her fair skin. I can't imagine what a week of August Italian sunshine will do for her, not just for her complexion but for her personality.

I read people for a living, and there's someone lurking beneath the surface of Avery...whatever her last name is. The woman who used to travel and be brave? I'm willing to bet she's still in there, and something tells me she's more beautiful than the woman I met on the plane.

Maybe I can get the real Avery to make a longer appearance than a few seconds passing the Florence Cathedral. That Avery was sexy. And there's nothing I like more than the challenge of helping people find their authentic selves. I've built my whole career around doing just that.

"Hey, you're West, right? Worked with Riccardo when his gig was still a startup?" A baritone voice pulls my attention from Avery to a group of couples sitting at one of the closer tables.

I doubt any of them will have a bed I can use, but I approach and offer a broad smile. "That's me."

The man who spoke stands and shakes my hand. "I've been meaning to get in touch with you for a while now. Hoping you could help me with a little project I'm working on."

As he offers me a seat and jumps into the details of his business, I look back up at Avery's balcony only to find it empty. I'm more disappointed than I should be, given I still don't know much about the woman.

I know her first name and that she smells like peaches. And that she gives some great hugs. I don't usually need more than that to enjoy some casual interaction, but Avery has presented a challenge I can't resist.

This week might be more fun than just a wedding.

CHAPTER 5
Avery

I figured out what's missing in my life.

If the answer is anything other than gelato, you're wrong.

What if I say cornetti and cappuccinos?

Close enough. I won't disown you. Though we both know Grandma Sue will be disowning both of us because neither of us said a sexy, rich Italian man. *laughing emoji*

About that…

TELL ME EVERYTHING!

And please say you have pictures!

Avery:

Okay, well, he's not Italian, but he definitely has sexy and rich on lockdown. And no, I don't have pictures because I am not a creep.

Dani:

I'm liking what I'm hearing! Also, we live in the time of AI and internet stalking. What's a covert photo between new acquaintances?

Avery:

Next time you're on a plane, you try taking a picture of the guy next to you and see how covert you can be.

Dani:

To be fair, Mason will just pose for the picture with me. No need for covertness.

Avery:

Ugh, yes, you think your new boyfriend is sexy. No need to remind me.

I doubt I'll see Benson again, but it was fun while it lasted. He shared his taxi with me! And I'm pretty sure he gave me his hotel room because there was a mix-up with mine.

DANI DOESN'T IMMEDIATELY RESPOND, which is fine even though I'm dying to tell her in detail about how unreal Benson is. There's no way he can be this kind, charming, *and* attractive without having some major red flags waving in the wind, but I'm pretty sure I dreamed about him all night after I passed out on the bed almost as soon as I got up to my room.

He wasn't in the lobby this morning when I headed out to find breakfast at this adorable little outdoor café. I thought about hanging around the hotel for a bit in the hopes of running into him, but that feels a little desperate. Avery Baldwin is not the type of person to get desperate.

Nor is she the type to contemplate a week-long fling, but here we are.

I sip my cappuccino and pop the last bite of my cornetto into my mouth, savoring the buttery bread. If I'm not careful, I'll be late for my guided tour of the Uffizi Gallery. Art isn't always my favorite thing, but this is Italy, and the gallery feels like the kind of place someone should go if they're here. But a part of me wants to keep sitting here at my table and watch the people walking by, locals and tourists alike.

I wonder what all their stories are.

My phone buzzes right as I'm getting up from my table and slinging my purse over my head—harder for someone to steal it this way. Opening my text thread with my sister, I keep to the side of the busy street so I'm out of anyone's path.

Dani:

> Sexy and creative and hardworking and kind…sigh. Am I nauseating or what? ;)

> Very gentlemanly of him! Though I'm a little disappointed the two of you didn't end up with only one bed. It happens in romance novels all the time but never in real life.

Avery:

> Does it mean I'm on the rebound if I wish it could be a real-life trope? Are they still called tropes if it's real life?

> Ugh, I shouldn't even be thinking about this guy when I'm only going to be here for a week. I don't know anything about him other than the fact that he's drop-dead gorgeous and heroic and smells like a rainy forest and has the kind of smile that saves babies from burning fires.

Dani:

> How does a smile save babies from burning fires? Is that a skill he could list on his resume? I might need a demonstration.

> Also, aren't all fires burning?

I cringe as I look back at my last text. Wow, that was a mess. I'm going to blame the nonsense on the fact that I slept for like thirteen hours last night and am running on nothing but bread and caffeine, none of which is doing me any favors when it comes to combating my jet lag.

Avery:

> I might be a little jet lagged. I tried to sleep on the plane, but freaking Benson was over there looking all manly the whole time.

> I'm going to stop fantasizing about him being interested in me, because that will never happen, and focus on myself the rest of this trip. Reset. Mostly I texted you to let you know I made it safely, and I'll be sure to eat some gelato for you.

Dani:

> Of course he could be interested in you! You're intelligent and gorgeous and passionate! And it's about time you started noticing other men. Men that actually have personality and depth, unlike You-Know-Who.

Rolling my eyes, I start typing a text in defense of Eric, telling her that he totally has depth because I wouldn't have started a business with him if he didn't. But I pause halfway through the thought and flip back to the texts Eric has sent me since I left. It's all work-related, and most of them are things he can easily figure out himself. I honestly can't decide if he's floundering without me there or if this is some strange way to tell me he misses me.

I bite my lip and consider that. Eric and I were together for six years, which is anything but insignificant. Does he really have nothing to say to me other than asking me where we keep the bookmarks? *Same place we've always kept them, Eric.* We used to talk about anything and everything, but it's been *months* since we had a conversation about anything that isn't our company. Even before we broke up. And while I love talking about our books...

I miss that. I miss having someone to talk to about the big things and the little things and all the things in between. But it's only been a couple of months since Eric and I broke up, and it's not like I can flip a switch and pretend our relationship didn't happen. Dani says it's time for me to move on, but what if I'm not ready?

What if I can't find anyone I can talk to like I used to with Eric?

Avery:

While I appreciate the praise (you're the best sister ever), it's a bad idea for me to flirt with some guy. It's not like we

Someone bumps into me, nearly knocking my phone out of my hand as I accidentally hit send. "*Scusi!*" he says. "Sorry, I didn't—Avery?"

Alarm shifts quickly to surprise as I meet Benson's gaze, all too aware of his hand cupping my arm to keep me upright. "Oh! Hi. Hey. *Hola.*"

His lips twist in a smirk. "That's Spanish, but I like the effort. Hi back. I'm sorry for running into you."

"I'm not." Oh goodness, that's not the kind of thing someone says out loud. "I mean I'm glad it's you and not some handsy Italian guy."

Both our gazes drop to his hand, which at some point in the last few seconds shifted from my arm to my waist. "Uh." He lets go like I've burned him and runs his hand through his hair. Rather than a suit like yesterday, today he wears a light blue button-down and a pair of chinos, looking very Italian. "Sorry."

"Don't be!" I grab his arm when I say this, which leads to another matching look down to where we're touching.

He clears his throat, and we both shift backward half a step as I register my phone buzzing multiple times. I look down, my face growing hotter with each of Dani's texts.

Dani:

We what? Have instant chemistry? Are going to run away together and start a cult? You can't leave me hanging like that. You know my imagination runs wild!

Avery?

AVERY?

AVERY!

At this point, I've decided you've been kidnapped by Mister Sexy-Benson and are experiencing your first good kiss in years. Enjoy!

Also, Mason says if that kiss doesn't involve gelato, you're doing it wrong.

"Everything okay?" Benson tucks one hand into his pocket and points at my face with the other. "You went all..." He trails off as if he can't think of any words to describe how I look right now.

My face is on fire, so I don't blame him for being concerned. I need to respond to my sister and make sure she knows that there is no way I would be making out with a stranger. Especially not with gelato. How would that work? I can only imagine it being incredibly messy, not attractive. "My sister is being presumptuous," I mutter and wave my phone in his direction.

His eyes jump to my phone, then go wide, and he grabs my wrist. "Did I see my name in your presumptuous sister's texts?" he asks, and his voice is flooded with amusement.

Oh, kill me now. "Of course not."

"Mister Sexy-Benson?"

Goodness, does this man have super vision? "Her words, not mine."

"What were *your* words?" I'm too embarrassed to resist when he eases the phone out of my hand and starts scrolling, reading through the conversation with a smile that keeps growing with each passing second. "Wow, Avery. Drop-dead gorgeous? I'm flattered, but I think you're being a little generous with that one. And I'm with Dani and need a demonstration of how a smile can save babies."

When he grins, I feel like I might implode. He knows full well the power his smile holds, and I will not give him any more power by agreeing with him. "Like I said in the text, all of that was jet lag talking."

"Now I need to know what your last text was going to say." He fixes me with a smirk, one of his eyebrows quirked up. I've never been able to do that with my eyebrows. Is it a genetics thing or a talent thing? "Why can't you flirt with me? That's just disappointing."

"Ha!" This can't be happening. I set out this morning thinking I wouldn't see Benson except maybe in passing or at a distance. This is a big enough city that the chances of us running into each other have to be astronomically low. Yet here he is, asking why I won't flirt with him.

Seriously, is Poppy onto something when she talks about fate?

When I don't answer, Benson leans in close enough for me to catch flecks of navy in his bright blue eyes. "If it helps, I'm definitely interested. Dani wasn't wrong about that."

"This can't be happening," I whisper out loud, pressing my hands to my cheeks to try to cool the heat that has been burning there since he appeared. "You're not being serious right now."

His expression falters, and I could swear there's a bit of uncertainty behind his eyes now. This guy has been nothing but cool and collected from the moment he first asked if I was okay on the plane, and nervousness was the last thing I would have expected from someone like him.

Putting some distance between us again, he drops his gaze to the stones at our feet. "I can back off," he says, his tone so much softer than what I've heard before now. "If I was reading something that wasn't there, then—"

"No!" Ah geez, do I have to sound so desperate? Taking a deep breath, I try to force my anxiety down to a manageable level. "I just... It's been a long time since anyone flirted with me."

He frowns. "What about that ex of yours?"

"We were together for six years. Flirting wasn't really a necessity by the end."

Chuckling, he looks down at my phone, still in his hand, and scans some of the texts again. "Flirting is always a necessity. Maybe you should follow your sister's advice and let yourself notice someone new."

Boy, have I noticed Benson. Though threads of attraction have been weaving their way through me since my first look at this guy, there are too many reasons why I shouldn't indulge them. "I'm not..."

Man, there was once a time when I didn't hesitate to say anything that was on my mind, but right now I'm terrified to speak the truth even though I get the sense Benson is an honesty kind of guy. He certainly didn't hesitate to tell me about *his* interest.

Benson nudges my arm with his own. "You're not what, Avery?"

I shrug. "I'm not a week-long fling in Italy kind of girl."

"But you used to be."

My eyes fly wide. "What? How do you know that?"

Laughing, he pulls up the camera on my phone and flips it to selfie mode. "Call it a hunch. What do you say we play with your sister a bit?"

I'm not sure I like the sound of that, but I'm too curious to argue. "How?"

He lifts the phone to take a picture of himself, which is genius. But then, too quickly for me to realize what he's doing, he tucks an arm around my waist and pulls me close, and then his lips are on my jaw.

What is happening?

The kiss lingers more than I expect it to, and I can't breathe or move or react in any way as I close my eyes and let my mind jump from one sensation to another. The feel of his hand on my ribcage. The smell of his cologne. The slight rasp of his scruff. The warmth of his mouth.

He might stay there for minutes or maybe it's seconds, but it isn't long enough. Slipping his hand free and stepping back, he keeps his focus on whatever he's doing on my phone as if kissing someone's jaw is an everyday occurrence for him. Maybe it is. Benson's still a stranger, and he might be the biggest player on the planet for all I know. He seems genuine, but maybe that's how charmers like him come across to everyone they flirt with.

Benson chuckles at something on my phone, and I lean in to see Dani's response. Multiple responses.

Dani:

Yes!!!!!!!!

> Mason pointed out that your boy-toy missed.

> Also, where's the gelato?

"Missed?" I ask in bewilderment. Benson did *not* miss. I still feel a spot of fire where his lips caressed my skin. "You didn't—oh." The realization hits me hard, and I drop my face into my hands. "She's the worst. I'm so sorry."

"I thought about it."

My hands slip, and I stare at him. "What?"

He shrugs. "I missed your mouth on purpose, but I almost didn't."

"Gah."

Laughing, he tucks my phone into his pocket and asks, "Where are you off to now?"

We're going to move on from the whole kissing comment like it's nothing? Okay. "Are you stealing my phone?"

"Temporarily. What's your plan for the day?"

It certainly wasn't to flirt with the swooniest man I've ever seen. I need to take control of this situation before Benson overwhelms my prefrontal cortex. The logical brain was not built to withstand a man like him. "Um. I was going to take a tour of the Uffizi Gallery, and I don't want to be late for my booking, so I'd like my phone back."

He looks at me for a long moment, though I have no idea what he sees. This interaction, every bewildering second of it, is the first time we've been face to face without distractions, and there's something in the way he studies me right now that leaves me feeling exposed. But it's not a bad feeling, which is terrifying in and of itself.

The more good feelings I have about this guy, the more likely I'll get myself into trouble.

"Who's your favorite painter?" Benson asks, folding his arms.

I tilt my head. "Is this a quiz?"

"Sure. Name one of your top artists."

If I could think of any, I would, but I will be missing out on this chance to impress the hot man. Though, it doesn't seem like I need to do that. He has already admitted he's interested, which is hard for me to swallow. This guy is sexiness incarnate, and I'm an uptight publisher who owns too many pairs of slacks and forgot how to go through life without a plan. "Honestly," I say with a shrug, "I don't know anything about art. I'm more of a literature and architecture kind of gal."

"That's what I thought. Come on." He holds out his hand.

I stare at it, trying to understand what in the world is happening right now. This man came out of nowhere, took a picture of us kissing—well, he did the kissing—stole my phone, and now he's looking at me with the kind of look you don't see except in movies and novels where the dashing hero grabs the innocent heroine and tells her to go with him if she wants to live.

Chuckling, Benson shifts closer, his hand still at the ready. "Relax, Avery. I'm just offering to help you live life in a different way from what you're used to. A little spontaneity won't hurt you."

"But what if it does?" I can't stop myself from asking. The more important question: what if letting go leaves me worse off than when I started? I can't remember when I started living with caution, but it has served me pretty well for a while.

Hasn't it?

"Whatever turned you scared," Benson says, his voice low, "it didn't follow you here to Italy. You have a week to be free and let the real Avery have her time in the sun." He quirks his lips up in that irresistible smile of his. "Don't waste it."

How is a girl supposed to argue against that?

TICKET
N
W
E
S
PASSPORT
Time To
Travel
HOTEL

CHAPTER 6
Benson

DISTANCE. *EMOTIONAL* DISTANCE. IT has to be my best friend right now or I might be walking myself right into the sort of attachment I've spent my life trying to avoid. But Avery is not making it easy on me as she admires yet another Florentine building.

I still don't know anything about her, but she has somehow made herself the most interesting part of Florence. All we've done is wander the city—my all-time favorite way to explore—but she has this way of seeing everything that gives her a sort of childlike quality.

Whoa. No. Definitely not that. I'm not looking at this woman like I would a child.

She's...innocent? Still not the right word. Not naive. Full of *wonder*.

Yeah, I guess *wonderful* is as good a word as any.

"Are you going to stare at me all day, or...?"

I smile wide at Avery's question, not at all embarrassed by being caught. Ever since we got to the Basilica di Santa Croce a few minutes ago, I haven't been able to take my eyes off her while she keeps her gaze on the sunbathed church. I figured taking her around the city would be fun, but this is more fun than I've had in a long time. Enough so that I lied to Riccardo and told him I had some work to get done this afternoon and would have to miss the winery tour everyone is doing.

Maybe it's crazy to skip out on the whole reason I came to Italy, but this week is a vacation for me, just like it is for Avery. I get so few real vacations that I want to make the most of this trip, and right now that means unabashedly admiring her. After the things she said about me to her sister? I'd be an idiot not to take my shot.

"Are you going to spend all day with me?" I ask instead of answering her question.

Tilting her head to one side, she looks from me to the basilica as crowds of people wander around us. People I've barely given any thought to even though I usually pay attention to who's around me. As far as I'm concerned, we're completely alone in the square. "I guess that depends on if you know of more places like this."

Did she really plan to spend all afternoon in an art gallery? I have nothing against art and the talent it takes to make it, but as soon as she told me her plans, my gut knew Avery wanted something more substantial. My guess is the gallery was her ex's idea and non-refundable, like her flights. The moment she said she was going to the Uffizi, the light in her eyes dimmed. Sure, the gallery has its own architectural points of interest, but nothing compares to places like this. The contrasting colors on the facade of the church are the epitome of Florentine vistas.

"Are you kidding?" I say and bump my shoulder into Avery's. "Have you forgotten this is Florence? You can't walk a block in this city without running into something beautiful." *Especially if you're walking with someone like Avery.*

Whether she catches my unspoken thoughts in my expression, Avery blushes and tucks an arm around herself. "For the record," she says, waving toward the basilica, "this was on my itinerary."

"For the record, it would have been a lot less fun if you'd come here without me."

"We're just standing here, Benson. I have a tour scheduled."

Then I'd better make this more interesting. Slinging an arm around her shoulders, I nudge her a few steps closer to the building, where a group has gathered around a tour guide who's talking about the building's design. I bend down and speak in Avery's ear. "There are a bunch of old dead guys inside that everyone likes to talk about."

She shivers, leaning into me. "That is the worst way to talk about da Vinci and Dante. A bunch of old dead guys?"

I chuckle. "If you already know who's inside, why bother putting it on your list?"

"Because I want to *see* it!" She waves an arm again, like that gesture speaks more than she could say with words. "I mean, look at it!"

I would, except I'm too busy looking at her as she once again becomes enraptured by the architecture. Her light auburn hair has been slowly slipping from the bun she twisted it into this morning, and a strand of it hangs right where my hand is resting on her shoulder. My fingers itch to start playing with that bit of hair, but I worry it will overwhelm her again if I pull a move like that. In all honesty, there are a lot of moves I've been wanting to pull since running into her earlier, but she's made it clear that my interest confuses her.

If I'm *really* being honest, it confuses me too. I'm no stranger to week-long flings, but usually it's with someone as noncommittal as me. Based on the fact that this woman recently got out of a six-year relationship, it shouldn't come as a surprise that she is reluctant to try something casual and temporary. What does come as a surprise is how much I'm still drawn to her.

Usually I run from her type.

But I'm helping her. She might not know that, but I'm trying to get her to come out of her shell and embrace the person she said she used to be. We're only here for a week, so it's not like I'm putting down roots, and this will be good for her and a challenge for me. We both win.

"What do you like about it?" I ask, doing my best to stay subtle as I breathe in her peach shampoo. I've asked the same question any time we've stopped, which has been often because Avery finds something interesting just about everywhere, from bridges to storefronts to massive Franciscan churches.

I may not know anything about *her*, but I'm learning what brings a smile to her face.

"I'm amazed that people can build something like this by hand," she says without hesitation. She's getting better at not holding back her responses, which is wildly attractive. There are few things sexier than confidence. "Like, so many places use one color, but everything around here is so vivid and symmetrical and unreal. How did they build something like this?"

"If you had been listening to the tour guide, you wouldn't have to ask that question."

The glare she throws at me makes me burst into laughter and garner a few additional glares from the people at the back of the tour group. "If you weren't such a distraction," she hisses, "maybe I would have been able to catch some of the history!"

"Ah, but that's one of my best talents." Unable to resist any longer, I run the loose strand of her hair between my fingers, then brush my knuckles along the back of her neck, enjoying the way goosebumps pebble on her skin. "I should have warned you that this adventure with me would include a whole lot of distraction."

She throws her elbow into my side. "Benson Whatever-your-last-name-is, you are the biggest flirt I've ever met!"

She doesn't remember my last name from when I said it to the receptionist at the hotel? For some reason, that bit of anonymity sends a thrill through me. At this point, she doesn't know anything about me—not my job, where I'm from, why I'm here. And *I* don't know anything about *her*. It's a fun game of mystery that I don't usually get to play because most of the women I meet are connected to whatever project I'm working on, so I tend to know *too much*.

"I have an idea," I say, choosing not to address her flirt comment. "You say you're not a week-long fling kind of woman, but what if you were?"

She tenses, shifting so I'm no longer touching her. "What are you proposing? I'm not going to sleep with you."

My eyebrows shoot up. I'm both surprised by her assumption and concerned that I've given her that impression. I'm flirty, but I don't go around diving into bed with every woman I meet. That sort of thing makes relationships too messy, and I don't need messy in my life. "Definitely not proposing that. Contrary to movies and stereotypes, not every man is out for sex. I'm not opposed to a kiss or two..." I cannot stress enough how not opposed to that I am, and my eyes slide to her lips as if I need to make myself extra clear. "But what I'm suggesting is you and I let things go where they go this week and keep the pressure off it all."

She narrows her eyes. "How?"

"I don't know you." I gesture toward her, then press my hand to my chest. "You don't know me. What if we keep it that way?"

"What would be the point of that? Some non-committal make-outs and that's it?"

She is seriously underestimating the fun of a good make-out. Still, I scoff and shake my head in mock offense. "Avery, it could be so much more than that."

"Without getting to know each other? I doubt that. Conversation is the heart of any connection."

"We've been talking for hours today," I point out, "but neither of us has given any details. That's what I'm proposing. We can get to know each other, but we'll keep the essentials out of it. Last names, occupations, where we live. Let's just..." How do I explain it? I'm not doing a great job of it so far because she's still staring at me with her eyebrows low and her shoulders tensed up. "Let's be ourselves. Not what the world has made us become."

How this is supposed to help me keep emotional distance, I have no idea, but I would be an idiot to miss this chance to spend as much time with this woman as I can.

Glancing at the basilica, Avery wraps her fingers around the strap of her purse and seems to be thinking through my suggestion. She hasn't shut me down yet, but her skepticism is in full force on her face. "Don't you have places to be this week, like I do?"

Just the wedding of a good friend to whom I owe a lot of my success. But that isn't until Friday, and I'm sure he'll understand if I skip out on a few wedding things. He didn't think I was showing up in the first place, so it's not like he planned on me.

"Nowhere important," I lie, and guilt worms its way into my gut. I shouldn't have made the decision to work on strengthening my relationships when all it takes to turn my attention elsewhere is a kind smile and a pair of warm brown eyes. Not *brown*. In the sunlight, like now, they're a golden amber with the smallest ring of green on the outer edge.

Dang, she's beautiful.

Avery lifts her eyebrows. "Not even with your friend? Isn't he the reason you're here?"

Not wanting to lie again, I nod, but I'm hesitant to tell her the reason Riccardo is here in the first place. I don't need her unleashing the waterworks again. "He's, uh, getting married on Friday."

"Benson!" She whacks my arm with impressive force, angry rather than sad. "You call that unimportant?"

"Compared to spending a week with you? Sure."

She rolls her eyes. "You're ridiculous. I'm not going to be the reason you miss your friend's wedding, even if I want..." Blushing scarlet, she trails off and watches a family who stop to take a selfie in front of the church.

With a grin, I take Avery's hand and lift it to my lips, bringing her attention back to me where it belongs. "You won't be. That's just one day. If you want to spend time with me, all you have to do is say so."

"Have you always been such a flirt?"

If she were anyone else, I would tell her that I'm never this flirty and something in her has sparked to life a new side of me. It's a line I've used many times before and usually works. But right now it feels true, at least the part about Avery sparking something inside me. I've never been this entranced by a woman, and I still haven't figured out what it is about her that intrigues me so much. It's more than the challenge she presents. More than her outward beauty.

"Yes," I say, letting my smile shift to one of self-deprecation. "It's a blessing and a curse."

"Blessing for you, curse for the rest of us?"

I gasp in mock offense and pull her hand to my chest. "You wound me, Avery."

"Someone should. I think your head is altogether too big." But she grins and shakes her head, that lovely blush making an appearance again. "You really want to spend all week with an uptight weirdo like me?"

"Neither of those are words I would use to describe you."

"You don't know me, remember?"

I don't think it will take much more persuasion to get her to join me, but I might as well pull out the big guns and list out the things I've learned about her so far. I lean in, dropping my voice so she has to lean too. "I know you love flowers and mosaics and that you enjoy romance novels and possibly are a bit of a classic literature snob on top of that. You have a thing for dogs and chocolate—not together of course—and ramble when you're tired, even in a text." I lift her fingers to my lips, then reach out with my other hand to tuck the loose strand of hair behind her ear. I have a feeling I'm going to be doing that a lot if she agrees. "I know you're beautiful, even when you're crying over a guy who obviously doesn't deserve you, and you smell like peaches and have a smile that brings your whole face to life."

That was too much. Avery is staring at me with wide eyes, and I don't think I've ever said anything like that before—it's enough to scare anyone off. *Good work, Bens.*

"Wow," Avery whispers after a long moment. "You..." I hold my breath, waiting for her to tell me I'm a creep and she'll be going about the rest of her trip the way she originally planned. "The only thing I know about *you* is that you speak Italian and aren't a very good friend."

I bark out a laugh, lacing my fingers through hers and lowering our hands. "I also know you have a snarky side that is majorly attractive."

"You like when I insult you?"

"I like that you're not afraid to say what you mean. To be yourself."

Something about my comment hits her in a way that dims her expression, leaving her muted. "I haven't... I don't remember the last time I was myself."

I knew it. There's more to Avery than a woman who has become scared to travel. There's a whole different side of her, one I've seen pieces of and who has been making more of an appearance as the day has gone on. I would have been interested in her anyway, but that side of her feels like the kind of person I would enjoy every moment with. "So be you this week," I tell her and take a few steps away from the basilica, our arms stretching out between us. "Let loose and don't let fear hold you back."

"How do I do that?" she asks. It's not an argument against my idea, and I'm calling this a win. But I need to ease her into things.

I grin and nudge her forward so we can start walking. "You start with the most obvious."

"Which is?"

I wink, recalling the conversation she had with her sister. "Gelato."

CHAPTER 7
Avery

BENSON DOESN'T LIKE CHOCOLATE. I knew there were people out there who have something painfully wrong with their taste buds, but I figured Benson was perfect. He has proven that to be true in the day and a half that we've been wandering Florence, but when we stepped into a chocolate shop after eating the most amazing pasta I've had in my life, he declined a sample.

A free sample.

"I am so disappointed right now," I tell him, shaking my head as I pop my own sample into my mouth. Oh goodness, I forgot how good chocolate is when it's made anywhere but the US. I might need to buy another suitcase just to bring chocolate back home with me.

Chuckling, he folds his arms and stands off to the side so I can see all the chocolate varieties on the shelf. "It's not my thing."

"What happened to letting loose and trying everything?" It's what he's been saying to me for a day and a half now. "I tried that lamp thing from the street vendor yesterday; why won't you try a little chocolate?"

He chuckles. "Lampredotto. And you loved that."

"What was it?" He wouldn't tell me before I tried a bite, and then it was so good that I didn't care. Now that it's been a day and I am pleasantly full of penne noodles and cheese sauce, curiosity is coming back. The lampredotto was some sort of meat sandwich, but the spongy texture wasn't something I've ever tried before coming here.

Benson's near-constant smile shifts into a smirk. "I don't think you want me to tell you. Eat your chocolate and enjoy your life of ignorance."

My stomach twists into a little knot, and suddenly I regret eating so many breadsticks. But they were so fun! Actual little sticks of hard bread, more like crackers than anything. I'd rather not get squeamish and lose them all. "Please don't tell me it was something like a cow's intestine."

"It was not an intestine." Well that's a relief, though something in his too-innocent tone makes me think I'm not far off.

Benson is way too good at playing innocent and teasing me into doing things I wouldn't have done if I had stuck to my itinerary. Last night, when I was so tired after walking around the city that I could hardly think straight, he convinced me to wander the Piazza della Signoria for over an hour to listen to all the different street musicians. He practically had to carry me back to the hotel, leaving me at my door with a kiss on the forehead and a promise of more fun today.

I might have squealed into my pillow after I was sure he was no longer in the hall.

He knocked on my door before dawn and only gave me time to get dressed and run a brush through my hair before he was hailing a taxi and taking us to the Ponte Vecchio to watch the sunrise on the river. "The bridge lights up at night," he said when I remarked how beautiful the spot was, and then he promised to take me one of these nights so I can walk across it and see the lights reflecting in the water.

I've eaten foods I never would have tried, wandered shops I would have been too scared to set foot in, and held hands with someone who is everything a girl could want in a man. I've said it before—there's no way Benson can be real. This is all some fever dream.

I'm not sure I want to wake up.

"You seriously have to try this," I say, forcing my thoughts back to the chocolate surrounding us. "You've been pushing me all day, so I should get a turn."

He shakes his head. "I've tried chocolate many times, Avery. I'd rather save it for someone who would enjoy it."

"How can anyone *not like chocolate*?" I lean up on my toes to get closer to his face, as if that might convince him he's utterly wrong. "Especially *Italian* chocolate."

Shrugging, he snakes one hand around my waist right before I wobble. He learned last night that my balance can be questionable when I'm on my toes, when I nearly bowled him over after trying to see over the heads of the crowd and get a better look at the cellist we were listening to. I fell right into him, and he caught me like the heroic man he is.

Or maybe he's touching me now because it's what he does. It's been pretty much nonstop contact since bumping into him yesterday morning.

The only time he doesn't touch me is when he takes pictures of me like some mystical Instagram husband. He's good at it too, finding the best angles and suggesting poses. His camera skills are the only reason I've let him hold on to my phone for the last thirty-six hours; I haven't touched the thing once since he stole it.

Honestly, it's been nice having an excuse to ignore the texts and emails Eric keeps sending. I told Benson to let me know if anything important comes up, but so far he's only told me about the conversation he's having with Dani because they're best friends now.

"You like chocolate," he says, pulling me in. It's not quite an embrace, but it's a whole lot more intimate than strangers standing close to each other. "And I like you. I think that should count for something."

"Not chocolate gelato?" Apparently this is a big deal for me, though I don't know why when literally everything else about this man is perfect.

"I'm happy with my amaretto."

"So you're telling me you're a hopeless case? Not even stracciatella? Tiramisu?"

"Look at you with your Italian words." He smiles as his fingers tighten against my side, digging into my waist to pull me closer. "We might make an Italian speaker of you yet."

"Where did you learn Italian?" I've been listening to him talk to shop-keepers, waiters, and locals for two days now, and I don't think there's a more attractive language. French has its moments, but a man speaking Italian? My kryptonite, for sure.

Benson presses his lips together, a bit of mischief entering his eyes as he glances around the busy chocolate shop. I've lost track of the number of things we've told each other about ourselves—never anything we could use to find each other after this week is over—but he always pauses whenever I ask a question, like he's scared to tell me things that make him more real. Maybe he wants me to live in this unrealistic bubble for the rest of my life, where he's perfect except for his stance on chocolate and I'm good enough for a guy like him to be interested.

"I like languages," he says, some hesitation in his words. "I have con-tacts all over the world, so it's nice to have at least the basics."

"You have more than the basics," I point out.

Nodding, he swings us both around to face the other direction as a big Italian man reaches for some of the chocolate that was behind me. The protective move, putting himself between me and the man, makes my heart swell, but Benson doesn't seem to notice the hearts in my eyes as he keeps talking. "I took Spanish in school because it made the most sense where I lived." He pauses again, his eyebrows pulling low.

Though I'm desperate for some of those details we agreed not to share, I hold back my curiosity and shake my head. "You don't have to tell me, Benson."

Relaxing, he moves us into the corner of the store so we're out of the way. More people have come inside, making the space feel crowded. "I picked up some French because a lot of the roots are the same as Spanish."

"Italian too?"

He nods. "Plus, when I started working with Riccardo, I was kind of forced into learning conversational Italian because a lot of his vendors are here in Italy."

"Riccardo is your friend who's getting married, right?" It's not the question I want to ask. I want to ask what kind of work he does because it's clearly lucrative. Benson hasn't let me pay for a single thing since we've started hanging out, and the only reason I've agreed is because I'm nowhere near as wealthy as my sister. Dani's book has made Rose & Quill a pretty penny, but we're using most of it to build up the company so we can grow along with Dani's popularity.

It's not that I'm into Benson for his money—I try to pay every time, and he always beats me to it. There's so much more to him than his wallet, as much as I love getting free pastries. Benson is indulgent and a hype-man and takes seriously good photos, and he is one of the most handsome men I've ever seen. But more than that, he knows how to hold a conversation. He is friendly with everyone he meets. He has a wealth of knowledge that seems to have no end and makes me want to ask him about everything he shows me rather than looking up facts on the internet.

I could sit and listen to him talk for hours on end and never get bored.

"Yeah," he says, tucking me closer to his side as his eyes dart around the shop. "He and Siena have been together for a few years now and are stupidly perfect for each other. Do you want to buy any chocolate? We should grab it before this place turns into a madhouse."

I can't decide if it's a deflection or actual concern for our wellbeing, but I snag a couple of bars and make my way to the front counter, digging into my purse as I go. If I hurry, I can pay for them myself before Benson—

He tosses a couple more bars onto the counter and hands over his card.

"You don't like chocolate," I point out, giving him an annoyed glare for beating me to the punch once again.

His grin brightens the whole store. "But you do." He says a few things in Italian to the cashier, who smiles back at him and hands him his receipt, holding the brown paper bag of chocolate out to me. As much as Benson thinks I'm starting to pick up on some Italian, he's dead wrong. Most people here speak English, and those who don't tend to talk way too fast for me to catch anything at all. But everyone is so much happier when Benson busts out his language skills, and I wish I'd had time to learn more before I got here.

I don't remember the last time I had free time.

"Do you speak any other languages?" I ask as we head out onto a street bathed in golden evening light. Maybe I can glean some more tidbits of Benson if I ask innocuous questions.

"The tiniest bit of German," he says, linking our hands together as we walk. "Enough Russian to think I'll be okay when I inevitably get into trouble there. Never could figure out Chinese, though."

"Oh, well, if that's the only one you can't get... I knew you had to have more than one flaw."

He chuckles. "I can't decide if you're impressed by me or just indulging me, Avery Grace."

A shiver runs through me at the sound of my name. "Did Dani tell you my middle name?"

Smirking, he tugs me down a side alley with the sort of confidence that makes me wonder if we're going somewhere specific. I didn't think we had an agenda. "You would not believe the sort of juicy gossip your sister is willing to share."

"I feel like you texting my sister is breaking the rules of anonymity." If he's allowed to get info, I should get the same chance, but I don't know if he *has* any siblings I could text. This man is a vault when it comes to personal history.

"Don't worry." We turn left, picking up our pace a bit. "She knows all about our plan and hasn't told me anything important."

"My middle name isn't important? What *has* she told you?"

Benson glances at his watch. "How do you feel about running?"

"Hate it."

"Too bad." He breaks into a jog, pulling me with him as we weave through the throngs of people wandering the busy street. I have no idea where we're going, but if Benson has a plan, it's probably a good one.

Except, he's like eight inches taller than me, so if we have to go much farther, I might ask to jump on his back and let him carry me. I'm about to suggest that when he rounds a corner and slows to a stop, a look of excitement on his face.

"Right on time," he mutters with another glance at his watch.

That's when I see the building we're in front of, with the giant orange dome and the green-and-white-patterned designs in the walls. It's the Duomo, formally called the Cathedral of Santa Maria del Fiore. It's the building that caught my attention so thoroughly during the taxi ride to the hotel, and it's the church I've been looking forward to the most. I smile wide. "Hate to break it to you," I say brightly, "but I have a tour scheduled here in like an hour, so we're technically earl—oh!"

The bells. Like before, their bold sounds seem to fill the entire city as they start up their vigil. There's no pattern or rhythm, the notes high and low and everything in between, and it is *magical*. But we're not in the right spot.

"Come on." I pull Benson to the left, apparently catching him off guard because he nearly trips as he stumbles after me. I'll have to come back and get a picture with the dome, but the other end of the church has the bells, and I want to experience this moment properly. I stop when we reach the other side, and my heart picks up in rhythm as I take it all in. The bell tower, like the front of the church, is peppered with arches and reliefs and Gothic tracery that give the stone a lacy feel. I'm not much of an art person, but it feels different when it's all made from stone rather than painted on.

"Did you know this building took almost a hundred and fifty years to build?" I ask, though I have no idea if Benson can hear me over the tolling bells. But his attention is fixed on me, so I turn back to the cathedral and keep talking even if Benson likely knows all the same facts about the Duomo that I do. "It's almost six hundred years old, and the guy who designed the dome revolutionized this type of architecture because he didn't use any scaffolding. And the bell tower was designed by an artist whose name I can't remember, but it's its own feat of engineering and design. It's all so amazing," I finish, turning to face the man next to me.

He's staring at me, his eyes bright as the sunset turns his brown hair to copper. His eyes drop to my mouth and stay there.

Swallowing, I keep talking because no matter how touchy-feely this guy has been over the last couple of days, he hasn't come close to kissing me except for that forehead kiss last night. But it's looking like that might change, and I don't know how to feel about that. "Can you imagine how brilliant everyone who made this place must have been?" I ask breathlessly. "To create something so magical out of nothing? What would it be like to be the sort of person who does something no one has ever done before? To see your vision turn into something real? I would love to someday create something I can be proud of, you know?"

Benson exhales. "You are incredible," he whispers, and then he's leaning in, his mouth only a breath from mine.

The bells stop.

The square goes quiet.

For a moment we're frozen in time, neither of us blinking, neither of us breathing, and I feel like I'm on the edge of a precipice, wondering which way we're going to fall.

A group of tourists starts clapping as the last of the bells' ringing fades. Benson pulls away, an unreadable look on his face as he slips his hand from mine and runs it through his hair. "Uh, I should head back to the hotel."

My heart sinks. "Oh."

Wincing, he seems to search the crowded square for some sort of explanation as he takes a step back, putting more distance between us than we've had since yesterday morning. "There's some wedding stuff tonight, and I should be there for that."

What happened to the guy who was willing to skip out on the wedding altogether? Did I do something wrong?

"I can take you back with me, but... You should do the tour," he says and holds out my phone, his fingers barely touching it so there's no way our hands can brush when I take it. Taking the phone back feels symbolic somehow, and I don't like it. I thought for sure he was about to kiss me, but something changed. Did the bells break the magic spell?

Oh goodness, what if they put us under a spell in the first place when we were in the taxi driving in? Benson has been way too attentive over the last couple of days—there's no way that's normal. This could have all been a fluke, and now Benson has been snapped out of the madness.

Looking down at my phone, I glance through the dozens of notifications waiting for me, most of them from Eric and some of the people we work with. There are a couple of texts from Dani, and the partial preview of her latest message makes me wonder if she's part of the reason Benson almost made a move.

Dani:

> It's been way too long since she last had a good ki...

"I'll..." I don't know what to say right now, standing in the middle of a crowded square with a ton of awkward tension between me and the man I was so ready to kiss a moment ago. "See you around?"

Grimacing, he gives me a nod that isn't at all reassuring. I didn't believe in magic spells before, but Benson's one-eighty just now has convinced me that all of this was the result of some strange wizard who needed a laugh. "Can you get back on your own?" he asks.

"I'll be fine."

"Right." He scratches his scruffy jaw, looking anywhere but at me. "Have...have fun."

Goodbye, whirlwind romance. You were fun while you lasted. I watch him walk away until he vanishes into the crowd, and then I pull up my text thread with Dani. There isn't nearly as much conversation as I expected, and most of it is pictures that Benson took of me. The last text does *not* say what I thought it did.

Dani:

> It's been way too long since she last had a good kindred spirit to spend time with, and from what I can tell, you're a lot like the sister I used to know. Thanks for getting her out of her shell. She looks happy.

The text was unread, so I don't know if Benson ever saw it, but nowhere in these back-and-forth messages are there any texts from my sister that could be classified as *juicy*. She did tell him my middle name, but not because he asked. It was in response to one of the pictures and she used my first and middle name as a reaction, complete with a million exclamation points.

Confused and a little disappointed, I pull up my booking for the Duomo tour and make my way to the entrance.

At least I'll end the day on a good note.

CHAPTER 8
Benson

"I am in so much trouble." A crowded rooftop restaurant is not the place to have this conversation, particularly because Riccardo is here with all of his family and closest friends, but I'm out of my depth here. Hence why I have pulled my buddy aside and said the most out-of-context thing I could say.

Riccardo lifts an eyebrow, leaning against the wall overlooking the twilit city. "What kind of trouble are we talking here?"

This is going to sound so stupid, especially from me. "I might be falling for Avery." Leaning my elbows on the wall, I stuff my hands into my hair and wait for him to pass judgment. When he says nothing, I look over and find him staring at me with one eyebrow raised.

"Who's Avery?"

Ah right, he hasn't been living my life the last two days. In fact, he hasn't seen me except for half a second this morning when I stumbled out of his second cousin's room, where I will unfortunately be spending the week. The guy seems nice enough, but his room only has a queen size bed. I'm man enough to share a bed when I have to, but Riccardo's cousin sleeps in the buff, and that sight was not something I needed first thing in the morning.

Or ever.

"The woman I met on the plane," I say, shaking my head.

"Wait, is she the real reason you bailed on the winery yesterday?"

"Yup."

"And you're falling for her?"

"Maybe."

"Where's she from?"

I laugh, feeling almost manic. "No idea."

"You spent all afternoon with her and don't know where she lives?"

Groaning, I stand up straight again and stuff my hands into my pockets. This restaurant has a fantastic view of Florence, though it doesn't quite compare to looking at it from the dome at the Santa Maria cathedral. I wonder if Avery stayed to do her tour or if my sudden personality shift messed her up. It's been a few hours at this point, but is she standing in the dome right now, gazing in my direction?

With a grunt, I shake my head and force my focus to Riccardo and his justifiably concerned expression. I've known Avery for *two days*. There's no reason I should be freaking out like this. "No, I don't know where she lives because we agreed to keep anything personal out of it."

Riccardo's eyebrow somehow rises higher. Impressive. "Out of what, exactly?"

"Our...relationship." That's not what we have. It's a fling. But based on the way I reacted this afternoon, it's more than a fling. It's...something. Why is it so impossible to find the right words when it comes to this woman? I'm better than this. "We're keeping things casual."

He scoffs. "You always keep things casual. It's your entire MO."

"But *she* doesn't. So we decided to take the pressure off and keep it all surface level on both sides."

"Uh huh."

He's not getting it, but I'm too wound up to keep explaining. "Just... I don't know where she lives, okay? Or what she does for work or her last name." Not that any of it matters. As soon as this trip is over, I'll be out West for a bit, then on to spend a few weeks in Alabama. That says nothing about my goals to expand my business, not just in the number of clients I have but into other countries as well. My job doesn't lend itself to settling down, which is exactly why I ran from Avery when things started to feel more...

Well, *real.*

"Let me get this straight," Riccardo says. "You met a woman on the plane, gave her your hotel room, decided to ditch your best friend to hang out with her, and you haven't tried to learn more about her? Seriously? And I know you're not getting any action because my cousin Nick said you were an excellent bed mate last night, so what's your goal here?"

I groan. "Please tell me those weren't the words he used."

"Verbatim, unfortunately." Though he chuckles, there's sympathy in his eyes. "We can try to find someone else with space."

One of Riccardo's coworkers has a sofa in his room, but having worked with the guy back when I was helping Riccardo start his trading company, that might be worse than Cousin Nick. And no one else I talked to has space.

"It's fine," I mutter. "Nick's sleeping habits aren't the problem here."

"Right. This is about you having feelings. A new experience for you."

I don't like the way his explanation paints me as cold and heartless, even if he's not wrong. Not about being heartless but about generally avoiding feelings. But I'll deal with the implications of my dislike of Riccardo's assessment some other time. "What do I do, Ricky?"

His eyes practically roll to the back of his head. "You tell her how you feel, you idiot."

Tell her that my plan to keep all things personal out of our interactions has failed because even the most inane facts about her are fascinating? Great idea. No chance of that backfiring at all. "I can't do that," I mutter. "She deserves someone who can stick around."

"You do remember you set your own schedule, right?"

"The whole reason my business works as well as it does is because I'm flexible and mobile. You know that."

"Sure," Riccardo agrees, "but you can adapt. Some might say that's your strongest suit."

"Change my whole life for a woman I met three days ago?"

Dropping his arms, he laughs and starts making his way back to where Siena is sitting. "You started this conversation, Bens. Not me."

He's right. The whole reason I ran away this afternoon is because I've already strayed too far into something I'm not equipped to handle. That moment in front of the Santa Maria del Fiore, when Avery was talking about her dreams and the bells were ringing and the sun was bathing her in a soft orange light, something flashed through my mind. Not a memory because it hasn't happened, but the mental image felt like something familiar. I imagined Avery on a hillside, with a spectacular sunset behind her and a white dress hugging her curves.

And I got spooked.

I watch as Riccardo slides into the seat next to Siena and kisses his almost-bride, and his smile is an outward manifestation of feelings I've never had. I've been pretty content with my life for a long time, willingly choosing an unsettled existence because I've never seen myself as the settle-down type. But maybe there's something to be said for finding the right person and keeping a promise.

I'm not anti-marriage. Never have been. My parents have been married for almost forty years, and my two brothers seem to be happy with their choices to marry young and have big families. But I've never seen that kind of life for myself. Not when I've always jumped from interest to interest since I was a kid. There's so much of the world to explore and experience, and something about a settled life is terrifying. What if I missed out on something amazing because I was in a stable career and stuck in one place?

Those fears are why I ran from Avery. If I start thinking about a future with her, how long before I feel too stifled and trapped and have to escape?

Tell her, Riccardo said, and he's right. Not about telling her about my growing feelings, but I should tell her why I ran away today instead of kissing her. She deserves that much, just as much as she deserves a guy who will stick around after the week is over.

I catch Riccardo's gaze and gesture to the door with my head, telling him that I'm heading out. He nods, mouthing, *Tell her*, as Siena nods beside him, and I can't help but chuckle as I take the stairs down to the street and start walking back to the hotel. He's a good friend, and I'm glad I made it out here for his wedding. He and Siena deserve every bit of happiness.

Avery does too.

She's not in the hotel lobby when I get there—why would she be?—and while I technically have her phone number because I sent myself some of the pictures I've taken of her over the last couple of days, I don't want to use it if I don't have to. Things need to stay casual between us, which means we can't have a way to stay in touch when we leave Florence.

There's a good chance Avery is still out and about in the city, unless I broke the part of her that is brave enough to wander without a plan, so talking to her might have to wait until morning. I'd rather it didn't. If she sleeps on the confusion she undoubtedly feels after my behavior today, she's going to overthink things and keep her distance from here on out.

That's a better scenario than keeping things going, but it's not the one that benefits me so I don't like it, as selfish as that sounds. I still want to spend time with her. I'm a little desperate for it, honestly. But when I've cleared the air, if she chooses not to associate with me anymore, I'll honor her decision. Even if it sucks.

Giulia is manning the front desk again, and she smiles when she sees me. "*Buonasera*, signore!" she greets, happy to speak Italian when her hotel is full of Americans and a groom who pretends he's a local despite barely spending more time here than I have. "Can I help you with any-thing?"

"Do you remember the woman I gave my room to?"

She tilts her head, studying me. "Sì."

"Have you seen her today? Is she here? In her room?" That sounds creepy, so I scramble to add an explanation. "I've been showing her around Florence, but I had to leave her on her own for a bit tonight, so I want to make sure she's safe."

"Ah." Giulia's expression turns to worry. "I have not seen her, no. Should we be worried?"

I want to say no, but the unease in my gut says otherwise. I like to think I'm generally concerned for the wellbeing of the people around me, but this feels different from anything I've experienced before. Swearing under my breath, I run a hand through my hair and grab my phone, deciding a text is better than wondering all night if Avery is safe.

"Buonasera, signora!" Giulia says, clear relief in her tone.

I look up, and a wave of the same relief washes over me at the sight of Avery standing a few yards away. "You made it back."

Avery frowns, glancing between me and the receptionist. "I am capa-ble of doing things on my own, you know. I would have been fine all week without you."

Ouch. But I deserve that. "Can we talk?" Ugh, those are the worst words in the world, second only to *it's not you, it's me*.

She gazes at the elevator almost longingly. "It's getting late."

"Please." I consider stepping forward and touching her arm, but that would defeat the whole purpose of the conversation we need to have. "It'll be quick, I promise."

Sighing, she looks down at the bag of chocolate in her hand and nods. "If it's quick. I need to get a good night's sleep tonight."

Man, I must have really done a number on her if she's worrying about early bedtimes while on vacation. She didn't care last night when I kept her out past midnight. I don't want to take the blame for subduing her more adventurous side, but I wasn't at all careful with our interactions over the last couple of days and likely gave her the wrong idea. I'm used to casual, but she isn't, and I should have realized we probably weren't on the same page.

"What do you want to talk about?" Avery asks.

I glance at Giulia, who is unabashedly watching us. "Let's go out onto the terrace. There's a nice bench out there by the fountain." I offer my hand to Avery, but she ignores it and starts walking. Weirdly, her disdain relaxes me so I'm not so keyed up and nervous. If she has already turned against me, we could go without this conversation and be fine.

I shake my head and follow her to the back door. Convenient as it would be to part ways now, I admire Avery too much to leave her hanging. I'd rather get the truth out there—some of it, anyway—and let her decide how we proceed. In my line of work, I make too many decisions for other people as it is, and I shouldn't do it here.

When she finds the bench, Avery sits on the very end of it in a clear display of wanting to keep distance. I hate it, but I sit at the other end. If we weren't stuck in an awkward silence backed by the soft splashes from the fountain, this would be the kind of romantic spot that would lead to a lot more than talking. But I'm probably not going to get a kiss from Avery tonight. Or ever.

"What's this about?" Avery asks again.

"How was the Duomo?"

She rolls her eyes and pulls a piece of chocolate from the bag, popping it into her mouth. "Can we skip the small talk?"

I like her even more when she's snippy. What's wrong with me? "Sorry, yes. I want to explain what happened earlier."

"When you ran away?"

Oh good, she thought it looked like running just like I did. Not embarrassing at all. "I…" What do I say? Years of using my words to build up dozens of businesses, and I've got nothing. "I overreacted."

She lifts an eyebrow a fraction of an inch. "To what?"

"To you."

The eyebrow drops. "Excuse me?"

"To how much I…" Nope. I'm not going there. I'm not going to tell her that I'm into her and then turn around and tell her that we're just friends, if that. "I was unfair to you. I knew this was only going to last a week, but I didn't act like I knew it. I was careless, and you deserve more than that."

"More," she repeats, grabbing another piece of chocolate. "In what sense, exactly?"

Okay, yes, I can see the confusion. I could mean any number of things. More touching? Yes. More personal details? Probably not. More honesty? That can be dangerous, but I always tell my clients that honesty and authenticity is their best asset. "I'm not the kind of guy who commits," I say. It's true, but it makes me sound…not great. "And I wasn't acting in a way that fits with that truth. So I'm sorry."

She seems to process my words, and then she softens. Her shoulders relax, the lines on her forehead smooth, and a corner of her mouth turns up. "Benson," she says, the sharpness in her tone gone now. "I agreed to keep it all casual. I knew this week wasn't going to turn into a whole relationship."

Right. Of course she knew that. I'm the one who got freaked out by a few feelings. Apparently I'm the only one who has a problem here. Here I was thinking I was leading her on, when it looks like I was leading *myself* on.

So how do I fix this without saying goodbye to her yet? For my own sanity, I need to make sure we don't have the same level of physicality that I allowed before. Assuming she wants to keep hanging out. I know what

I want—definitely not to part ways tonight and never speak again—but I have to leave this up to Avery.

I take a deep breath. "Even so, I was out of line. I'm sorry if I gave you the wrong impression."

"So you didn't want to kiss me?" Her eyes fly wide, and she looks as surprised as I am by her bold question.

I can't help but chuckle. "No, I wanted to kiss you." Her answering blush is a reward I don't deserve, but I treasure it. "Still do. But maybe we..." I can't bring myself to say the rest of that sentence, no matter that I should.

"Hold off on that?" she finishes for me.

"Yeah, that." But now I'm fixated on the idea of kissing, and my eyes slide to her lips.

She smiles, making herself more tempting. "It's probably a good thing if we don't kiss. I don't think you could handle it."

I force my gaze back to her eyes and find laughter in them. "Meaning what?" And why do I feel like she's feeding one of my usual lines back to me?

Her smile shifting into a smirk, she pulls out another piece of chocolate and says, "Meaning I'm just that good," before placing the chocolate on her tongue.

If not for that chocolate, I would kiss her right now and show her exactly what I can handle. At the same time, she might be right. This woman is a magnet, and kissing her would pull me in and leave me locked to her side for as long as possible. The thought of kissing her is tempting enough that I almost don't care that I would leave Italy with a hole in my chest.

I've never held on to anything like that in my life.

What has Avery done to me?

I clear my throat and stand. *Distance.* "Now that we've cleared that up, I need to buy you a cannoli because I still cannot believe you've never tried one. So we're going out." *That is the opposite of distance, Benson!*

Glancing at her chocolate, Avery gets to her feet and plants herself directly in front of me, her chin raised and a defiant look in her eyes. "No. I'm going to buy my own cannoli."

Is this her telling me that she doesn't want to keep hanging out? If it is, good for her. But I don't like it. "Of course you can buy your own cannoli. You can do whatever you want to."

"Yes I can. And I'm going to buy my own cannoli. But you can come with me if you'd like."

Smiling easily for the first time since leaving her at the cathedral, I hold my hand out to her and feel something fall into place when her fingers lace with mine. I wasn't supposed to hold her hand. That was half the point of this conversation, but I can't *not* hold her hand. It's dark out. She could get lost among the other tourists exploring the city. It hasn't bothered her before now, so it won't bother her going forward.

As we make our way through the lobby and onto the street, I curse my lack of willpower and hold on to her all the more. I started tonight's conversation so we could make sure we don't cross any boundaries, but something tells me we're going to push those lines until they snap. Even if she won't, I sure as hell know I will.

Non vedo l'ora.

CHAPTER 9
Avery

I CAN DEFINITIVELY SAY this is the first time I've crashed a wedding. Well, in this case a wedding *reception*. Even in my wilder days, I was more of an adventurer than a disruptor, and despite hearing a lot about Riccardo over the last few days, I have no idea if he'll be cool with me showing up to his party.

But tonight's my last night with Benson, and I don't want to waste it.

The last three days—and the two before it—were pure magic. True to his word, Benson was clear about his intentions, and while he quickly fell back into the physical contact we shared during our first two days in the city, he hasn't come anywhere close to kissing me. I'm both relieved and disappointed.

Relieved because I don't know how good I can be with casual kissing. Disappointed because I'm pretty sure Benson would kiss the same way he does everything else—with confidence and skill.

Strapping on my sandals, I move to the little vanity in my room and take in my appearance. I haven't worn makeup most of the week, choosing instead to be as natural and free as I can be. Tonight, I've put on some mascara and a bit of blush, but other than that I'm sticking with the status quo. Benson likes how I look when I don't put in a lot of effort. Like a couple of days ago, when I showed up in the lobby in a sundress and strappy sandals, my hair in loose waves down my back and not a bit of makeup on, he stumbled over his words as he said I looked like I belonged in Florence.

And this dress! It's one I bought for my wedding-crashing, and I'm proud of myself for choosing a vibrant green rather than sticking with the more muted colors that I've grown used to with my business attire. Snapping a quick mirror selfie, I send it to our cousins group chat—a chat I have been severely neglecting—but I need to hurry if I want to get to the reception in time to steal some cake.

And by 'cake' I mean 'a dance with the most attractive man in the universe.'

Benson tried to get me to come to the wedding in its entirety, but that was a line I wouldn't cross. He convinced me to slip into the reception if nothing else, and when the wedding is over we'll go out to one of the squares and listen to the street musicians again. I haven't seen him at all today because of the ceremony, and I'm buzzing with anticipation. A girl doesn't go five straight days with Benson as a constant companion without getting attached to his easy charm and broad smiles.

Tonight will be one last hurrah before I go back to reality in the morning.

My phone buzzes twice right as I reach my door, and I pause to see the response to the photo. One is from a younger cousin, Lucy, while the other is from Dani.

Lucy:

> That color is SO pretty on you!

Dani:

> Oo! Look at that gorgeous dress. Looks like things are going well with Mr. Sexy-Benson.

Oh crap. I should have known Dani would bring up Benson, and I am so not prepared for my cousins to learn about my Italian fling. Unfortunately for me, the group chat is thriving today.

> Who is this smokin' Avery and how do we get her to stay??? And who is Mr. Sexy Benson??? Details. Now.

Now I *really* don't want to go home.

Though the texts keep coming, I tuck my phone into my purse and head downstairs, my nerves growing with each step. I'm really doing this. Wandering into a wedding where I've only met one of the groomsmen whose last name I don't know. I still don't know any details about Benson, like his occupation or his family or where he lives. I don't know what foods he likes or what his hobbies are. I just know he's easier to talk to than anyone I've ever met, and he makes me feel powerful and beautiful and brave.

Riccardo rented out the back terrace of the hotel for the wedding, and the reception is in full swing when I arrive.

A string octet plays classical music in one corner while beautiful people in beautiful clothing linger around the candlelit space. I've been out here multiple times for various meals, but I've never noticed the floral smell permeating the space. Probably because I've only ever been back here with Benson, and he has his own delicious smell. The scent of the bouquets on the tables and hanging from the balconies along the sides of the terrace, mixed with whatever they served for dinner tonight, is intoxicating, and I feel like I'm living in a movie.

"You're Avery, right?" a soft voice says beside me.

I turn and gasp at the sight of the bride in her elegant A-line gown. She's absolutely gorgeous. "Um, yeah. Yes. I'm sorry, I know I wasn't technically invited, but—"

"No, we're *thrilled* you're here," a man says as he joins the bride, tucking an arm around her waist and pulling her against his chest. "Benson has been a total downer all day, moping around because he had to wait to hang out with you. I'm Riccardo." He holds out his hand, which I take with trembling fingers.

I don't know if I'm embarrassed about being caught or nervous about the idea of Benson being as desperate to see me as I am to see him. Being around him this week has started to feel as natural as breathing, and my morning felt...empty. We haven't talked about what will happen when I head to the airport tomorrow, and I'm not looking forward to it.

"Avery," I say, forcing a smile. "You must be Siena. You look absolutely stunning."

Siena smiles wide, leaning into her new husband. "Thank you. And Ricky's not lying about Benson. It's been a few years since he and Ricky worked together, but I've never seen him like this."

Oh, it would be so easy to innocently ask what kind of work Benson does. Benson hinted that Riccardo knows about the nature of our relationship, but Riccardo seems like the kind of guy who might enjoy spilling a few secrets. Knowing Benson's job might make it easier to find him. Knowing his last name would be even better.

But guilt builds in my stomach before I open my mouth. I can't ask Benson's friends about him. If I want to know details like that, I need to ask *him*.

So I ask something less specific. "He's a good guy, right? He's not putting up a front for me?"

Riccardo and Siena both laugh. "I have no idea what he's been like with you," Riccardo says. "But he's one of the best guys out there. He saved my bacon a few years back, and he's been one of my best friends ever since. He's loyal, no matter how much he pretends otherwise."

It isn't that Benson has come across as disloyal, but he certainly made it clear when he said he wasn't the type to commit. That's easy to believe; a guy like him would have been locked down long before now if he had any plans to settle down. It's the one part of him I haven't liked.

People make long distance work all the time. Why couldn't we?

Because you're barely two months off your engagement, I remind myself and fix my smile before it droops. "Well, he gave you a glowing recommendation," I tell Riccardo, "so I'll trust yours about him. Uh, where...?"

Siena points near the fountain. "I last saw him over there somewhere. He was texting someone."

"Probably working," Riccardo says with a roll of his eyes. "Avery, go save him from himself."

Is Benson a workaholic? I try to imagine that as I pick my way through the throngs in the direction Siena pointed. I haven't seen him on his phone much at all, and most of the time when he is, he's texting Dani. Which is weird. But they've both told me they've barely talked about me and have been talking "business," whatever that means. I trust my sister, and she says she trusts Benson, so I'm choosing to be cool about their strange friendship.

So tonight Benson is either working or texting Dani, but either way, he's not as desperate to find me as the newlyweds think.

"You look breathtakingly beautiful," a smooth voice says behind me, stopping me in my tracks. "Please tell me you're looking for me and not some Italian man to sweep you off your feet."

Grinning, I spin to face Benson, exhaling shakily when I see the look on his face. He examines me with a slow, searching look, from my head to my toes and back up again before meeting my gaze.

"Breathtaking," he repeats in a whisper and tucks some of my hair behind my ear.

He's one to talk. I saw this man in a tailored suit the first time I met him, and that was wildly attractive. He's been more casual throughout the week, wearing button-down shirts and chinos or fitted t-shirts and shorts. But Benson in a tuxedo? This man knows how to wear a tux.

Does anyone look bad in a tux? Probably not. But Benson has the height and the bulk and the jaw and the eyes and...where was I going with this?

A chuckle rumbles through him, and he reaches out and laces his fingers with mine, pulling me closer until we're swaying to the music. "How was your day?"

"I rescheduled that tour of the Galleria dell'Accademia so I could see the David statue."

"And?"

"I was so bored." I bury my face in his chest in my embarrassment. "I mean, the statue was cool, but I feel like I already saw it because of that replica in the Palazzo Vecchio we saw two days ago."

Benson tucks his arm around my back, holding me tight against his body. "What else did you do?"

I love so much that he's asking. Even more that he seems to genuinely want the answer. "I bought a bracelet at that jewelry shop we've passed by a few times."

He lifts our clasped hands to study the gold chain on my wrist. "It's nice. But it's not the one you were looking at."

The one I was looking at every time we passed the jeweler on the Ponte Vecchio was four times more expensive than this one and way out of my budget. I tried—and apparently failed—to be discreet every time I looked at it, worried Benson would try to buy it for me because this dude really has a thing for buying me things.

He let me buy a cannoli, but his shiny credit card has bought everything else. At one point he strong-armed me out of the way before I could buy a silk scarf for Dani. I would have died if he spent hundreds of dollars on a bracelet just because I like the star pattern built into the chain.

"I like this one," I tell him, twisting my wrist to look at the single gold star charm hanging from the chain. "The simplicity of it can be symbolic."

"Of what?"

"Me, I guess. Remembering that life doesn't have to have every moment planned. I don't know."

Humming, he spins us in a slow circle. "It's like a shooting star," he says. "You can't plan for them, and if you try, you'll be disappointed. But you also have to slow down if you want to see one. Let yourself be in the moment, without any distractions."

I'm certainly in the moment right now, my head resting on his shoulder and the buzz of conversations around us blending into the music and the sounds of the city. To think I was nervous about coming to the party... I should have known it was stupid to be nervous about anything when it comes to Benson. He really is the perfect man, and he will live on forever as a dream unless I figure out how to make this thing between us last beyond tonight.

"You really have a way with words," I murmur, feeling sleepy. I'm way too comfy in this spot, and I'm never going to want to leave.

Benson laughs. "Not around you. You make me forget everything I know."

I highly doubt that. This man was as good as any tour guide this week, with all his random factoids about buildings and statues and bridges. Sometimes I wonder if he doesn't get into relationships because there's no space in his head for frivolous things like love.

Or is love strictly a heart thing?

I used to think I understood love, but with the way things ended with Eric, I'm not sure I ever did. We were compatible, but that's not the same as love. I've experienced something totally different with Benson this week than I've ever felt with anyone, and I...

Wait. I tense as my thoughts catch up to me. Love? I can't fall in love with someone in a few days! But I've felt so safe and empowered with Benson that I might be well on my way. How could I *not* fall for this guy?

He has been a dream, the man I didn't know I needed in my life until he appeared.

I'm not wearing the bracelet Poppy gave me at the airport, but I've had it tucked into my purse all week because I keep forgetting it's there. Maybe it has more power than I've ever allowed myself to believe.

Speaking of Poppy, my phone hasn't stopped buzzing with texts, and I sigh as I think about the mayhem I will be going home to.

"You okay?" Benson asks, pausing our little dance. I don't know if it's because I tensed up or because of the sigh, but of course he noticed a change in my demeanor.

If I tell him I might be falling in love with him, I'll get another heart-to-heart chat by the fountain about boundaries, so I stick to the cousins. "You've caused me a lot of trouble, Benson Jay."

He chuckles and starts swaying again. "Using my middle name against me? I wish I hadn't told you."

"You know mine. It was only fair."

Offering a smile of allowance, he spins me out and back to his arms. "How have I caused you trouble? That's a pretty serious allegation without any specifics to back it up."

"You made friends with Dani, who told my cousins about you, and now they won't leave me alone."

His gaze drops to my purse, eyes sparkling with interest. "What did she say about me?"

"At this point, I'm afraid to look."

"What have I told you about fear?" Benson steps away and tugs me to the nearest table, pulling out a chair for me. Once we're seated, he holds out his hand, silently asking me for my phone.

The thought of Benson having access to my cousins is too intriguing to pass up. I place my phone in his hand and scoot my chair closer, tucking myself against his arm so I can see the screen.

As he scrolls, I see that the girls have been active, throwing out speculations about who Benson is and how I managed to find a man in Italy who can handle my plan-making tendencies. Jokes on them. Benson silenced that part of me almost instantly. At one point, Lucy decided Benson is a world-weary and mysterious artist with a tragic past, and I groan when I read Dani's assessment of him.

Dani:

> He's the second hottest guy in the world! (Mason is obviously the first). Also, he's capable of having a conversation that isn't about himself, his advanced degree, his extensive collection of tube socks… In short, he's the opposite of The Great Letdown, and I like him!

"Seriously, what have you two been talking about?" I wish he had kept my phone instead of using his to talk to Dani so I could go back and figure out what they've been saying without needing to interrogate my sister when I get home.

Benson's grin turns mischievous. "I need to have *some* secrets, Ave."

Oh, that nickname is a bad idea. Or maybe a great one. Nicknames are a step we haven't taken this week, which makes this moment feel all the more intimate. I try to keep my focus on the text and not the way my name on Benson's lips sounds like how chocolate gelato tastes.

"You have kept plenty of secrets from me," I say, "and you know it. Obviously you've been talking about my ex."

"He sounds like a tool."

"Dani has probably made him sound worse than he is."

"He let you go, so he's a tool regardless."

Heat flooding my face, I press my cheek against his shoulder and watch as he starts typing.

Avery:

> Hey ladies, this is Benson. No, I'm not an artist, and having a conversation is like breathing for

> me, so that's hardly a talent. Dani's only saying good things about me because I promised to buy a special edition of her next book. I wanted to let you all know that I've been taking very good care of your cousin and will be sure to return Avery better than how I found her.

I gasp and try to stop him from hitting send, but I'm too late. "Oh my gosh, they're going to think… I don't even know what they're going to think!"

"Am I wrong?" Benson raises an eyebrow as he shifts in his seat to get a better look at me, his arm stretching out across the back of my chair. "There's no question that you were great to begin with, Avery Grace, but you are not the same woman I met on the plane."

No, I'm not. That Avery wouldn't have bought a bracelet simply because she liked it, and she would have spent all day at the Galleria to get the most out of her ticket, even if she was bored the whole time. That Avery wouldn't be looking at Benson and wondering if it would be worth kissing him, no matter the heartbreak that will come with it.

Texts come in from my cousins immediately, making Benson chuckle as he starts up a conversation.

Poppy:

> Mr. Sexy-Benson or a different one?

Avery:

> The very same.

Poppy:

> I think I need a picture to be sure you're not phishing…

Sadie:

Uhh…taking care of her how?? That can mean so many things. And I agree photo evidence is required.

Avery:

And ruin my mysteriously handsome stranger status? Not biting. Dani can vouch for me.

Sadie:

Dani, is this true?

Lucy:

You realize you can't claim "handsome" without proof, right? As of now you're just a mysterious stranger. According to a lot of books and podcasts, those are also called "kidnappers." I'm expecting a photo of Avery with today's newspaper at any moment.

Sadie:

Also the fact that you won't give us any photographic evidence is concerning…

Lucy:

I for one would like to state that my bank account has a number smaller than my age, so meeting a ransom is going to be tough. I'll dip into my savings if I must, but don't expect much!

Benson laughs out loud as soon as he reads Lucy's last text, shaking his head. Unfortunately for Lucy, she's probably not lying about her bank account. Her mother's destination wedding plus frequent flights to Canada are likely hurting her financial situation. "There are so many ways I could take this," he mutters, thumb hovering over the keyboard.

I'm feeling more adventurous than usual, so I say, "What if you sent a picture of a small part of you? I can be in it so they at least know I'm alive."

Eyes dancing, he opens the camera and flips it to selfie mode, lining it up so only one of his ears is in the shot with me. I'm about to bust up laughing, so I cover my mouth with my hand right as he hits the shutter button.

"Perfect," he says and starts typing.

Avery:

> Wow, tough crowd. Reluctant to scrounge up a couple bucks to save your cousin from her incredibly handsome captor? For the record, I have plenty of my own money. *winky face* But if you insist…

He sends the photo, and the responses come quickly.

Poppy:

> Not what I had in mind…

Lucy:

> There he goes throwing that "handsome" word around again. *raised eyebrow emoji*

Poppy:

> Avery, if you're in trouble, text our safe word.

Lucy:

> Avery definitely looks more kidnapped than charmed by her mysterious stranger there…

"Do we have a safe word?" I ask with a laugh. "If we do, I don't know what it is. Maybe you should send an actual picture before they start looking up how to call the Italian police."

Benson takes a quick selfie of his forehead and sends that along with a text.

What are you talking about? That's my sexy ear. But if you need more…

Is that a six finger hairline? Are you "balding"?

"Ouch." He touches his hairline, which is not receding in any way, and I'm so tempted to run my fingers through his hair and assure him of as much. My hand is halfway to him when Dani finally jumps into the chat.

Ah, yes. The forehead. Many a relationship has started with the thought, "Man, that's a sexy forehead!"

You're not helping your case, mister.

I'm very much not okay with our cousin chat getting commandeered by a weirdo. Get outta here, Benson! And be nice to Avery!

Ugh… How come all the good stuff always happens when I walk away from my phone??!!

Dani:

> For the record, Benson really is buying the most expensive copy of my book, so I'm a fan!

> Unless he hurts Avery. Then he'd better be prepared for a world of hurt.

Benson turns to me and smiles warmly. "Your sister is pretty great. The cousins too."

"Yeah," I agree. "And you don't have to keep talking to them. They're a lot." I try to grab my phone, but Benson holds it out of my reach and starts typing one-handed. Oh, to have giant man hands.

Avery:

> Okay, fine. You've all convinced me. Or maybe Avery is ready to strangle me and steal her phone back. So for your peace of mind, I am willing to comply.

He looks at me with those dancing eyes and gestures with his head for me to come closer. I do, and he recreates the photo we sent to Dani on our first day in Florence, his lips pressed to my cheek. Only, this time it feels so much different. This isn't a stranger invading my bubble and catching me off guard. This is a man I've spent hours upon hours with over the last several days, to the point where I have no idea how I'm going to say goodbye to him when I have to go home tomorrow.

Once that picture is sent, he locks my phone and slips it into his pocket. "You need cake," he says and waves down a waiter.

What I need is to stop imagining a world where we can keep having nights like this forever.

CHAPTER 10
Avery

BENSON GRABS TWO PLATES from the waiter, one with a layered pastry-type cake covered in fruit and one with a square of chocolate tiramisu that looks so good I want to cry. Regular tiramisu is good, but this is chocolate on chocolate and sent straight from heaven. I have my fork at the ready even before Benson places the tiramisu in front of me. "Easy!" he says with a laugh as I dig in and stuff a bite into my mouth. "I nearly lost a finger to your chocolate addiction just now."

"Don't be such a chocolate-hating baby," I say through a mouthful of chocolate mascarpone. "Eat your own...what is that?"

"Torta Nuziale."

"What is that in English?"

Laughing, he picks up a fork and takes a bite of his dessert. "It's cake, Avery."

"Can I try it?" I reach my fork over, but he nudges my arm away.

"With that chocolate-tainted thing? Absolutely not." But then he gathers up another bite with his own fork and holds it toward me.

It seems we're at the feeding each other stage of things, and my heart starts beating a samba in my chest. Suddenly all my knowledge and motor function when it comes to how to eat from a fork is gone, and as I lean forward to accept his offering, I'm so nervous that when someone shouts something nearby, it makes me jump and miss the fork, leaving a splat of cream on my cheek.

Super classy.

But Benson practically invented classy, something he reminds me when he picks up a napkin and wipes the cream away. "Can't take you anywhere," he jokes. I know it's a joke because this man has taken me *everywhere*. I saw all of the best parts of Florence, things I wouldn't have seen if I had stuck to my plan, and Benson chose to do that for me. He gave up the chance to hang out with one of his best friends so he could give me an experience I will never forget.

I wish I had a way to thank him.

This time when he offers the bite of cake, it makes it into my mouth, and I smile as the tang of berries combines with the sweet pastry and cool cream. "That's amazing!" I say with my mouth still full, though I am intelligent enough to cover my mouth with my hand as I do. I am a lady, after all.

"Way better than yours," he agrees.

Seriously, what does this man have against chocolate? "You haven't tried it!" I scoop up as much tiramisu as I can onto my fork and hold it in his direction. "Just one bite."

He eyes it warily. "That is the biggest bite I have ever seen."

"Are you six? It's just chocolate. You'll survive trying it one more time."

"I'm not so convinced." He shakes his head, blue eyes dancing with amusement as he grabs hold of my wrist before I can move the dessert closer. "What if I'm allergic?"

I hadn't thought about that, and suddenly I'm worried I put him in danger by dragging him to that chocolate shop the other day. "Are you?"

He chuckles. "No. But I appreciate you being worried that I am."

"You really won't try it? Not even a little bit?"

He shifts my hand to my own mouth and lets go, shaking his head. "Not unless the outcome feels worth it."

What in the world does that mean? Is he waiting for the right chocolate or something? But what could be better than chocolate tiramisu?

Sighing, I eat the massive bite of dessert and savor the flavor before swallowing and admitting defeat. "I guess you can't be perfect. I had such high hopes for..." I trail off when I notice the way he's staring at my mouth. "What? Do I have something on my face again?" I swipe my tongue and taste chocolate, and I realize with horror I have mascarpone smeared across my upper lip. I grab a napkin to make myself presentable again.

Benson stops me, taking hold of my wrist before I can reach my mouth. His gaze darkens, filling my stomach with a flock of birds, and I stop breathing as his expression heats. I can almost see a battle happening behind his eyes, and I wonder which part of him is going to lose.

I don't have to wonder for long. He swears under his breath, and then he leans forward and covers my mouth with his, kissing the chocolate from my lips.

And this man is *thorough*.

Every thought flees my mind as he slides a hand behind my neck to pull me closer, his lips exploring mine until I can't breathe.

When he pulls away, his tongue running across his lip, I feel like I might implode.

"So?" I breathe, as if the only thing that matters right now is his opinion of the tiniest bit of chocolate he just tasted.

He grins. "Worth it." Then he's back, mouth crashing into mine. One hand in my hair, he uses the other to pull my chair flush against his without breaking from my mouth, and then he deepens the kiss, drawing a gasp out of me that gets swallowed up in the kiss. This man kisses exactly how I thought he would—confidently, skillfully, *deliciously*—and I'm floating. Italy has been one of the most amazing experiences of my life, but nothing in Florence compares to this right here. Right now. I could get lost in this kiss and never make it out again, and I wouldn't care.

When my hands roam from Benson's chest and up into his hair, he shudders and breaks the kiss, keeping our foreheads pressed together.

"You're going to get me into trouble," he murmurs and cups my cheek with his warm palm.

"You started it," I murmur back. I'm trying to breathe again, but I don't know if I'll be the same after that. Kissing Benson is unlike anything I've ever felt before, and learning that now... Reality is already sinking in, leaving me with a hollow feeling in my chest. Tomorrow, all of this will be over.

"No," Benson says, as if he can sense where my thoughts are going. He kisses me again, this time so softly that my heart throbs. "Dance with me," he whispers against my mouth. "Don't let this night end."

I nod. I will do anything this man wants me to do. For however long he wants me to do it.

After we send Riccardo and Siena to the honeymoon suite with cheers and tossed flower petals, we wander the streets of Florence hand in hand as the sky turns from inky black to a soft blue. We're both quiet, simply enjoying the moment, and Benson drops me off at my hotel room door just before sunrise. Neither of us speaks; I think we both got hit hard with the reality that our time is coming to an end, and talking would only make the morning come sooner.

I don't reach for my key, instead leaning up on my toes and pressing my lips to Benson's. He guides me back a step until I'm flush against the door, and the kiss heats between us, hands and lips and bodies pressed together. It's sweet and desperate and full of longing all at the same time, and it hurts when Benson breaks the connection.

I'm not ready.

"What if you change your flight?" he whispers before touching a kiss to the soft skin below my ear. "Fly back with me this afternoon." His lips move to my neck, beginning a trail down to my collar bone.

Shivering, I cling to his arms to keep myself from melting into a puddle. He has no idea how good that sounds and how much I don't want to leave Italy at all. But at some point this has to end, and we both know it. I need to be responsible Avery again. "No," I whisper.

His kisses pause, and he lifts his head to meet my gaze with heavy eyes. He doesn't have to speak for me to hear his question.

Pressing my hand to his cheek, I search for the words I need. "This week has been the best week of my life, Benson. All thanks to you. But it's going to be hard enough to leave as it is, and I think you were right all along. A clean break…"

His throat bobs, and he presses his hand over mine, curling his fingers around mine and pulling them to his lips. "You're right. But I don't want you to be right."

I won't suggest we try a long-distance relationship. I know him well enough to know he still isn't the guy who will commit. No matter how much he likes me, he's not going to try. He would have asked for my number or my last name or *something* if he thought this could go beyond today.

A tear slides down my cheek, and Benson brushes it away with his thumb. He shouldn't have bothered; more will come. "Keep being brave, Avery Grace," he murmurs and touches a soft kiss to my lips. "The world needs the woman you really are. Not the one you think you should be."

And here come the real tears. "She never would have come back if not for you. I don't… How can I thank…" I swallow as the emotions start to overwhelm me.

Benson pulls me into his arms, wrapping me up in a tight embrace that shuts out the world. I cry into his chest, hating that I fell so hard so fast. This wasn't supposed to happen. I wasn't supposed to come on this trip, I wasn't supposed to meet the perfect man, and I definitely wasn't supposed to open my raw and vulnerable heart to him.

What do I do now?

"I should go," he says, but he doesn't make any effort to move. Instead, he starts rubbing small circles on my back, his hand warm and soothing as the fingers of his other hand work their way into my hair. It's a testament to how perfect this man is. Instead of telling me I shouldn't be crying over a week-long fling, he's simply letting me cry and offering silent comfort.

Nothing in the world is ever going to compare to this spot right here, held in his strong arms and surrounded by his warmth.

"You can do anything," he murmurs as he finally pulls away. He brushes the tears from my cheek, then steps back, his expression as mournful as I feel. When he opens his mouth again, I hope he'll say we should keep in touch, but he closes it again with a shake of his head, hands me my phone, and turns around, walking away without looking back.

As he rounds the corner, I stare at the place he disappears, feeling like my entire world has been shaken, leaving me unsteady and fragile.

CHAPTER II
Benson

WALKING AWAY FROM SOMEONE has never been harder. I cross the hotel to Nick's room with heavy feet, like they are as convinced as the rest of me that I shouldn't have left Avery. Pausing with my hand on the door, I look back the way I came as if I might see her through the walls. It's a good thing I can't. I need to get a couple hours of sleep before I head to the airport and trek back to New York. I have less than a day at home, and then I'll be on a flight to my next temporary destination for almost a month, and that's the only reason I'm not rushing back to the woman who fills a space in me I didn't realize was empty.

I don't know how to make it work. I don't even know if I'm capable of a real relationship. I'm too transient, and my business can't function standing still. I've been doing this work for almost a decade, and I'm good at it. It makes me feel fulfilled and successful and valuable, and that's a hard thing to give up when I've spent my life jumping from one thing to the next, trying to find something that sticks.

But Avery makes me feel...something.

Of course I can't think of the right word. *Important, useful, wanted.* Like I matter.

Whole.

She makes me feel *complete.* And I can't do the same for her, so I need to walk away.

I slide my phone from my pocket and pull up her number in my contacts, gazing at the picture I set for her. It's from three days ago, and

Avery looks absolutely breathtaking. She always does, but that day we found ourselves at the Piazzale Michelangelo right at sunset. The hill overlooks Florence, offering a panoramic view of the city that can't be beat. But it's Avery who shines the brightest in the photo, her laughing smile so much more beautiful than the city behind her or the golden sky overhead.

I delete the contact, a pang settling in my chest even if it's for the best. I delete Dani's info as well, though I can't bring myself to block her number in case she texts me again. I don't want the temptation of trying to find Avery when I can't have her, but if the universe—or a presumptuous sister—wants us to find each other again…

Sighing, I pocket my phone and slip into the room, closing the door—and Avery—behind me.

CHAPTER 12
Avery

JET LAG IS THE literal worst, which is why I'm rearranging my entire apartment at three in the morning. My lack of sleep definitely has nothing to do with the gold bracelet I found tucked into the side pocket of my purse when I was cleaning my bags out after I got home. It's the bracelet I stared at so many times but didn't buy, and somehow Benson snuck it into my purse, likely before we had the conversation about it at the wedding.

Okay, so maybe I burst into tears when I found it and spent an embarrassing amount of time stroking the tiny little stars woven into the chain, but I'm fine now.

Totally fine.

I groan as I heave myself against the massive armchair I keep in my living room, trying to force it down the hall.

I've decided to turn my spare bedroom into a book room because it's not like I ever have guests, and I needed something to keep my mind off perfect men in perfect cities. Now the extra bed frame from the spare room is in pieces in my closet, the mattress is tucked under *my* bed, and my emptied bookshelves are ready to move from my room to the spare. I figured I should get the chair moved first since it takes up the most space, but I didn't anticipate this thing weighing a million tons.

I should have waited until Dani was back in town so I could use her help. And by Dani I mean the muscly reformed playboy she's dating. Heck, I would take any of my cousins and their men, even if I've barely interacted with the guys they're dating. Not that they're close enough to help. Sadie's new boyfriend lives here in Utah, but Chloe's in North Carolina now and Lucy fell in love with Prince Edward Island along with her new man. Though, who *wouldn't* fall in love with that place? Her boyfriend is cool, if unavailable to help me move furniture.

It's eerie the way most of my cousins have all found their person recently and dumb that I can't reap the benefits of their new relationships.

Maybe I'm just feeling lonely.

"It's the jet lag," I tell myself and give the chair another massive shove, managing to get the chair to slide a few inches along the carpet. At least it's moving, but with every push I can't stop thinking about how this whole endeavor would have been a cinch if Bens…

Nope. I can't let myself think about him. I said we would have a clean break, and I have to make that real. Changing my phone background to one of the few pictures I have of him—the one of him kissing my cheek at the wedding—might not be a great way to keep him out of my head, but I am a strong, independent woman. I can look at a picture of a handsome man without bursting into tears.

At least, I'll be able to do that tomorrow. Once I'm back at work and in routine and surrounded by distractions rather than left to my own devices (AKA scrolling through all the pictures Benson took with my phone). The only pictures I took were in rare moments when I was alone, so they're all lame. If Benson was there, I was too focused on him to care about immortalizing the scenery.

My foot slips on my next push, sending me tumbling to the floor. It's a good thing I'm on the ground floor of my complex and don't have downstairs neighbors, or who knows what they might have heard. Thumps and scrapes and the occasional crying probably sound questionable when taken out of context.

It's time for a break, even if I'm only getting started on the redecorating. I should be in bed, maybe with some sleep meds to get me back on the right schedule, but as soon as I fall asleep, tomorrow will come.

Tomorrow, I have to face Eric again. Despite being on the honeymoon he should have been a part of, I thought very little about my ex last week, and the space was...good. Nice. He's always going to be my friend and my business partner, but if I learned anything from Benson, it's that Eric and I lost our passion for each other, and I don't think either of us really cared.

Basically, Italy brought me some much-needed closure, and I have to hope Eric came to his own conclusions so we can move on with our lives. I think it will be good to have his friend, Sonny, in town for a bit to help us with boosting our marketing strategies. Sonny can keep Eric occupied and help us scale up our business, and I can settle back into my job and find a new normal.

Talk about good timing.

"Okay, Avery," I say, forcing myself back to my feet and rolling up my sleeves. The star-chain bracelet sparkles in the light, drawing my attention to my wrist and sending a sharp pang of longing through me. I shouldn't be wearing it while moving furniture, but seeing it next to the one I bought myself, I'm not sure I'll ever be able to take it off. I shake my head and focus on finding the will to move the chair that's twice my size. "You're going to get this chair in the room, and then you're going to move all your books because you were stupid enough to put them on your bed instead of the floor, and then you're going to go to sleep because you have to work in the morning."

Never mind that it's already technically morning.

I rub my hands together and take a deep breath. I'm strong enough to take care of myself, and I can move a chair. Easy peasy.

It takes me almost an hour with a multitude of breaks, both to give my muscles a rest and to pump myself up again.

The chair must weigh four hundred pounds, and I'm going to have to ask Grandma Sue where she got it because it seems to be made of solid oak. When she updated the furniture in her house right as I was graduating college and moving into my own place, I begged her to let me take the armchair because I used to spend hours sitting in it and reading books whenever I was at her house. When we were kids, it fit me, Dani, and Sadie all at the same time.

I miss reading with them like that. Sadie is only four years younger than me, but Lucy, Chloe, and Poppy are all young and close enough in age that before we grew close as the six of us, it tended to be three and three. Dani and I talk all the time, obviously, but it's been a while since I had a good book conversation with Sadie that wasn't work-related. I love having her as one of my contracted editors—she's amazing—but as I stand here staring at this old chair, I'm realizing how little I've treated her as a cousin rather than an employee.

It's so dumb. We've all been close since we were little—all of my cousins are more like extra sisters—and I hate that things have changed.

I've been a terrible sister.

Grabbing my phone, I take a moment to gaze at the picture of Benson and me, and then I pull up the camera and snap a picture of the armchair, sending it to Dani and Sadie. They won't respond—it's literally the middle of the night—but the nostalgia is hitting hard, and I want to try to be better.

Benson told me to be brave and be myself, and putting in a valiant effort is the least I can do to repay him for taking me under his wing last week and giving me such a magical time in Florence.

I grimace as soon as I hit send. I shouldn't be allowed to text when I'm under the influence of jet lag and heartbreak. Oh well. Exiting my messaging app, I take a few seconds to admire my lock screen again and then head to the master bedroom, ready to start moving books and get this book nook looking...hooky? It's the only word that rhymes, even if it makes no sense.

Exhaustion hits me hard on that last convoluted thought, and one look at the dozens of books littering my mattress in several stacks brings a tired tear to my eye.

This was a bad idea.

Sighing, I grab a blanket and trudge back to the spare room, settling myself in the oversized chair and bringing my feet up off the floor. I'll take a quick power nap, and then I can clear the bed.

I wake with a start, unsure where I am for a solid ten seconds. The lights are still on, but the room feels lighter than it should. Scrambling for my phone, I squint at the blurry screen for a long while before the time finally registers. I'm supposed to be at the office in less than an hour!

"Crap!"

Taking the world's fastest shower and tying my hair back in rushed braids, I dart out the door. After a week of ignoring Eric's texts and emails, the last thing I need is to show up at the office late. In the past, Eric and I made it a competition to see who could get there first. I've already lost today, hands down, but it'll be better if I don't lose by more than half an hour.

But as I make the short drive to work, my stomach starts rumbling, and I can't resist the pull of the Einstein Bros. Bagels up ahead. I've gotten used to my morning pastry and coffee. I'll be sorely disappointed—I don't think anything can beat my Italian breakfasts—but my stomach and sleepy brain will be grateful for this little detour.

Eric texts me while I'm in the drive through line, but at this point it's too late for me to do anything but wait my turn. I'm stuck here.

> Sonny is here and ready to get started. Will you be here soon?

Ah right, Sonny was showing up *today*. While we badly need the help of a consultant, I wish he would have delayed his arrival by a day or two so I could settle back in first. After the week I just had, full of aimless wandering and carpe dieming, I am going to have a hard time jumping into a scheduled, work-first frame of mind.

I'm fully forty-five minutes later than I should be when I finally whirl into the office, one side of a smear-loaded bagel and coffee in hand as I greet Lynda at the reception desk and scurry to Eric's office.

He's in his usual spot at his desk, a happy smile lighting up his face until he looks over at me and the smile fades. He looks...disappointed? I don't think Eric has ever looked at me like this, and a sharp pain stabs me between my ribs. "Finally," he mutters and gestures to the guy sitting across from him. "Ms. Baldwin—" *Whoa, what's with the formality?* "—meet Sonny, our new consultant. Sonny, This is my partner, Avery Baldwin."

I turn to greet the guy who was at one point Eric's best friend. I've heard plenty about him but never met him, and I'm curious to see who...

Sonny has stood to greet me, but his outstretched hand falters halfway. It's a nice hand, big and sturdy at the end of an arm that is well-defined and muscular. That arm is attached to a broad set of shoulders over a solid chest. The kind of chest a girl could lean into and feel at home. Sonny swallows, pulling my eyes up to his throat and his scruff-covered jaw that clenches when my gaze finally rises the rest of the way and meets his.

Benson.

It's *Benson*, in all his handsome glory, his blue eyes wide.

My bagel falls from my hand and splats on the floor. It's by some miracle I keep hold of my coffee rather than dropping it at my feet.

Two thoughts war for dominance in my mind as I try to process what's happening: *Aww, my bagel!* and *What in the name of Jane Austen is* he *doing here?*

TICKET
PASSPORT
N
W
E
S
HOTEL
Time To
Travel

CHAPTER 13
Benson

THIS ISN'T HAPPENING.

This *can't* be happening.

Because if that's Avery standing there with wide, horrified eyes, then the sudden fire in my chest is proof that I didn't shut the door on everything that happened in Italy as firmly as I was supposed to. If that's Avery, I thoroughly kissed my friend's ex-fiancée. Many times. If that's Avery, she is now, if only temporarily, *my boss.*

Crap.

Eric clears his throat. "Avie? You good?"

She blinks, glancing at him only briefly before dropping down and picking up the bagel which, unfortunately, landed smear-side down and left a blob of cream cheese on the industrial carpet. When she straightens back up and tosses the bagel in the trash, her expression is more guarded than it was a second ago. "Um. Hi."

I need to say something. Eric is staring at me, Avery has turned so pale that she might pass out, and my heart is thundering in my chest like I just ran a half-marathon. My brain is full of a sort of whooshing sound that is making it impossible to think clearly.

Focus on the job. It's what I always do, and it might be the only thing to save me from turning this whole thing into a complete disaster.

"Hey," I say and hold out my hand. "Benson West. It's nice to meet you."

That was the wrong move. Avery's eyebrows drop low as her expression shifts from shock to hurt to anger in rapid succession while she takes hold of my hand. Her skin is warm and soft, exactly how I remember it, and I catch a hint of her intoxicating peach scent that makes my whole body sizzle with memories of our last night in Italy. Instinct tells me to pivot and pull her in for a hug, maybe a kiss, because I haven't been able to get her out of my head since leaving her side at the hotel, but I resist.

There's a time and place for casual make-outs, and this is not it.

"So nice to finally *meet* you," Avery says, her tone sharp. She's still holding my hand, and it feels like she's trying to squeeze as hard as she can. "*Mr. Greer* has spoken so highly of you."

Eric's expression hardens when she uses his last name, though he's the one who did it first. All morning, he's been talking about his pragmatic partner, Ms. Baldwin, and I was imagining a straitlaced woman in her mid-forties. Not the spunky and adventurous woman I spent a week in Italy with. Either Eric has no idea who he was going to marry, or there's more to Avery's past than losing her courage to break free.

"Uh." Eric clears his throat. "Avery, if you're ready, why don't you give Sonny a rundown of our current marketing strategy?"

She just got here, I want to say. *Of course she's not ready.*

But Avery nods, pulling the only empty chair to the side of Eric's desk rather than next to me. She digs a laptop out of her bag and sets it on the desk. "What would you like me to call you?" she asks without looking at me. "Benson, Mr. West, or Sonny?"

Eric's the only person aside from my family who calls me Sonny anymore, and I asked him to call me Benson when I showed up at the office this morning. But he's not a guy who does well with losing old habits, which makes me curious about his reference to Avery by her last name. He called her that in all his emails too, so has he always called his fiancée Ms. Baldwin? Like, did he go around introducing her to his family and friends that way?

Super romantic, dude.

"Benson is great," I say, reminding myself that I have no say in any of Eric's relationships. Especially not this one. "And you?"

That earns me a glance. I got into the habit of using both Avery's first and middle name while we were in Florence, and she seemed to like it. But her pained glare makes me think I won't be allowed that liberty here. "Avery is fine," she says, typing in the password on her computer.

When it boots up, she turns the laptop so I can see and pulls up a basic PowerPoint, which makes me internally groan. I knew I had my work cut out for me when I accepted Eric's offer, but knowing Avery is the other half of the Rose & Quill duo, I'm sensing things are worse than I anticipated. It's nothing against Avery—I don't know her very well—but I do know Eric. Catching up with him for a few minutes this morning was enough to tell me he's the same guy I knew in college, which means he is exclusively by-the-book and rarely thinks outside the box, if ever. And the Avery I first met, the one who had planned to marry Eric Greer, can't possibly be the kind of person who might push the boundaries of his boxes and take some risks to make their company shine.

In the time since she walked into the office, she has lost some of the vibrancy that bloomed last week, like Eric is some life-sucking leech. He's a good guy—always has been—but there's no way he was ever right for Avery.

Avery starts going through the presentation, but I barely listen as she lists out a few different ideas she and Eric have had to boost their company. Normally, I try to incorporate as much of my clients' input as I can because authenticity is so invaluable when it comes to marketing and building a brand. But Avery isn't exactly being authentic right now. She is muted and monotone, constantly looking at Eric though he's scrolling through something on his computer and paying about as much attention as I am.

I'm going to guess these were all his ideas.

"What else do you have?" I ask as soon as Avery hits the end of the presentation.

My question surprises both co-owners. Avery's mouth slips open, and Eric looks over at me with his eyebrows pulled low.

"Else?" Avery asks at the same time Eric says, "Those are the optimal strategies."

I hold back a laugh and decide to focus on Eric first, since he seems to be the stronger voice in this partnership. "And they're great." I have no idea if they're great because I was too busy staring at Avery rather than listening to the strategies she was laying out. I look at her again now, wishing she didn't look so guarded. "But it's a good idea to throw out any and all ideas, no matter how unconventional."

She takes a breath and opens her mouth.

"We went through dozens of ideas before we landed on these," Eric says. "I know you're the expert here, Sonny, but you haven't worked with anyone in publishing before, so this is kind of new to you."

Technically, I helped revive a dying magazine last year and turn it into a thriving blog, but I keep that to myself. One of the reasons I came here was to revive my friendship with Eric, and I won't be able to do that if I push against him at every turn. Even if we didn't always see eye to eye, he was like family to me when we were younger and I felt alienated from my real family. He was there for me when no one else was and is the single reason I got my degree. I owe him a lot.

My stomach twists as my mind flashes back to the way I acted with Avery last week. It would be great if Eric never finds out about any of that.

Avery glances between Eric and me, hardly confident in her expression and posture, but this time she speaks up. "What if—"

"Oh, I should take this," Eric says, holding up his phone as he stands. "Avie, why don't you go into some more detail on that first plan."

The instant he's out of the room, Avery and I talk at the same time.

"Why are you here?"

"Is he always like that?"

Avery huffs and folds her arms. I wonder if she realizes her shirt is on backwards or if that was a deliberate choice. "Do you make a habit of gaslighting people? Or are you an evil twin?"

Chuckling, I fold my arms to match her. The real Avery is back now that Eric is gone, though *gaslighting* is a bit strong of a word. "Why would my twin be evil?"

"He wouldn't because you're the evil one."

"Do all sets of twins have an evil half and a good half? I don't have a twin, by the way."

She groans, tugging on the two wet braids hanging over her shoulders. "Why did you pretend not to know me, Benson?"

I wish that question was easy to answer. "Because we agreed to anonymity," I reply, even if it's not the right thing to say.

She grits her teeth, letting her eyes rove over me as if she's still wondering if I have a doppelganger out there somewhere. "What's the point of anonymity when I already know you?" she asks eventually.

I shake my head. "You know what I showed you in Italy." Which, to be fair, was pretty much the whole me. I don't often hide behind masks, particularly when it comes to dating.

Snorting an unamused laugh, Avery stands and plants her hands on the desk so she can look down at me as she speaks. "You graduated from the University of Utah twelve years ago and lived in an old house in the Avenues and once gift-wrapped everything Eric owned because you thought he was being too uptight during finals week."

Ah. "You know all that?"

"Eric has talked about you a lot."

"So you knew who I was the whole time." Was I a complete idiot, thinking I had found the perfect moment to let go of my past and just be me?

"Well, no." She softens, grabbing one of her braids again. "I've only seen a few pictures of you, and they were from your college years. You don't exactly look the same." Then her eyes go wide, and she points at me. "But you! You had my phone for two days straight, and you didn't put the pieces together?"

"I thought I was respecting your privacy by not reading any of the texts from 'Colonel Buzzkill.'" I put the nickname in air quotes. "Does Eric know that's what he's listed as in your phone?"

"What about all the emails from Rose & Quill?" she asks, skipping over my question.

I sigh. This conversation isn't going to end anytime soon unless I try to steer things away from Italy. "I figured you were on their email list or something because of Dani. And if I'm being honest, I was kind of distracted." *How is that supposed to help?*

Scoffing, Avery waves her arm over me. "Too busy flirting with the first random girl you bumped into?"

The question feels like a slap in the face. Is that what she thought that was? Did she miss the parts where I told her how interesting she was, how beautiful, how fascinating to watch when she found something that caught her attention? "Flirting with a woman who interested me, yes," I admit, "but we both knew it was a fling and wouldn't go beyond last week. That's over now."

Now it's Avery's turn to look slapped, and she sinks back into her chair. "So that's it?" she asks, her voice thin. "We have this magical week in Florence, and now we pretend it never happened?"

I swear under my breath, rubbing my jaw as the memory of her lips on mine hits me hard. *Magical* is a pretty apt descriptor, though it's not one I would have chosen on my own. "That's it."

"What if I don't agree?"

"It doesn't matter."

"Look me in the eyes and tell me you're not still attracted to me."

She needs to stop. She needs to stop being bold and passionate and fiery because every time she pushes back and shows me she's stronger than she looks, it makes the attraction that much worse. And I can't be attracted to her. Not now that I know who she is. Attraction will only lead to disaster. "I'm not doing this, Avery." My words come out somewhere between a sigh and a growl because a large part of me is mapping out the difference between the woman in front of me right now and the one who demurely explained her ex's terrible marketing plans. She's different when he's around, and not in a good way. I want to fix that.

But I can't.

Her eyes glisten with tears, but anger seems to hold them back. "Why not?"

"Because you're my boss."

"That's not true, nor is it a good enough reason."

I knew it wouldn't be. "Because of Eric then."

"Eric?" She looks out the open door, but their office is small enough that I'm assuming Eric went outside, or we would have heard his phone conversation.

"Yes. Things between us"—I gesture from her to me—"are a lot more complicated now that he's a part of this."

"Feel free to elaborate," she grinds out, glaring at me.

I'd rather not, but she'll keep pushing if I don't give her a good enough reason to let Italy go. "I may have stolen his girlfriend in college."

Her glare softens in her surprise. "That was *you*?"

"Ah, so he didn't tell you that part of the story?" *Lucky me.* "I'm guessing that means he didn't tell you about how she cheated on me less than a week later."

"He did tell me that, actually. But what does a relationship over a decade ago have to do with anything?"

I'm regretting this conversation with every passing second. Does she really want me to lay it all out for her? Isn't it obvious? "I'm not going to make moves on someone my friend was going to marry."

"The moves have already been made, Benson," Avery says sharply, but her face blossoms with crimson as if she's remembering the kisses we shared. Just like I am. "You can't pretend Italy didn't happen."

Oh, but I want to. I want to put this all behind me and do my job and forget how deeply difficult it was to leave this woman behind.

"And Eric and I *broke up*," she adds, as if that settles it.

"Barely," I counter. I don't know how long it's been—Eric didn't mention ever being engaged when we were catching up this morning—but I have some pretty clear reasons to think the breakup was recent. "You can't tell me there aren't still feelings between the two of you, because you were crying over the guy when we first met."

Avery gasps, but she doesn't have an argument. She never said if the breakup was mutual or if he made the choice for her. With Eric, it could have gone either way. "So it's okay for you to flirt with some other guy's ex, but not Eric's?" she asks, shaking her head. "Really classy, Benson."

"No one said I was perfect," I grumble. I didn't expect the sting of her judgment, and I don't like it. How can she not understand that this is totally different from flirting with a stranger?

Swallowing, she looks down at her hands, and it's only now that I notice she's wearing the bracelet I bought her. "I did," she whispers, sending a wave of guilt over me.

"Sorry about that," Eric says, whirling into the room and plopping back into his chair. "I swear, our printer is the literal worst, and I'm so glad we're switching to a different company. Did you guys get some good discussion going?"

We sure did, though maybe *good* isn't the right word for it. At least now I can say with certainty there won't be any tension between Avery and me anymore. Not the good kind, anyway.

I'm more disappointed about that than I should be.

TICKET
PASSPORT
N
W
E
S
HOTEL
Time To
Travel

CHAPTER 14

Avery

SONNY IS BENSON.

What is who?

Sonny. The marketing guy Eric hired. It's BENSON.

Benson, the guy you fell in love with in Italy? That Benson?

I did NOT fall in love with him! But yes, that one. He's HERE. And he's WORKING WITH ME.

Why are you saying this like it's a problem? Now you can either lay one on him and get a second chance romance or you can tell me what he drives and I'll egg his car. Sounds like a winning situation either way.

> **Avery:**
>
> This is in no way a winning situation! And have you ever tried to clean up eggs? It's awful.
>
> More to the point, Benson is acting like Italy never happened and treating me like I'm nothing but his coworker!

HE'S ALSO SITTING A few feet from me *in my office*, since the only available desk in Rose & Quill headquarters is the one Sadie sometimes uses if she's not working from home. It's in my office with me because there was nowhere else to put it, and I've never minded sharing my space with my cousin. Sharing with a large, overly attractive man with the most tantalizing scent that reminds me of dancing at an Italian wedding and makes me crave tiramisu?

I'm dying here.

> **Dani:**
>
> Do coworkers normally do that thing with the tiramisu? If so, you and I have had VERY different coworker experiences. (And I only have to clean the eggs up if I get caught...)

> **Avery:**
>
> NO EGGS. Besides, he's here to make sure we don't go under and you can keep publishing books.

> **Dani:**
>
> Yay for book publishing! Boo for him being a man who thinks he can lock his feelings away in a tiny little box and pretend like you're not soulmates.

> *gif of woman licking pudding off a spoon*

Avery:

> We are not soulmates.

> I regret telling you about the tiramisu.

Dani:

> From what you told me, you two are endgame and he was totally into you, so I don't see what the problem is here.

Avery:

> He pretended not to know me, Dani. He clearly didn't have feelings for me.

Movement catches my eye, and I look over right as Benson slides out of his suit coat, showing off his arms and shoulders—features I know better than I should. I wondered in Italy what he did to give him that definition, but now my curiosity is worse. How does a consultant keep up a fitness routine when he's constantly on the road, going from business to business and living out of hotels?

At least now I know why he doesn't commit. He's never in one place long enough to make any promises.

My phone buzzes, pulling my attention from the care Benson takes as he drapes the jacket on the back of his chair.

Dani:

> I'm calling bulls

> Sorry, Mason walked in and distracted me before I finished that text. You catch my drift.

Before I can form a response, a message comes through on my computer.

I am more than grateful for the interruption. More likely than not, Lynda wants to catch up and see how I'm doing now that I'm back from my trip. Grabbing my coffee in case this turns into a long chat, I avoid looking at Benson as I head into the hall, though I can feel his eyes on me.

This is going to be the worst month of my life.

"Rough morning?" Lynda asks as I approach her desk. Her smile is warm and familiar, and I'm gladder than ever that she agreed to work with us. She is always a bright spot in my day.

I flop into the chair she keeps next to her own and sigh. "How could you tell?"

"Your shirt is backwards."

Gasping, I look down and cringe when I realize she's right. No wonder Eric was giving me that disappointed look. "Jet lag," I say with a moan. "It wasn't nearly as bad going the other direction."

"You must have had something distracting you." For some reason, she offers that comment with a wink, and I sit up a bit, not sure I like the knowing glint in her eyes. "How was Italy?"

I groan. "You heard everything, didn't you?" I tend to forget how small this office is and how well the sound carries. It's why Eric often takes his phone calls outside on the little balcony we share with the next office over. I forgot about Lynda when I was arguing with Benson earlier, and we weren't exactly quiet.

Her smile turning sympathetic, Lynda pats my arm at the same time she hands me a butterscotch from the bowl on her desk. "Tell me all about it."

And I do. Keeping my voice low, I give her the rundown of the entire trip, starting on the plane from JFK and ending with my shock this morning. It feels good to get it all out there without anyone throwing in comments about how I should take advantage of the hot guy while I've got him. If anyone will understand why this is so complicated, Lynda will.

She was going to be my mother-in-law, after all.

"What am I supposed to do?" I ask, leaning my head on her shoulder and letting her wrap me in a warm hug. Her hugs are second only to my own mom's. "Am I supposed to forget everything I felt in Florence? I don't want to hurt Eric, but I also…"

"Oh, sweetie, Eric's a grown man. He'll be fine." She says that, but her voice is full of hesitation.

I lift my head to stare at her. "I'm fully aware that, as his mom, you're going to be biased. You can say what you mean."

"I did say what I mean. He made his choice to give you up, and he has to live with that decision. It might hurt him for a bit, but he'll move on, just like you did."

Did I move on? Sure, I happily gave up all control to Benson and let him kiss me senseless multiple times, but it was just a fling. I knew it was temporary and I wouldn't see him again.

But then he showed up. In Utah. To help *my company.*

Sighing, I drop my head back onto Lynda's shoulder and breathe in her subtly floral scent. She smells a little like the wedding did in Florence, only without the bonus of garlic and bread. "Even if I do feel something," I mutter, "it's not like it can go anywhere. He made it pretty clear where he stands."

"Did he?"

"You heard him."

"I heard a man who is confused and doesn't want to hurt his friend again." Lynda pushes me up again and pierces me with her mom-stare. The one that digs in and makes you feel like you can't hide anything, no matter how much you want to. "I heard a man who couldn't deny his attraction to you. I can't blame him. You're wonderful, Avery, and he knows it. But," she pats my cheek, "Benson has always been a lost soul."

Curious, I glance down the hall to make sure Eric and Benson are both still in their respective offices. "How well do you know him?"

"It's been a few years since I last saw him, but when the boys were in college, he spent most of his holidays at our house."

"Where's his family?"

"Here in Utah."

I frown. "So why did he stay with you?"

"Like I said. Lost. But it's not my place to talk, so that's all I'll say on the matter."

"But you're supposed to tell me what to do!" I complain. I shouldn't. I know all too well how fortunate I am that Lynda still treats me like a daughter even though Eric and I never tied the knot, and I shouldn't push the boundaries of our relationship. But I'm feeling as lost as Benson apparently is, and this situation is so unlike anything I've ever dealt with.

"Sweetie." Lynda tugs on one of my braids. "I can't do that, and you and I both know you'll do the opposite of whatever I tell you."

"I will not!"

She raises an eyebrow.

Rolling my eyes, I take a long sip of my coffee and stand. "Fine. I'll figure it out on my own. But don't be surprised when I come crying to you when it all falls apart. I don't..." I frown. "I don't know if I can trust myself lately. I wasn't myself last week, but I don't think I was myself before that either."

I feel like I've hit two extremes—the adventurous, let-it-all-loose woman in Italy, and the strait-laced rule-follower of recent years. The Avery I want to be is somewhere in the middle, but I'm not sure how to find her.

I also don't have *time* to find her. Right now, I need to focus on the company and getting us to a sustainable place. Dani and our other authors deserve my full attention, no matter how distracting Benson is going to be. It's not like he'd go for a relationship, so I'm going to have to do my best to ignore him.

"How are submissions looking?" I ask at full volume. Forcing myself into work mode.

"Overwhelming," Lynda replies with a smile. "But I think that's a good thing. It means people want to be a part of Rose & Quill."

It also means more to sort through to find the books that are worth our time. "Anything good?"

"I'll email you the promising ones. You have a better eye for those than I do."

I don't know about that. We've only published a couple dozen books since we started a few years ago, and Dani's is the only one that took off. Yeah, the others are doing better thanks to Dani's success, but would they have thrived on their own with a more established publisher?

Sometimes I wonder why I picked a career that holds me responsible for so many people's livelihoods, but then I can't imagine doing anything else. This is literally my dream job.

"Yes, send them over," I say and take another sip of coffee. "I need to catch up on emails, but I'm going to need something more fun to distract me."

Lynda's expression turns mischievous. "From the handsome man in your office?"

I narrow my eyes and point a finger at her. "From the more tedious work. Don't go making more out of this than there is, Lynda Greer."

As she laughs, I turn and head to the bathroom to fix my shirt, trying not to think about how my disheveled state could be part of the reason Benson changed his mind about me. It's stupid—aside from at the wedding, I wasn't exactly all dolled up by the end of the week in Italy—but my brain wants a reason for his shift in interest. It shouldn't matter, but...

But it really matters.

Once I look more presentable, I make my way back to my office but am stopped in the hallway outside my door by a soft question.

"How was Italy?" Eric meets my gaze from his desk, his eyebrows low and his lips pursed. It's the look he gets when he's sad, and guilt pools in my stomach. He was as excited about that trip as I was, though I don't think he would have enjoyed the way I spent it. He would have stuck to the schedule.

I do my best to smile. "It was nice. I think you would have liked the art galleries."

"Please tell me you ate a lot of chocolate like you planned to."

Benson coughs behind me, making my face burn red.

Nodding, I duck my head to try to hide my blush until my face cools down. "I did, yeah. It was amazing. I brought some home, if you want to try it."

"Only if you want to share. I know better than to get between you and your chocolate." He smiles when I look up again, but it looks forced. I don't blame him. This might be the longest non-work conversation we've had in months, and it feels like we barely know each other. It's amazing how six years can fizzle away after one decision.

Tapping my finger on my coffee cup, I try to come up with something else to say but have nothing. "Well, I should get to work. Lots to catch up on."

"Yeah," he agrees, but his expression is still sad. He doesn't seem angry about the trip anymore, if he ever was. Maybe he's still unsure how to coexist, like I am. I may have gotten closure in Italy, but that doesn't make this any easier. "I'm glad you're back," he adds.

I'm not sure I mean it, but I reply, "Me too."

When I turn around and step into my office, Benson is fully focused on his computer and doesn't acknowledge me. I know he was listening because of his well-timed cough, but if he's going to pretend he didn't hear that whole conversation, so am I.

It's not until I've fully settled and jumped into my bursting email inbox that he speaks. "There's only one good way to enjoy chocolate," he murmurs.

Heat floods through me, and though I turn to glare at him, he doesn't look at me. But there's the slightest hint of a smile playing at the corner of his lips, a bit of the flirty side of Benson coming out to play.

What am I supposed to do with that?

TICKET
PASSPORT
N
W
E
S
HOTEL
Time To
Travel

CHAPTER 15
Benson

I SHOULD HAVE GONE back to my hotel. I'm too tired and thrown by seeing Avery again to be good company, and Eric is a lot more enthusiastic about this dinner outing than I am. He's been talking nonstop since we left the office an hour ago, filling me in on the years I've missed, but I just want to go to bed.

But it was Lynda's idea for the two of us to go out to eat and catch up, and I can't deny that woman anything.

At least the food is good.

"I still can't believe it's been eight years since we saw each other last," Eric says, waving his chopsticks around. This is the third time he's said that. "Crazy how life flies by the older we get."

"Crazy," I repeat, shoveling a ton of ramen into my mouth in the hopes that it'll keep me from having to talk. I'd much rather let Eric fill in the silence in case I let slip something about Avery that I shouldn't. Being in that tiny office with her was torture, surrounded by her sweet scent, and every little noise and movement she made pulled my attention away from the work I was trying to concentrate on.

"And you haven't changed," Eric says with a chuckle. "I figured you'd have gotten married long before now."

If I really haven't changed, he should know better than to think that. Maybe I wasn't as committed to casual as I am now, but I've always been flighty, for lack of a better word. College was no different. If Eric hadn't managed to convince me not to change my major from business to graphic design our junior year, I would have never finished a degree, instead jumping around to different paths and never sticking with one thing.

I force a smile and shake my head. "Nah, you know me. Too many things to explore for me to settle down." A question sits on the tip of my tongue, and though I shouldn't ask because I already know the answer, I can't hold it back. I want to hear it from him. "What about you? No one catch your eye?"

Eric's happy expression falters, his eyes dropping to his bowl. "Oh, right. Well, Avery and I were a thing for a while."

He clearly doesn't want to talk about it. I should leave it alone. "Avery, your business partner?" I ask.

He nods. "We met at a book club, actually, and started dating long before we came up with the idea to start Rose & Quill. But that relationship ended a couple of months ago."

"What happened?" That's the question I really want an answer to. How did he give up a woman like Avery? I've only known her for a week, and I fell so hard that I've barely been able to sleep since leaving Italy. I'm not the kind of guy who falls! But I did for Avery, and were I anyone else, I don't think I'd be able to let her go.

Shrugging, Eric looks up and rests his arm on the back of his chair. "I don't know."

Come on, man. You have to give me more than that.

"I guess..." He shakes his head. "We both decided it was for the best. We were more invested in the company than we were in each other."

Avery was crying over this guy. *Sobbing.* Something tells me he wasn't aware of the full scope of her investment in that relationship. "And you still work together?" I ask.

"We have to. I can't handle it all without Avery, and she's not business-minded enough to run the place on her own."

I don't like that answer, and I tuck my hands beneath the table before he sees my clenched fists. Hiding my feelings is as much for Avery's sake as it is the company's. "Do you see your failed relationship affecting Rose & Quill?" I can't do anything to help them if the company is going to suffer under their estrangement, and if that's the case, I might as well head back home and put distance between Avery and me before I start coming up with ideas to spend as much time with her as I can.

I need to be building my business. Not building a relationship with a woman I can't have.

Shrugging again, Eric returns to his food. "We can make it work. We just have to figure out how to be business partners instead of romantic ones."

He makes it sound so easy, but I felt every ounce of the awkwardness between the two of them this morning. In the brief moments I talked one-on-one with Lynda while Avery and Eric took their lunch breaks, she confirmed how tense the office has been since the breakup. She also told me she heard most of my argument with Avery, which is...embarrassing.

I think the only reason Lynda's still being nice to me is because of our history.

"It's good to see your mom again," I mutter, hoping the change in subject will keep me from rehashing the argument with Avery for the dozenth time. Could I have handled things better? Of course. Do I regret shutting things down? Absolutely. Do I wish Eric hadn't interrupted us? I don't know.

Eric grins at the mention of his mom. "I'm so glad she agreed to help us out. She's surprisingly great at handling the customer side of things and communicating with our authors. But I'm pretty sure she likes Avery more than she likes me."

I laugh, and it's a good thing Eric laughs too because otherwise I would feel like a jerk. "Yeah?"

"Yeah. It's not like I can blame her. Avery is perfect."

So why did you break up? Eric said it was mutual, but I still don't know who was the first one to suggest breaking up, and that's going to drive me nuts. I need something to distract me. "Tell me about her." *Something that isn't that.*

Tilting his head to one side, Eric studies me for a long moment with narrowed eyes. "Why?"

Oh, come on. Does he really think I'm asking because I'm planning to make a move? I can't hold back an eye roll. "Because I already know one half of the Rose & Quill team, but I'm going to need to know about the other eventually." If I had thought this through, I would have realized this would be a great excuse to interact with Avery.

An excuse you don't need, I remind myself. Now, more than ever, I'm going to need to keep emotional distance in mind.

Thankfully, Eric accepts my reasoning without any more argument. "She's... Well, she's Avery."

"That's all you've got for me? I thought you dated."

"We were *engaged*." Eric frowns, as if surprised by his own correction. "But she's...she's the kind of person who can't be defined. You'll just have to get to know her."

Can't be defined? Avery is bold and spunky. Passionate and snarky. She's the kind of person who will fight for someone to get the most out of life and push them to love the things she does because they make her happy and she wants people to be happy too. She's a loving older sister and cousin and supports the people she loves in any way she can. When Dani told me about her book, she also told me that Avery has been her biggest cheerleader her entire life and tends to put others' needs before her own.

Of course, I don't say any of this out loud because Eric has no idea I've been around Avery before today, and I want it to stay that way. Does this count as lying to my friend? Maybe. But I don't see how admitting the truth will benefit anyone.

"How do you split the duties with the company?" I ask, hoping Eric will have something more concrete for this question than he did with the last one.

"Avery has the ideas," he answers immediately. "She's more of a broad thinker and handles the creative aspects, like working with the cover designers and formatters."

So why did none of the marketing ideas this morning sound like her? I spent my day going through the presentation and picking out anything useful to connect to the prior research I did while on the flight to Utah yesterday, but there wasn't much. All the while I had to pretend Avery wasn't sitting a few feet from me because otherwise I wouldn't have been able to concentrate, but that's neither here nor there. I failed at that part anyway.

"And you're the business side?" I guess, leaning back in my seat while the restaurant buzzes with activity around us. Tired though I am, this part of the conversation is quickly helping me settle into more of a norm. This is the kind of thing I can do in my sleep.

"I take Avery's vision and make it functional," Eric says, a hint of pride in his voice. "She has these huge dreams, which is great, but I make sure they're within the scope of our capability."

Eric said he and Avery care more about the company than their relationship, and I'm starting to see why. They seem to balance well, their opposing viewpoints leading to a middle ground that works. It's good for me to know as I go into this consultation, especially with my history with both of them. I've known Eric far longer, but I see some of myself in Avery. I can straddle these lines and help their company thrive, assuming I don't get distracted by thoughts of tiramisu.

My next question is one I'll have to ask Avery too, but I'm more curious about Eric's answer. "Why publishing?"

Eric chuckles, relaxing in his seat like I have, but his smile has shifted to something I don't think I've seen from him before. In a way, it reminds me of the way Riccardo looked in Florence whenever he was next to Siena, and it makes me queasy. Does he still have feelings for Avery? "Because Avery made me fall in love with it," he says, almost dreamily. "I was mostly a nonfiction kind of guy, but a friend invited me to a book club about six years ago. They were reading a fantasy, which wasn't really my thing, but I decided to go and meet some new people. And there she was. She convinced me to fall in love with reading because she made it look so...freeing. You know?"

I can imagine the moment. Eric, reluctant to try new things, stepping into a room and feeling out of his element. His gaze probably caught on Avery as soon as he walked through the door, and I'd bet she was talking to someone about the book, her eyes bright and her whole face lit up by her enthusiasm. If there were any other single guys at that book club, they would have seen the same thing Eric did, but he was the first one to make the move. Or the one who said the right thing. The one who won the jackpot.

What would I have said if I were there? Would she have seen me if I wasn't the only option she had? If I didn't have the romantic atmosphere of Florence on my side, would she have given me the time of day? Am I the kind of guy Avery would *want* to date?

Not likely. Not unless I were able to offer her more than casual, which I never will.

"But enough work talk," Eric says, pulling me out of my thoughts. "I want to hear more about you! It's been so long since we talked that there's this massive gap of time I know nothing about. You've built up this whole marketing consultant gig and made yourself a bigshot, and I'm surprised you've stuck with it this long."

"So am I," I admit, letting out a tired laugh. "I think it helps that every company is different. And it's more than marketing. It's kind of everything."

"You get the thrill of something new and the satisfaction of success, and you get to start all over again on the next one."

"Sounds perfect for me, doesn't it?"

He laughs. "How long are you going to stick with it?"

I don't think he means it as an insult, but it still feels like a slap. Yeah, I know I've struggled with committing to things my entire life, but I've been doing this for a decade. "I'm actually working on getting some bigger clients to help me scale up and start a whole firm," I say, doing my best to keep frustration out of my voice. "Bring on some more consultants and give myself a little flexibility."

Though his eyebrows rise high, like he thought for sure I'd be finding something new soon, he smiles. "Like your dad did with his law firm?"

Thank goodness for the waiter arriving with our check so I don't have to respond to that question.

A flash of discomfort crosses Eric's face, but then he reaches for the check. "We'll call this a business dinner."

I snatch the bill before he can touch it. "This is friends getting together," I counter. "I got this."

"Thanks." Eric visibly relaxes. As far as I know, Rose & Quill is bringing in decent money, mostly because of Dani's book, but I'm going to assume my pragmatic buddy doesn't love excessive spending. Not that two bowls of ramen is excessive, but he's smart to be cautious.

We're both quiet as we wait for the waiter to return with my card, which is fine by me. I'm eager to get to my hotel room and crash, though I'm wishing I had a whole weekend to recover from the last...year. I've slept in my own bed maybe a dozen times in the last six months, and while that's never bothered me before, I'm feeling it now. This is one of the reasons I'm trying so hard to scale my business. Give myself some room to breathe so I don't have to work eighty-hour weeks just to go to a friend's wedding.

"How is your family by the way?" Eric asks, wincing when my scowl hits him. "Sorry. I was curious if they know you're here in Utah."

I shift in my seat, thoroughly uncomfortable. What's taking the waiter so long? I thought for sure I'd managed to avoid this subject. "Uh, no. Not yet."

"Are you going to tell them?"

"Of course." But the words come out strangled. I *was* planning on texting my mom at some point and letting her know I was in town, but I figured I would wait a bit. Make sure my availability has an expiration date. If she finds out I'm here for the next month, she'll try to convince me to go to every family dinner and baseball game and piano recital. That would be as awkward for my nieces and nephews as it would for me, since they only see me for the occasional holiday, a day or two at a time.

"Things are still rough?" Eric wrinkles his nose in sympathy. I must have been making a face, or maybe he knows me too well.

"They're fine," I say with a heavy sigh. "But McKay has like six kids now, and Kimball is a partner at Dad's firm so he's as perfect as always."

Eric frowns. "From what I can see, your company is already pretty successful."

"But not the right kind of success." I shake my head and run a hand through my hair. "They're still waiting for me to get a real job and find a pretty wife who will keep me close to home. That's never been my path." An image of Avery flashes through my mind, but I ignore it. No matter how thoroughly she imprinted on my heart, that path leads to a dead end. Even if I do manage to hire people to consult with me, it'll be years before I can stabilize things enough to have any free time.

No woman in her right mind wants a relationship with a man who's never around, and that's fine.

"Maybe you haven't met the right girl," Eric says with a shrug.

I chuckle. Maybe he shouldn't say things like that when he's as single as I am. He *did* meet the right girl. Then he gave her up and made her cry.

The waiter finally returns with my card, and I get to my feet, more than ready to go to bed. We make it outside before Eric speaks again.

"Hey," he says, offering a warm smile as well as a handshake. "It's nice having you around again. Kind of feels like old times. Thanks for agreeing to come out here and help."

I look at his hand for a few seconds, then pull him into a hug that he quickly returns. It's a greeting we skipped this morning, instead jumping right into talking, but I've missed this guy more than I realized. I've missed the way things used to be, before life pulled us apart and I was on my own. "Thanks for asking me to come." Even if I have to fight my attraction to Avery while I'm here, this trip is going to be good for me. I can feel it.

By the time I get to my hotel room, I am completely spent. Normally, I like to settle in and unpack, but I simply change out of my suit and collapse into bed, eager for a full night's sleep.

It doesn't come. I spend the night wide awake, mentally wandering the streets of Florence, the imaginary smell of chocolate in the air.

TICKET
PASSPORT
N
W   E
S
HOTEL
Time To
Travel

CHAPTER 16
Avery

THE EARTH RUMBLED UNDERFOOT, trembling and knocking loose rocks from the cave's roof. Mira tightened her hold on her blade, resisting the pull of magic that swirled through the air around her. The sky, once gilded with sunlight, turned dark with storm clouds, and Mira's knife began to glow in the sun's absence, the only light left on the bloodstained battlefield.

"Don't move," Kael whispered, his words falling thick and heavy. The gleam of Mira's knife brought his battle-worn face into sharp relief as he stared at the cave's entrance. "If we move..."
She didn't need his warning. Not when the earth shook again, this time with heavy footsteps. Lungs heaving, heart racing, she gripped her knife and cursed her hands for being slick with blood and sweat. She couldn't afford to lose her hold. The blade was her only hope, and its light seemed to pulse in time with her breaths, growing brighter with each footstep.

The creature emerged all too soon, first its smoking snout and fiery eyes, followed quickly by a body of jagged scales and leathery wings, enormous limbs and deadly talons that scorched the ground with each step. As it stepped into the howling wind, it turned that flame-cursed gaze directly on Mira, as if it knew she was the one who had awoken it. It knew she was the only one who could conquer it.

The beast seemed to smile, and Mira's knife glowed brighter, as if in defiance.

Kael's hand slowly gripped hers as he looked at her with terror. "Don't," he begged. "Mira."

But Mira had no choice. As much as she wanted to turn and run and never look back, this had always been her destiny. "I love you," she whispered, squeezing his fingers before prying herself from his grip.

"No!"

She lunged, and the light from her blade exploded into a blinding arc that tore through the storm and—

A hand grabs my shoulder, and I shriek, head flying back and colliding with something hard. Eric reels back, hand pressed to his nose, and it only takes a second before blood starts dripping, bright and red and *oh my gosh what just happened*?

I tug my earbuds out of my ears. I turned on some music in an effort to ignore the man sharing my office this morning and actually focus on work, and it clearly worked a little too well because I'm suddenly very aware of how loud my music was as the world goes quiet around me.

Well, almost quiet. Benson has a hand clapped over his mouth, poorly stifling laughter as he looks from me to Eric and back again.

"Eric!" I gasp, scrambling to grab some tissues and toss them at him. He's moving to the far end of the room as if to put as much distance between me and him as he can, so the tissues float uselessly to the floor. "I'm so sorry! You snuck up on me!"

"He said your name like six times," Benson says, still chuckling.

"This isn't funny!" I snap, grabbing more tissues. This time I get out of my chair and bring them to Eric, though my stomach churns a bit at the sight of so much blood. Did I *break his nose*?

Eric groans as he takes the tissues and wads them beneath his nose. "Phillip Rogers is here," he says, his words coming out muffled enough that I'm not sure I hear him right. His wide-eyed expression makes me think I did.

"What?" I ask, tempted to creep down the hallway and see if I can get a glimpse of the lobby. "He's *here* here?"

"Who is Phillip Rogers?" Benson asks.

Ignoring him, Eric nods. "He's *here*," he confirms, which is nice because I'm still not sure I believe it. "And he's only here for like twenty minutes." He pulls the tissues away but quickly presses them back to his nose when he realizes he's still bleeding. Swearing, he glances at the door. "What do we do?"

I gape at him. "You're asking *me*? You're the one who's been sending him emails and calling his office for the last six months!" When Eric first started reaching out to investors, I told him Rogers was a waste of time because he's the kind of investor who notices legit companies, not makeshift LLCs who don't know what they're doing. There was no way he would ever pay attention to us. But I guess I was wrong? "Why is he here? And why is he only here for twenty minutes?"

Eric shrugs. "He said he was in the neighborhood and had some time to kill before another meeting. Go talk to him!"

Dizziness washes over me. "What?"

He gives me a little shove, thankfully with the hand not covered in blood. "This could be our only chance."

"Only chance for what?" Benson asks, coming up beside me. He has his phone in hand and a web page pulled up with Rogers's picture front and center. "Are you looking for investors? Why?"

"Because we need stability," Eric hisses, dropping his voice to a mere whisper. "And Phillip Rogers loves companies like us. He could put a lot of weight behind our name, and his money and influence would help us build better relationships with vendors and venues, even advertising agencies." He looks at me again, his eyebrows dipping low. "Avery, I can't go back out there like this!"

And I can't go out there at all! This isn't my area of expertise, and I am the last person who should be trying to pitch our company to a guy whose net worth is more than I can dream of. My sheer terror must be written all over my face because Eric's shoulders drop in defeat.

"No." The word comes out of Benson's throat in a growl, and he puts his hand on my shoulder. "If this guy's help is something you want, you can't let this opportunity pass you by."

The only reason I'm not crying right now is because my whole body feels like it's shutting down. "I...I don't... I can't..."

"Just show him the presentation you showed Sonny yesterday," Eric says, and then he's gone, rushing to the bathroom and leaving my office silent except for the whoosh of my blood pulsing through my ears.

I might pass out.

"That presentation wouldn't even convince my parents to invest in us," I whisper, shutting my eyes tight as if that might shut out this situation. My panic rises, leaving me dizzy. "How is it supposed to convince Phillip Rogers? I'm going to mess this up and scare him off and we're going to run out of money and Dani's going to hate me because no one will be able to read her book and—"

"Avery Grace!" Benson's gentle shout cuts me off, bringing my gaze to him. His lips are pursed, his brow furrowed, and when he realizes he has my attention, one of his hands rises to stroke my hair. The gesture feels so familiar that it hurts, and I stare at him like I'm seeing him for the first time. "Will you calm down? If you're half as passionate about Rose & Quill as you were about random architecture in Florence, then you'll be fine. Tell Rogers why you love this place, and he'll have no choice but to want to join you."

Easy for him to say. Benson is the kind of guy who oozes confidence, and I doubt he's ever felt unsure of himself. "I don't—"

"Come on." He grabs me by the elbow and starts dragging me out of the office and into the hall.

I fight him, grateful that the lobby is offset from the hallway and hiding me from view as I struggle, but I can hear Lynda's soft voice conversing with a rich, masculine baritone. "I can't!" I argue. "This isn't my area of exper—"

"This is *your company*, Avery. No one is more expert than you." Benson groans quietly when I dig in my heels, turning to glare at me. "You didn't hesitate to try the lampredotto," he says on a breath. "You're being ridiculous."

"That was cow stomach," I whisper back. "This is my *career*. My whole life!"

"So don't abandon it!"

Fear and guilt and worry all mix in my stomach, leaving me queasy and wondering if I'll be next to rush to the bathroom. But Benson takes advantage of my weakness and tugs me forward, hard enough that I fly past him and stumble into the lobby.

Phillip Rogers stops mid-sentence, looking from Lynda to me with his eyebrows high. He matches his picture, a solid man with a solid dark beard peppered with gray. He's wearing a bird-patterned button-up shirt, dark-washed jeans, and Vans, which isn't what I would have expected from a businessman of his esteem, and his casual attire suddenly makes him feel much less intimidating.

"Miss Baldwin, I presume," he says, and the British lilt of his smooth voice is almost soothing.

He is not at all what I expected.

Benson nudges me from behind, breaking me from my surprise.

"Yes!" I squeak, holding out my hand. *This is my company. I'm the expert. I can do this.* I'm not sure I believe my inner thoughts, but I do my best as I say, "It's so nice to meet you. Unfortunately, Eric got tangled up in something, but I don't want to waste any more of your time. I know you don't have much to spare." I gesture to the door to the balcony, where we keep a table and chairs for moments like these.

When we get outside and settle at the table, I realize Benson has followed us, so I reluctantly make the introduction. "Um, Mr. Rogers, this is Benson West. He's..." Should I say he's here to help us build our business, or would that interfere with Rogers's interest? Eric would know the answer to that, but he's too busy bleeding.

"I'm an old friend of Eric's," Benson says, grasping Rogers's hand in a firm handshake. He sits next to me, far too close for my comfort because it's already difficult enough to concentrate without his fresh scent filling my nose. "I'm in town for a few weeks to help maximize the marketing strategy of Rose & Quill in the coming years and ensure the company establishes themselves as a strong contender in such a competitive market."

Rogers lifts a thick eyebrow. "An outsider?" He clearly doesn't approve.

But Benson smiles and glances between me and Rogers. "A friend hoping to be useful," he corrects. "My focus is on building scalable marketing frameworks that not only amplify brand visibility but also translate directly into measurable growth, because the books R&Q are producing are already a cut above most and selling themselves."

Where in the world did that come from? I gape at Benson, trying to understand how the carefree and flirty man I knew in Italy got replaced by a completely different version of him. He's like Batman swooping in out of nowhere to save the day. Or Bruce Wayne? Batman if the vigilante part of him dressed like Bruce Wayne. Gah! His initials are even B.W.! *Ridiculous.*

"We were just discussing a new approach to marketing to set Rose & Quill apart from other publishers," Benson continues, and he shifts his gaze to me. "Why don't you tell Mr. Rogers what you were telling me?"

What? We weren't talking at all! As my panic starts building again, I stare at Benson and silently beg him to say something else. Anything.

But he simply grabs my hand under the table and offers a brief smile that seems to say, "You've got this." It's the same look he gave me all the time in Italy when he was pushing me to break through my self-imposed inhibitions.

But trying mystery meat street food and convincing a big-time investor to give my little company a chance aren't the same thing. I don't know if I've got this, but I don't have much of a choice. Benson said Rogers needs to see my passion for this company, which I have in spades, so that shouldn't be too hard to show. I take a deep breath and squeeze Benson's hand, as if that might give me some of his strength.

"As you probably know," I begin, turning my focus back to Rogers, "Danielle Baldwin has taken the world by storm with her debut, *Of Curses and Pomegranates*, which pushed Rose & Quill into the public eye sooner than we expected, but we're hoping to use her popularity to boost our other authors and build a strong brand around her success."

Rogers tilts his head to the side, studying me with an inscrutable expression. "How so?"

That's a good question...

"Collaborations," I say, which is the first word that pops into my head. Luckily, I've had ideas around collaboration, though I've never been brave enough to suggest them to Eric. Not until we're more established. But I need to share ideas now, so I start talking. "We're looking into doing multi-author box sets and short story collections, as well as cross-promotions and group signings. We can use her social media following as well, by..." My mind goes blank, and I grimace.

"By pairing her with other R&Q authors in fun ways," Benson says in a way that makes it sound like he knew exactly what I was going to say. "We'll encourage them to make content together that resonates with their different audiences. Things like improvised poetry contests between the authors, with the readers and followers choosing the winner."

"Yes!" I say, sitting up straighter. That's brilliant! "Or having them write scenes on the spot where their characters meet each other in situations suggested by followers."

Benson grins. "Maybe we could have authors host a quarterly book club and interview each other."

"Knowing our authors, that could get hilarious."

"Even better."

"You're right. We want our authors to be able to show their personalities and be authentic, rather than perform for social media."

"The goal is to create genuine connections between the authors and readers," Benson says.

"Make it personal," I add. "No matter how big we grow, we want our readers to know that they are the reason we exist."

"The best authors are the ones who connect with their readers, and that will be the driving force behind Rose & Quill. We can capitalize on Dani's success to connect all of our authors to more readers and wider audiences, at the same time boosting their confidence and establishing their personal brands."

Rogers clears his throat, and the sound feels like a bucket of cold water dumping over my head. I almost forgot he was sitting across from us; I was caught up in Benson. But when I look at Rogers, he smiles warmly, eyes jumping between Benson and me. "Sounds like you have some interesting ideas," he says, and I'm pretty sure he sees that as a good thing because his smile is so genuine. "I'm afraid I can't stay, but I will certainly be in touch. I think we could do great things together, Miss Baldwin."

He offers his hand, which I take with trembling fingers. Benson gives him a much more enthusiastic shake and offers to show him to the door, which is good because I don't think I could stand if I tried.

I think that went well? Rogers said he would be in touch, which has to mean I didn't scare him off. *I think we could do great things together.* That's what he said. Even when I try to come up with a worst case scenario, those words have to mean good things. And I have Benson to thank for the good outcome, since there's no way I could have convinced Rogers on my own. Not when I ran out of stuff to say so quickly.

I grab my phone, still a little dazed by what just happened.

Avery:
Do you remember me telling you about that investor Eric has been trying to get? Phillip Rogers?

Dani:
I think so?

Avery:
I think I just convinced him to invest with R&Q…

Dani:
That's huge!!!

Avery:
I'm not sure it's real. Eric is bleeding in the bathroom, and I only had a few minutes to convince Rogers to be interested.

Dani:
I'm sorry… What?

Avery:
Oh, right. I might have broken Eric's nose.

Dani:
It's about time! But also, what happened? And please tell me you have video!

Mason also wants video.

Avery:

No there's not video! It was an accident! And that's not what's important here. *I* convinced Rogers to invest. ME!

I frown as I read the message I sent. That's not true. Yeah, Eric wasn't here to throw out facts and figures like he usually is, but that doesn't mean I can credit this win entirely to myself. Not when I would have floundered without...

Dani's next text pops up.

Dani:

Fine, but please know that the next time it happens, I expect video or to be present for the event.

But focusing back on Rogers, that's amazing! Tell me everything! How did you do it?

Avery:

It's not going to happen again. I know you don't like Eric, but he's still my business partner. As for Rogers… It wasn't just me.

Benson helped.

And a feeling deep in my gut tells me that the two of us working more closely together might be a good thing. Which means I might be in trouble.

CHAPTER 17
Benson

I MISSED THESE MOUNTAINS more than I thought. It's something I've realized more the longer I'm here. I started spending a few minutes out on the balcony each afternoon, but it's too hot to work out here or I would bring my laptop out and make this my office. In part because of the view but also because it would put some distance between me and Avery, something that has become increasingly hard to come by.

It's been a week since I showed up at Rose & Quill. Six days since Avery and I talked to Phillip Rogers, who sent over a term sheet only a day later to get things moving with an investment plan. Eric has been in constant conversation with the company's contracted lawyer over the last several work days, leaving Avery to her own devices.

And Avery's devices have started to involve me in almost everything.

I sigh, taking in the view of the Wasatch Front from my metal chair. Though the Rose & Quill offices are small, they're certainly in a good spot, and there are moments when I wish I could sit here all day and simply take in the majesty of the mountains. I can think out here, unlike in an office with Avery sitting a few feet away and pulling me into conversations every few minutes.

They're not bad conversations. In fact, she has quickly started deep diving into the marketing ideas we presented to Rogers, turning them into actual plans that will make my job easier. Every time she comes up with something new, she tells me about it and asks for input, which leads to more ideas. I love brainstorming with her and playing off her energy, but that's exactly the problem. I'm enjoying it too much.

This is going to end in a few weeks. And it's going to end badly if I'm not careful.

"Is this where you go when you're hiding from Avery?" Eric's voice breaks through my thoughts, full of amusement.

I look over at him as he settles in one of the other chairs. His face is still a bit mottled with purple from Avery's impressive headbutt last week, but it's healing. He's lucky she didn't break his nose, but I'm not sure I'll let him live this down regardless. Witnessing that debacle was the highlight of my time in Utah so far. "I'm not hiding. How's the face?"

He grimaces. "Sore. I'm hoping the bruising is all gone before the conference in a couple of days so I don't have to explain to people that my partner hit me in the nose. And I don't blame you for hiding from Avery. She can be a lot sometimes."

Defensiveness rises in my throat, but I swallow it down. Ever since Eric missed his chance to schmooze Rogers in person, he's been throwing out little comments about Avery, like taking out his frustration on her is going to make himself look better. I'm pretty sure it's his stress talking, but that doesn't stop me from wanting to counter him every time. The only thing holding me back is the worry that he'll read too much into my defense of his ex and start to think something is there that isn't.

Something that *can't* be there.

I force myself to focus on the first thing he said, rather than telling him I would happily spend all day with Avery if not for him. "Conference?"

"Oh. Right. I'm driving to Denver tomorrow for a publishing conference in the hopes of making some good contacts with vendors. As soon as we started negotiations with Rogers, I booked a ticket."

A ticket. As in one. "You're not taking Avery with you?"

"She hates this sort of thing."

Based on the million and a half ideas she was throwing around this last week, I highly doubt that's true. A publishing conference sounds like the sort of place Avery might thrive, where like-minded people share ideas. Since she's full of them, a publishing conference is exactly the sort of place she should go.

"Are you sure both of you shouldn't go?" I ask, rubbing the back of my neck.

"And leave you here on your own?" He scoffs. "That feels like a waste of good money, and you're not cheap."

"I wasn't..." The words fade on my tongue. I wasn't going to charge him for my services, and I thought he knew that. Apparently not. Does he not see this as a friend helping a friend? Are we relegated to business associates now? That defeats the purpose of me coming here, since the only reason I agreed to consult for R&Q was to have the chance to rebuild our friendship, and I had to turn down two different proposals to be here.

Clients who not only would have paid me but would have had more clout than what I usually deal with. In other words, clients who would have brought me one step closer to turning my one-man-show into something my dad might actually approve of.

Grunting, I shift in my seat and tell myself to focus on the problem at hand and not outlandish hypothetical situations. "Does Avery know when you're leaving?" I ask, though I really want to ask him if Avery knows *if* he's leaving. She hasn't said anything about the conference, and I can't imagine her sitting quietly if she knew about it.

Eric shrugs. "Not yet. I figured I'd let her know before I leave for the day so she isn't wondering why I'm not in the office tomorrow."

I don't remember him being this much of an idiot. "Dude."

"What?"

"She's your *partner*."

"Business partner," he clarifies, sharper than I expect. "And I know that. It's why I trust her to keep an eye on things while I'm gone."

"You didn't think to *ask* her about going to the conference?"

He frowns at me, as if my question makes no sense. "I'm an owner of R&Q just like she is. It's not like we're dating anymore; I don't need her permission to make business decisions."

Yeah, he's *really* an idiot. "Can I give you some advice?" I say, by some miracle not clenching my jaw as I speak.

"As my friend or as a consultant?"

Never mind. I lock my teeth together until my frustration ebbs. I would blame the heat for my increasingly bad mood, but Eric has been extra annoying this week, and I can't help feeling he clipped Avery's wings at some point so she can't fly to her full potential. Based on some of the ideas she's had this week, I'm pretty sure the main reason Avery had a shell to break out of in the first place was because of Eric.

I can only imagine what this company could be if he didn't hold her back.

Taking a slow breath, I keep my tone neutral as I say, "Can't I be both?"

Shrugging, he gets to his feet, as if he's considering running away before I can tell him my thoughts. "I guess."

"Don't keep secrets. Not from her. Going after each other is the surest way to send your company spiraling, and you and Avery have a good thing here."

He seems to consider that for a second, but he doesn't have a reply before he pulls open the door.

Voices spill out from inside, full of happiness and laughter, and I frown. "Who's here?"

"Hmm?" Eric glances back. "Oh, it's Sadie Ashcombe, one of the editors we work with."

And one of Avery's cousins, I silently finish for him, remembering something Lynda said the other day when we were talking about the contractors working with R&Q. Curious, I hop to my feet and follow him inside, stopping outside Avery's office, where the two women are chatting. Sadie is sitting at the edge of the desk I've been using, and Avery looks happy—happier than she's been since I've been here in Utah. I don't like the way my mind starts revisiting some of my favorite moments in Italy, when she shared that bright smile of hers with me.

A sense of challenge rises up in me as I think back to the woman I first met on the plane. The one muted by her ex/business partner. R&Q won't thrive if Eric is knocking Avery down every time she tries to take a step, but I have to be careful about mentioning their dynamic if I don't want him to think I'm sticking my nose where I shouldn't.

This is the first time in a long time that I don't have any ideas on how to fix an obvious issue, and I don't like that.

"Avie," Eric says, interrupting my thoughts by stepping in front of me and blocking my view. "You got a sec?"

"Oh." Avery sounds disappointed. "Yeah, sure."

"I should get going anyway," Sadie says.

"Hey, are you going to be at Kaden's thing?"

"Can't."

"Seriously?"

"Sorry, Ave, but I have a thing with Max. Besides, it's Kaden." Sadie skirts around Eric but pauses when she catches sight of me, her expression turning shrewd as she takes me in. "Hello, handsome. Who might you be?"

A bit of a blush brightens Avery's cheeks as she looks from me to her cousin. "Uh, Sadie, this is Benson. He's the—"

"I know exactly who he is." Sadie's lips twist up in a knowing smile, which doesn't surprise me because she was part of my short-lived text conversation during Riccardo's wedding. "You're prettier than your picture."

A laugh chokes out of me at the same time Eric scoffs. "Thanks," I say, though I'm trying to figure out her intent behind the comment. She's not flirting with me, like most women do when they meet me, and she still has that examining look. Based on the bite in her tone, I'm not sure she meant it as a compliment.

"Avery?" Eric nudges her into his office and closes the door behind him, leaving Sadie and me alone in the hallway.

I fold my arms. "So you're—"

"Let's get one thing straight," Sadie says and steps into my space, looking up at me with narrowed eyes. "If you do anything to hurt Avery, you're going to have the entire cousin group out for blood. Understand?"

Holding back a smile, I nod as seriously as I can. "I'm here to work. Not to date."

"Then stop looking at my cousin like she's the last bite of gelato."

Desire sparks to life in my gut as memories of Italy surface again. I force it down, hoping it doesn't show on my face. "I have every plan to keep a professional distance. You don't have to worry."

She looks me up and down one more time and doesn't seem all that impressed with what she sees. "I have a guardian moose on my side, so you'd better watch out, Benson."

That catches me off guard, and I frown. "A guardian what?"

"You heard me."

I have no idea what a guardian moose is, but I'm going to guess I should be wary. "I'm not going to do anything to hurt Avery."

"Better not," is all she says before she waves goodbye to Lynda and disappears out the door.

Lynda pokes her head around the corner and smirks. "Sounds like you've gotten yourself on the wrong side of the Hayes family's favor."

Chuckling, I put my hands in my pockets and join her in the lobby so I don't accidentally overhear anything from Eric and Avery's conversation. He'd better be telling her about the conference, though I worry about how she's going to react. "Seems to be my usual MO," I say and lean against her desk. "You know families and I don't get along."

She swats my arm. "What do you call me?"

"My saving grace." I pick up her hand and press a kiss to her knuckles. I mean that. Lynda taking me in during holidays is one of the big reasons I didn't quit college halfway through, particularly because she invited me over all the time during the summers too, when guilt brought me back home to live with my own family between school years. "Heaven knows why you put up with me as much as you did."

Tutting, she pats my cheek. "Benson, you are a much better man than you think you are. You were then, and you are now."

"You're making me blush, Mrs. Greer." All jokes aside, I feel her praise in my bones, and my regret for coming here isn't as strong as it was a moment ago. "But thanks, Lynda."

She grins. "So what have you done to get on Sadie's watch list?"

I'm about to answer when Eric's door flies open, followed shortly by Avery's slamming shut. I curse under my breath—she didn't take the news well—but I don't get a chance to fill Lynda in before Eric is storming toward us, his suit coat and briefcase in hand.

"I need to go pack," he says without looking at either of us.

Then he's gone.

"Oh dear," Lynda says and touches her fingers to her lips. "That clearly didn't go how he hoped. I'm guessing he told her about the conference?"

I raise an eyebrow. "Are there no secrets kept from you?"

Shrugging, she settles at her desk and starts clicking out of her open windows. Whether she's leaving because it's the end of the day or because she plans to follow Eric, she's going to leave me here with Avery. *Angry*

Avery, which is someone I haven't met. "This office is small," she says, as if that explains everything. "He's also my son."

And a mama's boy, I don't say out loud. He always has been. He probably told her he was going to the conference the minute he booked the ticket.

I rub the back of my neck and consider following her lead and sneaking out, except my laptop is in Avery's office and I need it for a video call with a potential client tonight. "Is she going to be okay?"

Sighing, Lynda pats my cheek again. "She'll be fine. She's stronger than she thinks she is, and it will be for the best if she stays here."

"Will it?" My eyes travel to the hall, though I can't see Avery's door from here. With her angry reaction, I'm more convinced than ever she would have loved to go to that conference, and if she stays here...

That means she's staying here with me.

"I need to run. Will you check on her once she's had some time to process?" Lynda pats my cheek a third time, grabs her purse, and slips out the door before I can formulate a response.

Not that I could say anything but yes.

I give Avery five minutes of privacy, during which I pace the hallway and search the internet for how to console an angry woman. I don't learn much at all, as most of the advice people have given is to run far away and let her cool down before approaching. I'm not the only one who finds an angry woman intimidating. It's suddenly painfully obvious that I have almost never had to deal with heightened emotions, as most of my life is spent charming people and keeping them happy.

When I can't keep myself away any longer, I knock softly on Avery's door. She doesn't respond, so I say, "It's me. Want to talk?"

Her door flies open a moment later, and I take a step back when I see her wild eyes. She hasn't been crying, like I thought maybe she would be, and there's nothing but righteous fury in her expression. "Did you know?" she demands, hand still on the door like she's ready to shut it on me as soon as I respond.

It's a bad idea to assume I know what she's talking about, but I do it regardless. "He told me right before he told you."

She softens at that, a bit of hurt entering her gaze. "It's sold out. I tried to buy a ticket, but..."

Part of me wants to tell her to go anyway and try to get in under Eric's name before he can show up, since he would have registered it under Rose & Quill. But that's the Benson who was in Italy, not the one who is here to make sure R&Q thrives. "I'm sure Eric will share any notes he takes," I say lamely, wincing when her gaze turns sharp again.

"All I've ever wanted—my ex mansplaining my own job to me." With a huff, she stalks back to her desk and drops into her chair, and her eyes go distant as she stares at her screen.

I lean against the door frame, wishing I knew the right thing to say. But as often happens with this woman, I'm at a loss for words. The right words, anyway. "For the record, he's an idiot for not bringing you with him."

She rolls her eyes. "Is he salty because of the whole bloody nose thing? It was an accident!"

An impressive accident that still makes me chuckle when I think about it. "I couldn't tell you," I say honestly. "But there's a chance you're right. Regardless, he made the wrong choice."

"I wish I could..."

"What?"

Looking up at me, she bites her lip for a second, then sighs. "It's stupid, but I want to go back to the way things were. When we were together."

Oh boy, I don't like the sharp pain now stabbing me in the ribs. "You want to get back together with him?" Whether she wants to or not shouldn't matter, but I hate that idea more than I hate the way Eric shut her out with this conference thing.

Avery snorts and shakes her head. "No. That's over. Probably should have been over sooner than it was."

The relief that washes over me is...concerning. "So what do you mean?" Somehow I manage to sound aloof and unconcerned when I ask that.

"I mean we had a good partnership when we were together. We were both more willing to compromise because we didn't want to damage our relationship if we had arguments about work things." With another heavy sigh, she stands and grabs her purse. "Now there's nothing to hold our frustrations back, and I'm worried it's going to ruin us."

"Then it's a good thing I'm here." I frown as soon as I say that. What does that mean? "Because I can, uh, bridge the gap." But only for a few weeks, and then I'll be off helping someone else's company.

Avery looks at me for a long moment, her expression inscrutable. "So it's just you and me for the next few days."

My heart thuds in my chest. "And Lynda," I add, almost desperately. Not twenty minutes ago, I was telling myself I need to find a way to put some space between Avery and me if I want to focus and make a proper plan for Rose & Quill.

But I don't want Avery to think she's alone when I know all too well how much that can wear on a person.

Avery huffs out a laugh and nods. "And Lynda," she confirms. "Maybe you and I can make some solid marketing plans while Eric is gone."

Lynda can help, I want to add, though Lynda only deals with the office and the customer service side of things. Maybe she would be interested in brainstorming with Avery? Without Eric across the hall, I won't have that steady reminder to stay in my lane, and I'll have to be extra diligent about keeping things professional, like I told Sadie I would do.

From the little I've interacted with Avery's cousins, it's clear they're not a family I want to cross.

And letting myself get close to Avery again? That will undoubtedly hurt her.

"Maybe," I say because Avery is waiting for an answer. But I need to change the subject. "Are you heading home already?"

Glancing down at her purse in her hand, she shrugs. "I shouldn't. I'm behind on social media posts, but I'm not exactly in a work mood right now. Honestly, I should just…" She stops herself, her eyebrows pulling low.

My curiosity is too strong to ignore. "You should what?"

Her jaw tightens as she looks at her computer. "I've been wanting to hire someone to handle our socials for a while now."

I tilt my head, sensing more. "But?"

"But Eric always says it's unnecessary." She stands a little taller, looking more like the confident woman I didn't want to say goodbye to in Florence. "Clearly Eric isn't always right, and I'm as much of an owner as he is. I can hire someone if I want to."

Though I shouldn't be, I can't help but be attracted to the fierce look in her eyes as she talks about going behind my friend's back. Fighting a grin, I fold my arms and nod thoughtfully. "You totally can. I was going to recommend it anyway. You have too much on your plate as it is."

Her eyes jump to mine. "Yeah, I do."

"Want me to post a job listing for you before I head out?"

Sighing, she rolls her eyes. "I can do it in the morning. But thanks." Her head cocks to the side as she studies me for a moment, and then she says, "Do you want to go grab some dinner with me? I don't want to be here, and I don't want to be alone. We can talk about the job listing and how stupid Eric is."

Yes. The word almost flies from my mouth, but I manage to swallow it. "Oh. Uh." I resist the urge to palm my face for that brilliant response. Is that all I have to say? *Pathetic.*

Avery must think so too because she rolls her eyes and pushes past me, heading for the doors. "Forget it."

I should let her go. Her frustration is exactly the sort of thing that can keep our relationship in the professional sphere. But what I should do is not often the thing I end up doing. "I want to," I assure her, hot on her heels as she reaches the stairwell. "But it's a bad idea."

"Colleagues have dinner all the time."

"You and I both know we're not just colleagues."

Coming to a sudden stop in the middle of the stairs, she whirls to face me. But she's on a lower step than I am, so her face is level with my sternum. Groaning, she stomps back up the stairs until we're at eye level with each other, which only adds to my attraction. "What does that mean, Benson? Either Italy meant something or it didn't, but you can't have it both ways."

I open my mouth, but I have nothing to say. Not anything she wants to hear. But words rise in my throat, like they're desperate to be free, and I find myself saying, "Of course Italy meant something."

I curse under my breath as Avery's eyes fill with tears because she obviously reads between the lines.

"But not enough," she whispers.

I let her continue down the stairs without argument. She doesn't look back, and I don't move. She's wrong. Our connection in Florence means more than anything has meant in a long time, but it also terrifies me because I don't know what to do with it. I'm only here for a few weeks, which is the case everywhere I go. What can I really offer her? And that says nothing about Eric or Lynda or my family here in Utah.

It's all too complicated, which means things have to stay professional, no matter how hard it will be.

CHAPTER 18
Avery

I CAN'T SAY I'M surprised by today's turn of events, though I wish I didn't have to deal with everything all at once. First a text from Grandma Sue, cordially inviting the whole family to a party to celebrate my youngest, most annoying male cousin, Kaden, graduating from Harvard. Then Eric telling me he's going to the Books and Bows conference without me even though I've brought that conference up for the last three years, telling him I want to go. And then Benson...

As I get to the front counter of my favorite restaurant, ready to order takeout, I pause before giving my order. I meant it when I told Benson I don't want to be alone right now. Especially not at my apartment, where there are still books everywhere. I haven't been able to move the bookshelves on my own, so I'm stuck in an overwhelming limbo. I'd hoped one of my cousins would be able to help, but Sadie will be busy for the next few days, and Poppy is always working. I don't have any non-family friends because my life has been Rose & Quill for the last few years.

So it looks like I'll be in limbo for a while. Being at my apartment is kind of depressing until I can get it all sorted, and I'm already in a bad mood.

Instead of ordering my food to go, I ask for a table. I can wallow with strangers instead of wallowing by myself.

Once I'm settled at one of the only open tables, close to the lobby, I grab my phone and pull up the cousin chat so I can try to set the story straight about Benson before Sadie makes any conjectures. I haven't told my cousins that he's here, and by some miracle Dani hasn't blabbed. Yet. I need to make sure they don't think he and I are going to be a thing, and I start typing.

But movement at the door catches my eye, and my stomach does a little flip, as if I know who's coming inside before he does.

Sure enough, Benson steps into the lobby, his eyes on his phone as he gets in line. My body reacts immediately, sparking to life at the sight of his sleeves rolled up and top two buttons undone. He's more dressed down than he's been all week, and those forearms...

Mentally slapping some sense into myself, I return my focus to my phone. Benson doesn't want anything to happen as far as a relationship goes. He made that very clear in the stairwell, even if he also made it clear that he wasn't entirely unaffected by our Italian fling. This man may claim to be the king of casual, but he felt something for me, and it feels like the only things standing between us are his friendship with Eric and a strange sense of professionalism that wasn't present in Florence.

Was that the real Benson? Or is it this stuffed up, no nonsense consultant who has no problem smiling and flirting unless it's reciprocated?

Gah! When I'm trying not to think about him, I'm thinking about him. I hate this. I hate the hard line he's drawn. I hate that Eric suddenly seems determined to stand between me and the things I want.

Or maybe he's always done that and I was too blind to see it. That feels more likely, which means I have Benson to thank for this shift in my dynamic with my business partner.

"It's probably a half-hour wait," the hostess says, and I look up to see that it's Benson she's talking to.

Benson lets out a heavy sigh, like this is the worst news of his life. Half an hour isn't that long, and there are about a million other restaurants in the area he could try. But instead he sits on one of the vinyl benches and pushes his hands into his hair, elbows on his knees. He's still holding his phone, and a dangerous idea sparks in my mind.

Why does he get to decide our relationship and where the boundaries lie? Why does Eric get to choose whether I go to a conference I have been dying to go to? Why do I never make choices for myself? Even in Italy, I did whatever Benson suggested I should do. While it was fun, I wasn't being true to myself.

I start a new text thread, adding in the number I stole from Benson's email signature the other day.

Avery:

> Are you going to sit there looking like the weight of the world is on your shoulders, or will you come share my table with me?

He slowly sits up again and looks at his phone, and his brow furrows as he reads the text I sent. Then he looks up. The moment his eyes lock with mine, his face softens and leaves me feeling both excited and terrified. Will he join me? Or is he going to keep his distance when there's no good reason for him to?

He stares at me for a second, and then his eyes shift back to his phone as he starts typing.

Benson:

> That's a bad idea.

I roll my eyes.

Avery:

> You said that already. And you're wrong.

Benson:

> What if I'm not?

I see the moment he realizes I've turned his own words against him. His eyebrows dip low, his jaw clenches, and the hand not holding his phone curls into a fist on his knee. Maybe it was a bad idea, but I can't let myself regret saying it.

"Benson," I snap when he still doesn't move. "Come sit with me."

I'm so done with men not listening to me.

He sighs again and stands, slowly making his way over to my table like I'm asking him to give me everything he's got.

"This seat taken?" he asks, a bit of growl in his voice.

"Yeah. By you."

He settles in the chair, his eyes on the table. "Avery, this is a—"

"Bad idea. You and I are going to disagree on that."

Chuckling, he lifts his gaze to meet mine and seems to choose his words carefully. "When did you get so bold?"

"When I met a guy in Italy who refused to let me hold myself back."

Something lights up in his countenance, his frustration dissipating as he looks at me with a hint of a smile. "Sounds like a nightmare."

"He was kind of the best thing to happen to me." I hold eye contact with him, catching every bit of the surprise that enters his eyes. Benson can deny our chemistry all he wants, but I'm tired of keeping up this charade of disinterest and pretending nothing happened between us. It happened, and I'm not willing to let it go.

Then, to my complete and utter shock, Benson blushes. I didn't know he was *capable* of blushing, and the crimson that rises up to his ears bolsters my confidence. "Avery."

"You picked my favorite restaurant."

He tilts his head to one side. "What?"

"Here." I gesture to the crowded dining area. "This is my favorite place to eat, and you chose to come here."

A small smile plays on his lips again, and he relaxes a bit as he picks up the menu in front of me and starts perusing. "I've eaten here before."

"But you still chose to come tonight."

"It doesn't mean—"

"Do you believe in fate, Benson?"

He looks up, his eyebrows lifted. "No."

"Liar."

"I believe in coincidence, maybe, but not—"

"What are the odds you and I sat next to each other on the way to Italy? That you happened to see me in the line for a taxi? That we were staying at the same hotel? And then you show up here to help *my* company?"

He doesn't have a response, which hopefully means he has no argument. I'm not sure I believe in fate either, but there has to be a reason we've been pushed together like this. I can't let him brush me off anymore if I'm going to take control of my own life.

"You can lie to yourself that we don't have a connection," I tell him, "but I won't. You're going to have to deal with that."

Taking a slow breath, he sets down the menu and leans forward, locking his gaze onto mine in a way that makes me shiver. "Do what you want," he says coolly, "but it won't change the boundaries I need to keep."

"Need to?" I counter. "Or are choosing to?"

"Does it matter?"

Maybe not to him, but it matters to me. It will tell me if I have any chance with this man. In all reality, I should cut my losses and accept that he isn't willing to put in the work or make sacrifices, which is a pretty terrible start to a relationship. If Dani were in my position, I would tell her to set the guy loose and move on to someone who won't leave her heartbroken.

But I guess I'm not as careful with my own heart as I want her to be with hers.

Before I can say any more bold things, our server comes to take our orders, and her smile turns flirtatious when she looks at Benson. To my delight, he barely gives her a passing glance as he tells her his order, his eyes fixed on me as if he's worried about what I'm going to say or do during this dinner.

Good. He should be worried. He's not getting off the hook so easily.

"So," I say when we're alone again. "What's your favorite food?"

He narrows his eyes. "Why?"

"Because I'm trying to get to know you, Benson. Believe it or not, you didn't tell me much about yourself when we were in Florence."

He groans, sitting back in his seat. "I don't want to do this, Avery."

"But I do, and I just got majorly hurt by my business partner, so you should be nice to me."

He mumbles something under his breath that sounds like a colorful insult directed toward Eric, and everything about his body language is uncomfortable right now.

Maybe I'm being *too* bold. He's allowed to set boundaries, even if I don't like them, so I change my question. "Actually, I want to hear how you and Eric became friends."

"Why?" he asks again, though this time it carries more curiosity than irritation.

"Because the two of you are so different."

"Hasn't he told you all about me?"

"Yes, but I'm pretty sure your version of the story is going to be different from his."

Benson folds his arms, making his white shirt strain against the ridges of his body. There are suddenly so many other questions I want to ask him, like what his workout routine is like and if he likes living out of hotels and what he does when he leaves the office at the end of the day. I want to know if he has any siblings and if he's ever played a competitive sport and why he chose consulting out of all the things he could be doing with his life.

"We were paired for a project together our freshman year," he says, surprising me with the response. He doesn't look happy to be talking about his life, but it's nice to see he knows me well enough to know I won't let him brood in silence while we wait for our food. He's picking his battles, telling me that Eric is one of the safer topics of conversation.

I wave my hand, urging him to continue.

With a sigh, his arms relax and he keeps talking. "I drove Eric nuts because I didn't care about the assignment and kept focusing on a different side of the topic we were supposed to be researching."

I vaguely remember Eric telling me about how he met Sonny, how this eighteen-year-old kid with boundless energy taught him so much patience. "You failed the project," I say when Benson falls silent.

Nodding, he lets out a soft laugh. "Yeah. Eric was furious and wouldn't look at me in class after that. But then he stopped me on campus a few weeks later and asked for help on an assignment in one of his other classes because he couldn't make heads or tails of what he was supposed to be doing, and he figured since I had a different way of looking at things, I might be able to understand it. It was...nice. To be seen that way." He shakes his head, his eyes distant, like he forgot about that moment when Eric cornered him after class. "I was failing a couple of my classes, so he offered to help me study in exchange, and we figured out that we balanced each other out pretty well. He kept me on track, and I helped him think outside the box and brought some fun into his life."

This feels different from the way Eric told it, though I can't put my finger on why. "So you decided to be roommates after that?"

He nods. "Yep. Stayed with his family a lot too. Best friends until I got a job out of state and we fell out of touch."

Of all the questions I could ask to continue the conversation, I want most to ask about his family and why he spent so much time at Eric's house instead of his own, but something tells me I shouldn't push him too hard. He proved in Italy that he can be as stubborn as me, so I'm going to have to take a more delicate approach.

"Okay," I say, keeping my voice light. "Now tell me about the time you almost got him arrested."

The smile that breaks across Benson's face lights the whole restaurant, telling me I made the right choice. "He told you about that?"

I shrug. "Briefly, and only because he accidentally let it slip one night when we were hanging out with some of his college friends."

"That night was wild."

I lean forward, matching his smile and loving the way he fully relaxes across from me when I do. "Tell me everything."

I could talk to Benson for hours. When the subject is only marginally personal, he talks easily, like he did in Italy, and I think he's glad to let out some frustrations when it comes to Eric. He doesn't say anything outright about his thoughts on the conference nonsense, but I'm pretty sure he's on my side of things, which boosts my mood significantly.

He tells me about all the stupid stuff he did in college and how often Eric had to bail him out of trouble, and he talks about how instantly Lynda accepted him as part of the family without asking questions. Now that I know what his job is, when we get on the subject of other places he's traveled, he goes into a lot more depth than he ever did in Florence, talking about some of the companies he's consulted for.

He's kind of amazing, going places I never would have thought to visit simply because he found someone who wanted his help. I traveled whenever I could before Eric, but not the way Benson does it. I was a tourist. He's an explorer.

No wonder he knew the best way to experience Florence.

When I buy him a slice of berry cheesecake, hoping he'll keep talking for another hour or so, he finally shuts his mouth and narrows his eyes at me. "Are you plying me with non-chocolate dessert, Avery Grace?"

I put on an innocent expression. "Why would I do that when you've been blabbering just fine on your own?"

"Don't you have enough dirt on your business partner to last a lifetime?"

I do, but that's not why I want him to keep telling me stories. I'm learning so much about him, things I never could have guessed and things he probably doesn't realize he's been telling me. Like, now I know that he has a habit of including other people in conversations, especially when they're on the edge of a group. Now I know he is serious when he needs to be and always honest, even when it's to his detriment.

I put my chin in my hand, elbow on the table, and smile at him. "I can never have enough dirt on Eric, but I like the way you tell stories, Benson."

His lips twist in a smirk that only sort of masks his surprise. "You do?"

"Of course. I thought the same thing in Florence when you were giving me fake history lessons."

Snorting a laugh, he shakes his head at me as if he isn't sure what to do with that admission. "Not all of my history lessons were fake."

"True, but the fake ones were way more fun than the real ones. Which makes me wonder how many of these consulting stories of yours are exaggerated because you can't help but flirt with me."

"I haven't been flirting with you."

Sure he hasn't. This man's default setting is flirtatious. "So sitting and talking to me for three hours is something you do with all your clients?"

He swears, smile dropping as he pulls his phone out of his pocket. He grits his teeth and starts typing while every ounce of happiness disappears from his expression.

I frown. "What's wrong?"

"Nothing."

"Obviously."

"It's..." He scowls as he finishes typing, then shakes his head. "I was supposed to meet with a potential client tonight, and I totally forgot."

"This late?" It's almost nine.

"The company's in Australia."

Crap. That sounds like a big deal. "Is it too late to have the meeting?" I ask as guilt settles in. It's my fault that he missed it, since I'm the one who convinced him to join me for dinner.

He shrugs. "If I didn't have to grab my laptop, maybe I could make it work, but I left it at Rose & Quill."

"Oh. I'm sor—"

"Don't." He reaches across the table and grabs my hand, which catches me so off guard that I freeze. As much as we've been talking over the last few hours, there has been zero physical contact. In fact, I've barely touched Benson since Italy, and he feels so familiar that it hurts. "It's not your fault. I let myself get distracted." Something burns in his gaze, like there's more he wants to say, but when his phone buzzes on the table, he breaks our contact and starts reading, his shoulders falling. "Well, lost that chance..."

He may have said it's not my fault, but I'm not sure I agree with him. "They won't let you set up another meeting time?"

"It's fine. I'm not hurting for clients."

But something else is hurting him. "So this won't cost you your job or anything?"

He chuckles, though the sound carries no amusement. "Nah. I have more than enough to keep me busy. Too bu..." He cuts himself off and looks at me. Was he about to say he's too busy? Over the last several days, he's spent as much time brainstorming with me and indulging my ideas as he has doing whatever he does as a consultant. He hasn't seemed to mind, but what if I've only been making his job harder?

"Benson."

"I should go." He looks up as our server arrives with the cheesecake and sets it in front of him, and a line forms between his eyebrows as he stares at the dessert. "I, uh..." He pulls out his wallet and tosses a few bills onto the table, leaving the cheesecake behind as he slips from his chair and makes a beeline to the door.

The old Avery would let things end here. She would recognize that she made a mistake by distracting him and let him have his space. But I'm not that Avery anymore, nor do I want to be, and being bold tonight felt *good*. Even if Benson left in a rush, he was having a good time before he remembered his meeting. He seemed happy.

He pushed me to be better in Florence. I think I need to do the same for him. Somehow.

TICKET
PASSPORT
HOTEL
Time To Travel

CHAPTER 19
Benson

I'm such an idiot. My conversation with Avery at the restaurant keeps running through my head as I lie in my hotel bed, keeping me awake though I'm desperate for some sleep. I let my guard down, and she wiggled her way through the cracks in my shields and put me at ease in a way only she can. What is it about this woman that makes me think I can be a different man?

My phone buzzes with a text, and shock jolts through me when I see that it's Avery.

Are you okay?

It is way too late for me to be texting her, but my thumb starts swiping out a reply. Stupid thumb.

I'm fine. Sorry for the way I left.

Is there anything I can do to help you get that client back?

Technically, I don't know when I would have fit the client in to begin with, but I was going to try. They're big enough that they could push me into the next level and give me connections with other international companies, which is exactly what I need to grow my business into something self-sustaining. But this particular client needs someone as soon as possible, so I would have had to cut my time with Rose & Quill short.

I would hate to leave Eric so quickly, idiot though he is, and it's too late anyway now that I've missed the preliminary planning meeting. The client told me they would hire the other person they've been talking to because of the time constraints, so I'll have to find someone else to give me the boost I need.

While I'm disappointed by this setback, I'm more upset that I so easily stepped over the line I wasn't supposed to cross. All it took was one text from Avery; I couldn't have said no to joining her for dinner if I'd tried. She makes it so easy to forget the reasons I should keep my distance, and talking to Avery is...easy. It has been from the beginning. Everything about being around her is easy.

Benson:

> I promise it's not a big deal.

Avery:

> Are you sure? Because if it's going to make paying your rent difficult or anything like that, we can give you a bonus for helping us.

She's worried about me paying rent? She clearly has no idea what people in my line of work make, but that also might mean she herself is strapped for cash and thinks everyone else is too. But that wouldn't make sense. I've seen what Rose & Quill brings in, and their numbers aren't small. It's why someone like Phillip Rogers would be interested in investing in the first place.

I groan and roll over, folding my pillow in half to make it easier to see my phone.

Benson:

> What is your salary, Avery?

Avery:

Huh?

Benson:

How much are you getting paid as CEO and Creative Director?

Avery:

I don't see how this is relevant.

I try to picture where she is right now, if she's sitting at her kitchen table eating that cheesecake I wish I hadn't ignored or if she's in bed, like I am. "Don't picture her in bed," I mutter to myself and type out a text.

Benson:

I can look it up when I get to the office tomorrow, but I'm going to guess it isn't enough.

Avery:

We're being cautious with our salaries.

She was cautious in Italy too, which is part of the reason I tried to buy her things whenever she seemed to be silently telling herself she didn't need something she wanted. Which makes me wonder again why she thinks I might be struggling to pay my bills. She knows what I spent on her in Florence.

Benson:

One, you should be getting paid more, so that's my first order of business tomorrow. And two, I live in a tenth-floor two-bedroom condo in the middle of Manhattan and have already paid off the mortgage. I'm perfectly fine.

Her response takes longer to come in than I'd like, but I use the time while I wait to see if I can log in to the R&Q spreadsheets on my phone. It's not the greatest setup on this small of a screen, but I can see enough to confirm Avery isn't being paid what she should. Thankfully, Eric's salary is equally pitiful, though I half expected to learn he's been paying himself more than what he's giving her.

He may be an idiot sometimes, but he's not a tool.

When Avery's text finally comes through, I almost drop my phone in my effort to open it as quickly as I can.

Avery:

> Right. I forgot you're both rich and handsome.

I lift myself up on one elbow, staring at the words on the screen. "Avery Grace, are you flirting with me?" She called me out on my unintentional flirting at the restaurant, but this brazen compliment is new coming from her.

What am I supposed to do with it? Ignore it. That's what I should do. But my thumb has other ideas.

Benson:

> Like I said, I don't need the Australian job.

That's not entirely true, given I haven't found any other international companies with the size and influence I need to expand my business, but I'm not about to tell her that.

Avery:

> That sounds like a heist. Like The Italian Job?

Benson:

> That's why I'm so handsomely rich, obviously. Consulting is just a cover.

Avery:

> Ah, it all makes sense now! Did I get in the way of the treasure you were going after in Florence?

Benson:

> Who says I didn't get her?

I curse as soon as I hit send and hope she doesn't read too much into my response. Jewels can be referred to as 'she,' right? This is what I get for letting my guard down around this woman. My phone buzzes once, then again, and I'm almost too afraid to look.

Avery:

You says.

But if you ever decide not to be a stick in the mud, you know where to find me.

I stare at the words on the screen until my vision starts to blur. She is...bold. Bolder than she was in Florence, where she let me take the lead on everything. Sure, she got braver as the week went on, but she still went with whatever I planned for her, down to crashing the reception. While she's been pulling me into conversation and brainstorming at the office this week, she hasn't openly flirted like this.

And I am finding this side of her a little too attractive. What is it about confident women that I can't resist?

I can either shut her down, or I can play along, and I know which one would be more enjoyable. She knows this can't last, so she knows any flirting I do is for the fun of it.

I groan. Does she know that? Things are different now that we're not bound by anonymity and an end date. She's made it clear that our week in Italy meant more to her than what it was supposed to, so if Avery is flirting with me right now, it's because she wants something to exist between us. Something I can't give her. If I give into the temptation she's presenting right now and flirt back, there's a high chance she's going to end up hurt when I have to leave.

I should end the conversation here and go to bed. Hopefully to get some actual sleep. But the idea of shutting this down and being nothing but colleagues with this woman makes my chest ache, like I can't breathe.

"That's a good sign that this is a bad idea," I mutter to myself, my stomach twisting as I type out another text. I'm going to regret this. But the screens and distance between me and Avery are making me feel reckless, and that feeling is not something I've ever been able to suppress easily.

Benson:
> I think the real stick in the mud here is the woman who has been going to work at six in the morning.

Avery:
> I was thinking about sleeping in tomorrow.

Benson:
> No you weren't.

Avery:
> Well now I'm definitely sleeping in.

Benson:
> I'll believe it when I see it.

She doesn't respond for a minute, during which I pull up the pictures I have of Avery because I haven't been able to delete them, no matter how many times I tell myself I need to. I'm already making a mistake by texting her late at night, so I might as well make things worse and get a reminder of how truly beautiful she is.

When Avery's next text comes in, I stare at it for a long time.

Avery:
> What do you do when you're not at the office?

> Obviously you hike, because you and Eric went up the canyon last weekend, but what else? When you left yesterday, did you go straight to

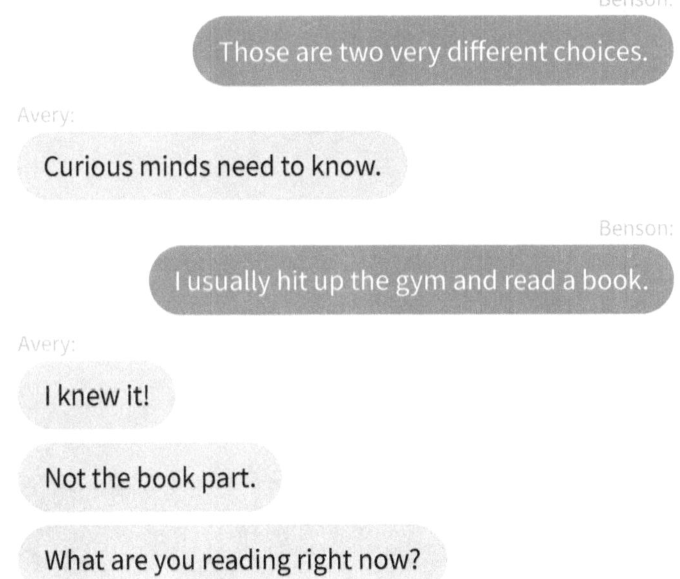

She's doing the thing we avoided in Italy, asking for details. Instinct is screaming at me to get the heck out of here and put up the walls that have kept me safe for the last thirty-five years, but...

But the grass is so much greener on Avery's side, and I won't be able to see it if there's a wall in my way.

I sigh and settle in, getting comfortable.

I glance at my nightstand, where Dani's romantasy novel is waiting for me. I didn't let myself dive back into it tonight because I knew I would stay up too late to get to the end, though at this point that argument is pretty moot because I'm not sleeping anyway. Do I dare admit I'm reading a romance? I could say it's to better understand the company and the book that pushed Rose & Quill into the big leagues, which wouldn't be a lie. But I'm also genuinely enjoying the storyline and the compelling way Dani crafted her characters.

I should tell Dani as much, but idiot that I am, I deleted her number that last night in Florence.

I settle on a different truth.

Benson:

I've been reading a lot of Sanderson lately.

Avery:

Fantasy? Really?

Benson:

Should I be offended by your shock?

Avery:

You don't strike me as a fantasy guy.

Benson:

What kind of guy do I strike you as?

Avery:

The kind who reads self-help books and listens to podcasts.

Benson:

I do that too, but not when I want to unwind at the end of the day.

Avery:

Huh.

Huh. That's all she says, which means I have no idea what she thinks about my reading preferences. It only makes me wonder again about what might have happened if she and I met at a book club. Eric caught her fancy without being a reader, so either she's not a fan of fiction readers, which feels unlikely, given her choice of career, or there was something else about him that caught her eye. I wonder what it was.

Before I cave and ask, I type out a different text.

For a second I worry I've overstepped, but then she sends a winking emoji. But it's the one that's also blowing a kiss, and my breath catches in my throat. I won't pretend I'm fully versed in emoji language, but that one feels like it means more than a regular wink. It's flirty and bold, like she was at the restaurant tonight.

"Avery Grace, what game are you playing?" I mutter and try to figure out what I can say to that. With my casual approach to dating and women in general, I rarely flirt over the phone, so this is out of my wheelhouse. Giving up on any sort of a clever response, I search through the bank of emojis to try to find one that might work as a reply.

I settle on the "rock on" symbol, the one with the pinky and forefinger held up, and lock my phone before I get even more caught up in this conversation. It's probably the wrong thing to send, but what else is new? I never have the right words when it comes to Avery Baldwin.

TICKET
PASSPORT
N
W
E
S
HOTEL
Time To
Travel

CHAPTER 20
Avery

I PACE MY BOOK-STREWN living room while waiting for one of my cousins to respond. I sent that text last night when they were probably all asleep, but it's morning now, and I'm desperate for an analysis. Surely one of them has some sort of emoji hieroglyph dictionary in their brain, right?

I'm old enough that when I started texting, emojis weren't a thing. Benson's older than me. So either he is more versed in emoji meanings than I am, or he has no idea how to say what he wants to say.

"This is why we use our words," I grumble at my phone.

Is it because I sent the kissy emoji? I thought it was fun and flirty, but it must have crossed the line. While I still don't know what the "rock on" emoji means, it's safe to assume that Benson wasn't interested in flirting back.

I've delayed going to work this morning as long as I can, hoping for some assistance before I have to see Benson, but if I don't leave in the next few minutes, I'll actually be late. Not that I have a set time I need to arrive—kind of the perk of owning my own company—but I'll feel terrible if Benson is there by himself. Lynda will look after him, but—

My phone buzzes on the counter where I left it, and I leap over a pile of books to see which of my cousins is going to save me. Instead, I find a text from Lynda.

Lynda:

> Hey sweetie, I woke up this morning with an awful head cold, and I'm going to need to call it a sick day. I'll monitor customer service emails from here unless you need me to come in.

Avery:

> Oh my gosh, no, please stay home! Do you need me to bring you anything?

Lynda:

> Avery, honey, I don't need you mothering me. I'll be fine. *kissy face*

There, see? A kissy face doesn't mean anything crazy! Then again, Lynda is of the generation who tend to use emojis completely wrong, so maybe that isn't a point in my favor.

Groaning, I grab my keys and head out to my car. I almost stop for a bagel to delay things more, but my conscience doesn't let me make the turn. I'll have to face Benson sooner or later, now without a Lynda buffer, and I will have to find out if I can stick to my guns or if the sight of him will make me retreat.

The texts finally come in right as I'm pulling to a stop in the parking garage.

Sadie:

> So the thumb isn't extended which means it's not an I love you… Is he a Texas Longhorns fan? I'm just as confused by that as you are. But I LOVE that you're getting your flirt on! You go girl!

Dani:

> It means he's VERY bad at emojis. *crying laughing* You should send him one back and see what he does. Also, yay for getting your flirt on!

Poppy:

> Maybe they are devil horns because he's being bad by flirting with you??? I'm not sure I can allow you to like a bad emoji-er.

Lucy:

> Umm… I've got nothing. I'm going with Dani and saying he's very bad at emojis. This is better than a romance novel!!

Well that was maddeningly unhelpful. I obviously won't get anything useful from Dani or my cousins, so I square my shoulders and head inside, my feet growing heavier with each step.

I find Benson standing in the doorway leading to the balcony, a mug of coffee in his hand and his eyes fixed on the view of the mountains. Here in Riverton, on the west side of the Salt Lake Valley, we have a pretty good vantage point, and Benson tends to take a few minutes every day to sit and look at the Wasatch Front.

"Do you miss it?" I ask.

Benson jumps with a curse, coffee splashing from his mug onto his shirt and staining the pastel blue fabric with a large spot of brown.

"Oh!" I wince, mortified. "I am so sorry."

"Are you always this quiet?" Exasperation makes his voice breathy, but there's a hint of amusement dancing in his eyes as he gingerly sets his mug on Lynda's desk and starts unbuttoning his shirt.

Is he going to strip down in the middle of the lobby? I can't decide if I love that or hate it.

"Um." I grab a tissue and hold it out to him, but he only stares at it while he finishes with his buttons. The undershirt he has on underneath is just as soaked, and his face clearly says, *It's going to take more than that.* "Hang on."

As my embarrassment continues to intensify, leaving me dizzy and overheated, I open the closet door behind Lynda's desk and flip on the light. We keep a bunch of books on hand in case we need something quickly and don't have time to head to the warehouse twenty minutes north of the office, but there should be some merch in here somewhere. We made way more than we needed to for Dani's first post-viral event.

"Ah ha!" I find the box I'm looking for and start digging, hoping I can find something that will fit Benson for the time being.

"What is all this stuff?"

I squeak and bang my head on the shelf above me. Though Benson grimaces sympathetically from the doorway, it only takes a second before he's laughing. Snorting, I join in, and soon I'm laughing so hard that I have to sit down.

"Payback?" I ask when I can breathe again.

Benson, wearing only his undershirt now, smirks and shakes his head. "How petty do you think I am, Baldwin?"

Baldwin. He's never called me by my last name before, and it feels like a wall has slid into place between us. I hate it.

I toss a shirt at him. "I wouldn't know. You were pretty perfect in Italy, and I'm still waiting to learn more about who you really are underneath all that charm." Oh hey, that sounded pretty good!

Eyebrows lifting, he holds the shirt up to take a look at it. "Dani's book?" Before I can answer, he grabs the back collar of his undershirt and lifts it over his head in one swift movement.

And I am not prepared. I don't know if anyone in the world could prepare themselves for the sight suddenly in front of me. I knew Benson was built, and he dazzled me with his biceps all the time in Florence. But this? Seeing the ridges of his torso without any pesky fabric to block the view? This man is basically a Roman god. Neptune, Apollo, Mars. Any of them. All of them at once.

Benson tugs the shirt over his head, regrettably pulling it down to cover his abs. "So is all of this swag and stuff?" he asks, apparently clueless about my ogling. Thank goodness. "What sort of things do you use this for?"

"Signings and preorders, mostly." My words come out a bit garbled even though he's fully dressed again. Maybe it's the fact that he opted for a pair of dark wash jeans today instead of slacks, and with the *Of Curses and Pomegranates* shirt and all its dark colors, his blue eyes are really popping.

It isn't fair how beautiful this man is, especially because I still don't have any idea what his parting emoji from last night means. What if Sadie's comment about the "I love you" emoji is right, and he just picked the wrong one? There's no way, but what if...?

He starts rummaging through totes and boxes, like he's taking stock of everything we've shoved into the storage closet. "There's a lot of good stuff in here."

Including you. He's repping that shirt so well that I want to sneak a picture and put it on our socials. He could sell everything we've got by standing there and looking pretty.

"I'm thinking we could do something with all of this and generate some buzz for R&Q and help get the ball rolling." He has a look on his face that is much like the one he had when we were talking to Phillip Rogers, like his focus has fully shifted into marketing mode. He looks...excited. More excited than he's ever looked.

He really loves his job.

I can't help but smile as he gathers up a few bookmarks, a copy of *Pomegranates*, and a tote bag, setting them on top of a box. He scans the shelves again and picks up a novella from a different author, as well as a couple of stickers. "We could make it a whole social media campaign," he mutters, practically talking to himself now. "I could reach out to some of my contacts in other states to do the same thing, so it isn't just here in Utah."

"Do what, exactly?" I ask, tilting my head.

Benson's eyes widen, but then he grins. "Little Free Libraries," he says, dumping all of his treasures into the tote and holding it toward me. "For one. Put swag bags in a few of them around the country and let your followers try to find them."

That's a pretty good idea. "And for another?"

Pulling up a box to sit next to me, Benson bites his lip as he keeps grinning. "I've been thinking about the R&Q brand, particularly last night."

"Did you sleep at all?" I almost reach up and touch his face. Now that he's up close, the dark circles under his eyes make him look exhausted. It's worse than the day after he arrived.

"Not even a little bit," he says with a chuckle, apparently in a great mood despite his lack of sleep. "Hence the coffee."

"That you didn't get to drink," I say with a wince. "Sorry."

"Don't worry about it." I'm pretty sure he means that. Or maybe he's so tired that he has no ability to regulate his emotions and he's stuck on happy. "Anyway, brand."

I grin. This sleepy and excited version of Benson is fun. "What about it?"

"You're still new enough that you don't have something that defines you aside from being Dani's publisher."

"We mostly publish fantas—"

"But what makes you different from the other fantasy publishers?" He grabs another copy of Dani's book and holds it in front of his chest, once again making me want to take a picture because dang, this man could sell water at a public drinking fountain by standing next to it and smiling. "What sets Rose & Quill apart? I've been studying other publishers, both similar in size and at a scope you should be aiming for, and I've been coming up with some ideas for how you might differentiate R&Q from your competitors beyond the quality of your books."

His words surprise me more than I expected them to, though this is the sort of thing I should have expected from a consultant. Either I've been taking too much of his time brainstorming marketing ideas and haven't given him a chance to do his job, or he was especially busy last night.

"Oh?" I say breathlessly. I don't know if I'm overwhelmed or excited to hear what he's come up with. It's probably a mixture of both.

Benson studies me for a moment, and then he chuckles and grabs my hand. "Okay, relax. Most of the concepts I've been working on have stemmed from your ideas."

My cheeks heat. "Really?"

Nodding, he squeezes my fingers in a way that helps me feel more stable. "Of course. If you were doing this on your own, you would have already done most of these things because you're a natural marketer."

He doesn't explicitly say Eric has been holding me back, but...

Unexpected tears prick my eyes, and I tilt my head down before Benson sees how much his words mean to me. I focus instead on our hands and the way he so easily laced his fingers between mine without any hesitation, like he did in Italy. If he really wanted to keep a professional distance between us, he wouldn't do this.

I clear my throat. "So, what else could we do with the swag?"

"The other day, you brought up mentorships as you bring on new authors, but what if you went beyond that?"

I look up. "What do you mean?"

His smile has turned softer. Warmer. I'm pretty sure this closet has exactly zero ventilation because it's a million degrees in here and all I can smell is Benson's clean scent. All I can feel is his thumb rubbing mine. "I mean you could go further than helping authors you've acquired. You could have your established authors, like Dani, host seminars or workshops for aspiring writers and give them the tools they need to get picked up by a publisher, whether it's you or someone else."

"But wouldn't that be helping our competition if they go elsewhere?"

"Not if you give yourself right of first refusal for a first book. Put it in the workshop contract. And everyone who signs up gets a signed book and swag."

"That would fit our focus of fostering community," I say as I catch on to what he's saying. My thoughts start building on each other, growing my excitement for this idea. "Not only are we creating a kinship between our authors, but we would also be encouraging external support. Our readers will see that the authors actually care about people, not just sales."

"'A rising tide lifts all boats,'" Benson says with a nod.

"That's kind of genius, Benson," I say, looking down at the tote he handed me.

He laughs. "That's why they pay me the big bucks. Except you, of course."

I frown, looking up at his face again. "I'm not paying you big bucks?"

"No. You're not paying me at all."

Wait. Is he telling me that I not only lost him a client last night, but I'm also not paying him to help our company? My jaw drops, but based on his growing smile, he finds my shock amusing. "Benson! We should be paying you!"

He laughs, shaking his head. "I'm doing this as a favor to an old friend," he says, and then he lifts my hand to his lips, pressing a kiss to my knuckles. His eyes slowly drop to our hands, resting there for a long moment before he meets my gaze again with a heated look in his eyes. It's the same look he gave me in Italy right before he kissed me, and my breath catches in my lungs as he slowly leans closer.

Maybe I'm not well-versed in non-romantic business relationships, given I started a company with my boyfriend, but that is not the kind of look someone gives their coworker if he isn't hoping for something more.

"And I'm doing this," he says, his voice husky, "because his co-owner is super cute when she's calling me a genius, and she makes it so hard to remember my rules."

I gasp, suddenly desperate to ask if he did mean to use the "I love you" emoji as my cheeks flame. But Benson is on his feet and leaving the closet before I draw in enough breath to speak.

"I have a call with your website designer in a minute," he says as he disappears into the lobby, "but if you want to check out some Little Free Libraries while I'm on the call, it might be a good idea to scope out the options if that's a direction you want to go with the swag."

While I'm more than happy to move forward with this idea, how am I supposed to recover after that moment we just had? He's left me feeling like I'm made of jelly. There's more to this being bold thing than I anticipated because I never expected Benson to cross the line he so clearly drew on Monday. He seems far happier when he's letting himself be authentic than when he's pretending there's nothing between us.

So maybe I should listen to my cousins and keep "getting my flirt on." Maybe it won't go anywhere beyond the next couple of weeks, but I'm not willing to waste the opportunity to try. I'll be bold and hope he'll take a chance on a future with me.

Benson has his laptop in hand and is on his way into Eric's office when I finally get up and move to my office. "I'm going to commandeer Eric's desk while he's gone," he explains before I can ask. "That way I won't be a distraction. You still need to hire a social media manager, remember?"

Be bold, Avery Grace. "You are literally a walking distraction, Benson. You're switching offices because you're worried about *me* distracting *you.*"

Though his eyes go wide, he quickly shifts his expression to a smirk. "So that's how you're going to play, is it?"

I fold my arms. "I'm not playing, Bens."

His lips quirk up. "I know you're not."

"You're coming with me to check out the libraries." I am genuinely impressed with my forceful tone.

He lifts an eyebrow. "Am I? Also, when is Lynda coming in?"

"Of course you are. It was your idea, so you get to see it through. And she isn't. She called in sick, so it's just you and me today, West."

The knuckles on the hand gripping his laptop turn white, and Benson processes what I said for a long time before he finally swallows and nods. "Great."

"I'm going to reach out to some of our biggest influencers and see if any of them are interested in doing our socials," I tell Benson, though I'm not sure why. I'll do it regardless of what he says. It's not the way Eric would go about hiring a media manager, but if Eric can make universal decisions, I can do things my own way.

He smiles again, like he can't help how much he is enjoying my newfound gumption. "That's a great idea, Avery."

Heat rises in my face, pushing me to keep being bold. "Let me know when you're free, and we'll go do that library tour."

Benson's jaw tightens, and I brace myself against him telling me no. But he nods. "Okay. I'm, uh, going to take that call now."

"You do that."

The instant he's out of sight, I let out a little giggle that is way more understated than I feel.

"I heard that!" Benson calls across the hall.

I don't even care.

TICKET
PASSPORT
HOTEL
Time To
Travel

CHAPTER 21
Benson

Is this how I made Avery feel when we were in Florence? Like I've been picked up by a whirlwind and am on the ride of my life whether I want to be or not? I tend to be a pushy person as it is, but I took a lot of pleasure in nudging Avery to do things she wouldn't have done on her own, and there's a chance I may have been a bit heavy-handed. Or maybe a lot heavy-handed, which would explain why Avery is not holding back this morning.

This is an experience I'm not sure I'll survive. The woman next to me is fearless, funny, and flirty, and she knows it.

And I have never been more attracted to her.

The instant I got off the call with the designer, Avery was at Eric's office door, her purse at the ready and a wicked gleam in her eyes. Though I half-heartedly suggested I should stay at the office in case anyone came in, she didn't have to try hard to convince me to join her and practically dragged me to her car, asking me rapid-fire questions that were so unconnected to each other that I answered each one almost by reflex.

Which high school did you go to?

Did you have any pets growing up?

What's your favorite late night snack?

What kind of workouts do you do?

It has been twenty minutes of nonstop inquisition, and the questions are likely only the start of things. I have no idea where she's taking me or if we're even checking out Little Free Libraries, but I have next to no motivation to do something about it. I'm here for the ride, whirlwind be damned.

"So you grew up in Logan, right?" Avery asks as she pulls into a coffee shop parking lot. "What do you miss most?"

While I'm grateful for the coffee stop, since I didn't get to drink my last cup, I'm less grateful for this subject. The other topics were easy. This one is anything but that. "Not much," I mutter as I slip out of the car.

"You don't miss anything about Utah?"

"Utah, sure. But not Logan."

"What's wrong with Logan?"

Nothing except for unmet expectations and a childhood full of being told I'm a disappointment and an enigma.

Holding the door open for Avery, I pierce her with a stare that is meant to intimidate her but lacks any strength because I'm so tired. "What are you doing?"

She stops and looks up at me, her expression falsely innocent. "What do you mean?"

I sigh. "What's with all the questions? I'm trying to keep a professional distance between us, and you—"

"If you call what happened in the storage closet professional, I'm worried about how you treat your other clients."

Narrowing my eyes, I try to come up with some kind of argument. I come up blank. I have definitely never held a client's hand before or looked at her like she was the oasis in my desert. I've certainly never come close to kissing a client.

Avery keeps talking. "I'm trying to get to know you, Benson." Folding her arms, she gives me the kind of look I was trying to give her just now, only hers is effective and makes me shift back half an inch. "Do you always hide behind surface level?" She pauses, her expression softening as she adds, "Doesn't that get lonely?"

If she had stuck with the surface level question, I could have denied it. I could have told her I've made friends all across the country. While that's true, her second question proves she knows me better than I thought. Eric got the full me, back when I was desperate for connection, and Riccardo is my closest friend more recently because he's the kind of person who naturally encourages vulnerability and honesty. But beyond those two?

Not many people know me.

I didn't dislike that until right now, when I'm looking down into the warm brown eyes of a woman who has been tempting me to be open since the moment she cried next to me on the plane.

Avery's obviously waiting for an answer, standing firm in the doorway and blocking someone's exit, so I mutter a lame response that doesn't answer her question. "It's easier," I say and nudge her inside.

She scoffs as she gets in line. "For whom?"

I can't help but chuckle, grateful for the distraction from the realness of our conversation. "Did you just say *whom*?"

"It's the right word."

"Maybe, but no one says it."

Rolling her eyes, she fiddles with her purse with the look of someone formulating a plan to keep me talking, which means I didn't deflect anything at all. All my teasing accomplished was reminding me how much I like this woman. A rock settles in my chest, making it hard to breathe. I *really* like her, and it's getting harder to remember my goals and the reasons I need to keep things casual.

"Where did you grow up?" I grind out, desperate for a topic that doesn't involve me and will last longer than a few seconds.

She looks up, narrowing her eyes. "South Jordan."

"So we're in your stomping grounds?" I try to picture Avery spending all her time in this area, though I don't know the west side of the valley all that well. The University of Utah, where I went to school, is on the east side, and Eric's family has always lived south of here, in Lehi. So while I've spent plenty of time on the freeway that splits the Salt Lake Valley, there was never a reason to come out West.

Strange, living twenty-two years in the same state and never exploring parts of it that aren't all that far away. If this were a place like Florence, I would have seen most of the valley by now.

"What's your coffee order, Benson?" Avery asks, pulling me out of my thoughts.

I stumble over my answer. "Oh, uh, iced Americano?"

"Is that a question?"

It wasn't until she asked that, even if my tone was uncertain. I can't hold back my amused smile. "Are you judging my coffee choices, Avery Grace?"

Though she fights her smile, her lips curve upward. "Maybe. But only because it's the most boring order in the world. And I thought you were exciting."

I fold my arms, lifting one eyebrow. "Well, what's your order?"

"Cappuccino, obviously."

I snort. "That made sense in Italy, but here? It's a million degrees, and you're basically one foam heart away from being a romcom cliché."

"What's wrong with that? At least I'm not boring like *someone* I know."

"Eric?" I wrinkle my nose. "You're right. He's incredibly boring, and you dodged a bullet there." Her answering laugh almost distracts me from the fact that she's handing over her card. I realize just in time and grab her wrist. "I've got this."

Her playful scowl loosens the rock in my chest. "I can buy you coffee, Benson."

"I know you can." I hand the cashier my card, still gripping Avery's arm. "But until we get your salary fixed, I'm not letting you pay for anything."

She snickers. "It's a company card, Bens."

Bens. I like when she calls me that, just like I like touching her. Wrapping my fingers around her wrist isn't in any way romantic, but I held her hand in the storage closet this morning, and that reminder of how it felt to hold her in Florence has left my palms feeling itchy. Any point of contact I get sends a shock of electric current through me.

I drop her arm and clear my throat. "Even so, I've got the coffee."

"Fine. Then R&Q will pay for lunch."

A swear slips off my tongue, making Avery laugh again. She's going to be the death of me. "You're going to make professional distance impossible, aren't you?"

"Yep." The amusement in her eyes, combined with a bright smile, makes her look so alive and happy. "You set the tone in Italy. Now it's my turn."

I have to stick to my guns. I *have to*. Letting myself think I can have this—have *her*—is only going to make things harder when I have to leave. If I thought it was hard to walk away in Florence, that's going to feel like a walk in the park compared to what's coming. Because Avery's going to make me know her. She's showing me the parts of her I didn't let myself know before, and each new thing I learn about her makes her all the more interesting. All the more beautiful.

I can't fall for her, but I'm pretty sure it's already too late.

TICKET
PASSPORT
N
W
E
S
HOTEL
Time To
Travel

CHAPTER 22
Avery

"There are only three boy cousins," I explain to Benson as I turn onto a side street. "Sadie's brother, Brody, who is the only grandkid older than me. Chloe's brother, Gavin. And…"

I've been telling him stories about my childhood as we've driven from one Little Free Library to the next, and we got on the subject of my extended family when one of the libraries had a book we used to read all the time as a kid. He's been rereading the text thread when he chatted with my cousins during Riccardo's reception while I've told him more about them, and I can't decide if he's enjoying this conversation or not because he's been so quiet.

Maybe even thoughtful.

I wrinkle my nose and sigh as I name the last of my male cousins. "And Kaden."

"What's up with Kaden?" It's the first thing Benson has said in at least half an hour that wasn't a grunt or a hum, and I suppose I should thank Kaden for getting the man to talk again. He hands me my phone, but not before I notice he had switched to looking at pictures in my camera roll instead of the text thread.

Pictures of Italy.

While I'd rather comment on where his attention has really been, I don't want to push my luck. "Aside from Poppy, he's the baby of the family, the only son of the only son."

"What's wrong with sons?"

I turn onto the street with our next library option and scoff. "Absolutely nothing! But Kaden? He's kind of a terror. When he was a kid, he peed in my favorite pair of UGGs."

Benson snorts. "UGGs? Seriously? I thought you were cooler than that."

I whack his arm and then pull to a stop on the curb, shifting the car into park. "It was the 2000s. Of course I had UGGs. But Kaden peed in them, and they were never the same." I slouch in my seat, losing some of the lightness I've been feeling all morning. Whether intentionally or not, Benson is good at making me forget about reality whenever he's around. "Our Grandma Sue is throwing a party for him this weekend because he graduated from Harvard a few months ago, and it's been so long since I had time to go to a family function that I need to go."

"But?"

"But none of my cousins can make it, which means it's just going to be me and all the adults."

"And Kaden," Benson points out with a chuckle.

I groan. "And Kaden."

"Is he that bad?"

I drop my head against the headrest and sigh. He's not really the reason I don't want to go, but I'm not sure Benson will get the real reason. "No one understands why I called off my wedding so close to the day," I say quietly, "so I've been avoiding everyone, but that isn't helping anything because I'm the oldest granddaughter, and there's always been that expectation to set an example and be involved." Not that I've always been good at that...

Benson lets out a soft chuckle, shaking his head. "I'm the youngest." It's the first time he's mentioned his family, a subject I tried to steer clear of for fear of spooking him, and I hold my breath, waiting to see if he'll say any more. "Trust me, it doesn't matter where you are in the family for expectation to weigh on you."

I wish he would keep talking because there's some weight to his comment, but my boldness does not extend to pushing him about topics he actively avoids. Without anything to say, I want to take his hand in a show of solidarity. To offer comfort. To grab on and never let go. But he opens his door and slips out of the car, and I'm pretty sure we're done with that topic of conversation.

It's okay. I'm slowly peeling back the layers of Benson West, and if I keep at it, I might find the gooey center of a man who is willing to take a risk. Or maybe I won't. Maybe Benson will always be afraid of commitment, but at least I'll know I tried.

That's all I can do now.

As I get out of the car and follow Benson to this latest library, my jaw slides open. "It's gorgeous!" I say, almost reverently. The owner took an old London phone booth and turned it into a bookcase, and it's almost magical seeing all the books stacked behind the glass door. "This is hands down my favorite one so far."

Benson chuckles, hands in his pockets. "I don't know if we'll be able to top this." But there's something in his voice, something he isn't saying, though it's hard to tell what he might be thinking because his eyes are on the phone booth.

I fold my arms. "But?"

He looks at me out of the corner of his eye. "But there are probably tons of people who come to this one. What if we picked a smaller library that might not get as much traffic? People don't get any money from having these libraries, but I'm sure they would love visitors all the same. Get the book circulating a little more, you know?"

"That's...actually a great idea."

"Don't sound so surprised."

"Too late. The more I learn about you, the more interesting you become." I grin when he blushes. It is remarkably fun to be the cause of a reaction like that, and now I understand why Benson so shamelessly flirted with me in Florence. I feel powerful and free. "But you're right. Choosing a smaller library would both bring other libraries in the area some attention, and it would also make the hunt more fun. Hopefully garner some good publicity."

"My thoughts exactly."

"In that case, I liked the library before the last one we looked at."

Benson nods, finally turning his head to look at me. "Busier neighborhood, so neighbors won't have to worry too much about increased traffic, sturdy and clean box housing the books to protect against damage, easy to find. I think that's a great choice."

"Great." Except, that means we don't have any good reasons to stay away from the office. I glance at my phone, not sure if I want the time to move faster or stop altogether. "It's too early for lunch," I mutter.

"Yeah," Benson agrees. He doesn't make any moves to return to the car, which I'm taking as a sign.

"But it's nice out today."

He glances at the sky. "Yep."

"It would be a shame to be cooped up in the office all day."

A smile plays on his lips as he shakes his head at me, like I'm the most ridiculous person he's ever met. "What are you trying to say, Baldwin?"

"Want to walk around for a bit? I hear it's good for clearing the head and making it easier to focus." Mostly, I'm not ready for our conversations to end, and if we go back, I'm worried he'll shut himself up in Eric's office the rest of the day.

Sighing, he holds his elbow out for me to take.

"So, tell me," I say and loop my arm through his before he changes his mind. "When you've been doing your own thing and aren't listening to me blabber on, what have you been working on?"

"No one in the world thinks you blabber."

"Eric does."

"Well Eric can be an idiot. I love listening to you talk."

The warmth that blossoms in my chest rivals the growing heat of the day. It's September, but summer is still in full force. Yet Benson somehow makes me feel warmer than the sun ever could.

I lean into him, tightening my hold on his arm as we walk. "Thanks. But sometimes I wonder if you and Eric are really friends when you say things like that."

He chuckles. "Idiotic tendencies aside, he's one of the best guys I know."

"Before yesterday, I would have said the same thing. But he's been…" I don't know the right word to describe how Eric has been acting ever since I got back from Italy.

"Different," Benson mutters. "Yeah, I was wondering if that was the case."

"Maybe he'll be back to his calm and content self after the conference."

"Maybe." He doesn't sound all that confident. "And to answer your question, I've been trying to build a solid business plan with standard operating procedures, working with Rogers on maximizing his investment, getting some tools set up so you and Eric have better performance metrics. Things like that. Anything that will make your job easier when I'm gone."

Ah yes. When he's gone. The reminder settles heavy in my stomach. I'm dreading that day, especially because I don't know if he would want to stay in Utah even if he does agree to a relationship, and I'm not sure I could handle long distance. The couple of days in between leaving Italy and Benson showing up here were bad enough. Do I want to put my hope in a man who travels for a living? During my earlier questioning, I got the clear sense that he is rarely home.

And yet I don't want to imagine a life without Benson in it now that I've gotten a taste of having him in my life.

"You've been able to do all that even when I keep talking to you?" I ask, trying to distract myself before I sink into a pit of despair. That's being dramatic, but I don't care. I'm going to let myself feel all the things because I'm tired of holding it in.

"I happen to be incredibly efficient," Benson says. He pulls his hand out of his pocket, severing our connection and leaving me disappointed. But then his fingers lace with mine, and the disappointment fades. "And I meant what I said. I like talking to you."

We round a corner as we fall into silence, walking hand in hand through a random neighborhood in South Jordan like we've done this a million times. It's not nearly as exciting as Florence, but there's a peace in walking side by side with another person.

My phone buzzes in my purse, interrupting that peace, and my watch shows an unknown number. Normally I would ignore it, but with Lynda out sick, I worry it might be business-related. Letting go of Benson's hand, I dig into my purse and answer the call. "Hello?"

"Avery!" The familiar voice is louder than necessary, forcing me to pull the phone away from my ear.

"Poppy?"

"You're going to be at Kaden's little party thing, right?"

"Uh, why?"

"Because I have to work, but I have something to give to him."

"Why don't you just give it to your mom?" I mouth an apology to Benson, who shrugs and puts his hands back into his pockets as he turns to study an impressive rosebush.

Poppy heaves a massive sigh. "Because she won't think it's an appropriate gift. You're my only hope, Avery."

I have never wanted an excuse to miss that party more than I do now. Not only do I *not* want to hang out with all my aunts and uncles while everyone praises Kaden for graduating college, something most of the rest of us have also done, but I'm not sure I have the mental capacity for Poppy right now.

I hold back a groan. "What's the gift?"

"It's a secret."

"Great."

"I'll bring it by your apartment tonight after my shift ends, but you have to promise me you'll give it to him personally so you can tell me his expression when he opens it."

Now I really don't want to go to the party. "Poppy, I don't think—"

"Pretty please? You know I only have people's best interests at heart. That's why I gave you that bracelet to help you find love when you went to Italy."

Benson chokes and starts coughing, and I look at him with wide eyes. "Bug," he gasps, gesturing to his mouth. I'm not sure I believe him, but Poppy is talking again.

"On that note, did you figure out the emoji debacle? I don't think Benson would have texted you devil horns when he is obviously in love with you, but I still don't—"

"I need to go, Poppy," I say, cutting her off because Benson has given up on pretending he isn't listening to every word and is now staring at me, a mixture of wariness and amusement in his eyes. I forgot how light his eyes get in the sunlight, shifting from bright blue to a pale gray. "Text me when you're leaving the airport, okay?"

"Will do!"

"Wait, what number are you calling from?"

"Oh, I forgot my charger today so I borrowed someone's phone in exchange for one of my crystals. See you soon, Ave!"

She hangs up, leaving me standing in the middle of a stranger's sidewalk and wishing the ground would swallow me up. "How much did you hear?" I ask, eyes on my feet.

Benson clears his throat. "All of it. Or none of it, if that would make you feel better." He tilts his head to the side, his tone hesitant as he says, "Your cousin gave you a bracelet to...find love?"

I grimace. "She's big into crystals and things," I remind him. "And she works at the airport and could probably tell how, uh, conflicted I was? About going to Italy without Eric. So she gave me a bracelet." It's coincidentally still in my purse, so I pull it out to show him, as if that might make that conversation with Poppy less embarrassing.

Benson takes the bracelet from me, running his thumb along the leather band. "You never wore it in Florence."

"Yeah, well, I wasn't looking for love..." I leave my sentence open, not willing to admit to stronger feelings than interest by using the word 'but.' Even if I want to. I don't know Benson well enough to love him.

But if he ever opens up to me, I'm a goner.

Benson's long fingers curl around the bracelet, and I wish I could tell what he's thinking right now as his eyes meet mine. He takes a step closer, moving in until I have to look up to meet his eyes. "Avery. What Poppy said about me... I..." His eyebrows bunch together as he pulls his phone from his pocket, staring at the screen for a second before he lifts it to his ear. "Eric. Hey."

You've got to be kidding me. If Benson never finishes his sentence because of this phone call, I might have to consider actually breaking Eric's nose. He's already the main reason Benson won't act on his feelings for me, and if he's going to get in my way from all the way out in Colorado, so help me...

"No, I'm out on a project," Benson says, glancing at me. A pause, and then, "It's a marketing thing. Yeah, she's— Eric, she's literally in charge of marketing." He turns and takes a couple of steps away from me, but I can still hear every word he says because he's getting increasingly frustrated. "You and I sat down and wrote out the duties of the COO and CEO, and marketing was on her side of the list. You know that."

When did they do that? Eric and Benson haven't spent any time alone at the office, which is kind of strange, now that I think about it. I thought Eric would monopolize Benson's time, given their close friendship, and if Benson is so determined to keep on the other side of a professional boundary line, he should be working more with Eric than with me.

I'm not convinced Benson's trying all that hard to maintain his own boundaries.

"What is that supposed to mean?" Benson asks sharply, stuffing his hand into his hair. "You know I would never do that again."

I shouldn't make conjectures, but I'm almost certain of what's happening on the other side of that phone call. Eric doesn't like me doing any marketing without him because he likes keeping my "wild ideas" in check, and he thinks Benson is making a move on his ex. Cat's away, mice play.

Yesterday's frustration bubbles back up, and I'm gladder than ever that one of the women I reached out to this morning about handling our socials is extremely interested in the job. I have a video interview set up with her this afternoon, and she said she's available immediately. She even lives in Utah, which would make training so much easier.

"You shouldn't be driving while on the phone," Benson says, a bit of growl in his voice now. "Yeah, I know what your imagination is telling you, but it's not true. Promise. Then maybe you should have brought her with you." He hangs up and swears under his breath, his head bowed and a hand gripping the back of his neck.

"That sounded fun," I say bitterly.

"Why is he being like this?" Benson asks without looking at me.

I'm pretty sure it's a rhetorical question, but I answer anyway. "Because he likes when things go his way."

"That's not how life works."

"Says the guy who has everything he wants."

He finally turns his gaze to me, eyes piercing me with their intensity and leaving me feeling both chilled and overheated. "Not everything," he mutters.

My breath catches in my throat. It doesn't have to be this way. He doesn't have to keep his distance, and we can figure out a way to—

"I promised," he says with a shake of his head, as if he was reading my thoughts. "I can't ruin this friendship."

"He's not being a very good friend," I argue. Especially if Eric is interfering with Benson's happiness just because he didn't get the girl in the end. *Eric* was the one who said we should split up. He doesn't get a say in my relationships anymore, and he certainly shouldn't get a say in Benson's.

Benson clenches his jaw as he slips his phone back into his pocket. "Maybe not," he agrees. "But he's one of the few friends I've got. He's..." He shakes his head, nothing but pain in his expression. "He's family, Avery. I can't lose..."

My heart aches as I stand here, almost close enough to touch this man but not quite. It's as much an ache for Benson as it is for myself. He *is* lonely. He can say all he wants that he loves his job and loves being on the road all the time, but I'm nearly certain he is desperate for a place to truly call home.

"We should go back to the office," Benson says with a heavy sigh, and I reluctantly agree.

There's no point in trying to push Benson to open up. Not right after he promised to keep his distance from me. Besides, I need to mentally prepare myself for a visit from Poppy, which is not for the faint of heart.

CHAPTER 23
Benson

Do you want to guess what Poppy brought me to give to Kaden?

I shouldn't respond. If I were smart, I would ignore any non-work texts from Avery and work from the hotel from here on out. There is plenty of desk space for people in my situation, and with Lynda out sick—I checked with her, and she's going to be out tomorrow too—I shouldn't be alone in the office with Avery.

Not when it would hurt my friend, who clearly hasn't moved on the way Avery has.

Though I'm exhausted and should go to sleep, I'm lying wide awake on my bed with nothing to do but sit with my thoughts, which is never a good idea. I should go for a run in the hotel gym. Lift some weights until I feel like my arms might fall off. Swim a few hundred laps in the pool until I'm pruney and wiped out.

Instead I text Avery.

I'm afraid to ask. Tarot cards? Essential oils? Chakra balancing singing bowl?

What is a singing bowl?

My phone goes silent after that, and fear creeps into my limbs as I wait for another text, like I can't move forward unless this conversation moves forward. My eyes slide to the bracelet I inadvertently stole from Avery. It's sitting on my nightstand next to Dani's book, which I still haven't finished even though tonight would be the perfect night to find out how Hypatia and Petros are going to defeat the Fates and be together.

I put the bracelet in my pocket when Eric called, not thinking, and I didn't remember it was there until I got back to the hotel and changed into workout clothes. It slipped from my jeans onto the floor, and I stared at the light pink stone for a full minute, as if the bracelet might tell me what to do. According to Poppy, who sounds like a force to be reckoned with, it will bring love.

It's the last thing I need sitting on my nightstand as I go to sleep, but I'm already thinking of carrying it in my pocket tomorrow.

"What is wrong with you?" I ask myself on a groan and run a hand down my face.

My phone buzzes, and I swipe it open immediately.

Avery:

Poppy told me to tell you that you need realignment in your life.

What does that mean? Like, go to a chiropractor? Something tells me that's not what she's trying to say, though I could use an adjustment. It's been a while, and plane seats are never as comfortable as I want them to be, even in business class.

Avery:

She also wanted me to ask you what you meant when you sent me *rock on emoji*

I snort and roll over onto my stomach, tucking my pillow underneath me.

Benson:

Honestly, I have no idea what that emoji was supposed to mean.

Avery:

Oh.

Benson:

Disappointed?

Avery:

Not necessarily.

Poppy says she's incredibly disappointed and you need to work on your emoji game.

Benson:

Noted *crying laughing emoji*

I'm supposed to tell you that that emoji isn't cool anymore. *crying laughing emoji*

Her use of the "uncool" emoji makes me smile, and already I feel lighter than I have in hours. Eric's phone call put me in a bad mood, and I'm pretty sure this is the first time I've smiled since then.

He's not being a very good friend, Avery said about Eric today. While she's right, she's also wrong. She's wrong because Eric sent me a text when he got to Denver this evening that reminded me why I came back to Utah in the first place.

Made it to CO. Sorry for being pushy earlier. I worry about you being this close to your family and doing something impulsive like you used to, and I don't want you or Avery to get hurt. We have to look out for each other, right?

Like we did in college. I owe the guy a lot, and the least I can do is let him grieve his relationship in peace without stepping on his turf. Deep down, he's still a good guy, and he'll go back to the considerate and emotionally stable man he's always been once things at Rose & Quill calm down a bit and he has more time to process his lingering feelings for Avery.

My phone lights up with a call, making me jump, and I stare at Avery's name for a long moment before slowly sliding the answer button. "Hey?" I cringe when my greeting comes out as a question.

"Hi."

"Uh, what's up?"

She laughs, and it sounds nervous. "Poppy just left."

"Okay?"

"And I need to talk to someone more my speed before I feel like a complete doofus."

She wanted to talk to me? She heard my side of the conversation with Eric, and her expressions said it all. She knows the promise I made, and she knows I won't let this go anywhere. But she still wants to talk to me, which makes me feel...something. Relieved? Terrified? Compelled to do anything she asks of me?

Probably that last one.

"Because we're friends," she adds, a little breathless.

I have never hated that word as much as I do when it comes to Avery Grace Baldwin. "Friends," I repeat dumbly. "Why do you feel like a doofus?"

"The goal is to *not* feel like a doofus."

"Ah, right. But why would you—"

"Because Poppy is so smart, but she says things and I have no idea what she's talking about, so I have to smile and nod and pretend I'm not completely out of my depth with her. The other cousins talk to her all the time, but I always feel like we're speaking different languages."

I sit up as she speaks and wait until I'm sure she's done talking before I say anything. "So you feel like a doofus when you talk to her," I say to sum up for her.

"Ugh, yes! It makes me feel like the worst cousin in the world."

"You're not."

"I am! I used to take care of Lucy all the time while her mom was at work, but now I barely talk to her. I was a miserable pain at Chloe's wedding. Lately almost all of my conversations with Sadie have been about editing and deadlines, like she's just an employee instead of family."

I can't help but smile at the dramatic way she delivers these lines, which is the only reason I know she's not entirely serious about what she's saying. If she was, her voice would be quiet and broken. But dramatics aside, there's real pain in her words, and I want to do anything I can to soothe that pain.

"I haven't talked to any of my cousins in fifteen years, maybe more." Those words hurt to say, but this phone call isn't about me. "And I have spent so little time with my nieces and nephews that I genuinely can't remember the names of the youngest three. You're not a bad cousin, Avery."

She's quiet for a long time, and I don't bother filling the silence. She's bound to have a lot of questions, but I won't give her more information until she asks for it. Talking about my family is never easy, but if I'm lucky, showing her how terrible I am with my family should make her feel way better about her own interactions.

"You have nieces and nephews?" she asks, and her voice has gotten small, like she's worried I'll end the conversation if she pushes too much. It's a fair worry to have because there's always that chance.

But tonight, I want to tell her. I take a deep breath, too tired to try to keep my personal life under lock and key anymore. Eric and Lynda know about my family, so what's one more person? "Yeah. Ten of them. Kimball—he's my oldest brother—has four kids, and McKay has six."

"Wow."

"Yep."

"And...you don't remember all of their names?"

I chuckle at the edge of judgment in her tone. She's right to judge, but this is my reality. Or maybe I only *think* she's judging me and she's simply trying to understand, which is way more likely when it comes to her. "In my defense, McKay has two kids under the age of three, and Kimball and his wife like to get creative with their names. I've only met some of them once or twice."

"Are you going to go see your family before you head back to New York?"

I should have known she would ask a question like this. Maybe answering honestly will give her a reason to stop pushing the line and keep this connection between us from strengthening. Ha! Avery is too stubborn for that. "If I do, it will be right before I fly out," I say.

"Do they know you're in Utah?"

"Nope."

"Benson!"

I wince. "I've only been here for a few days, and R&Q has kept me plenty busy."

"Too busy to send a text?"

"I'm not sure I like your tone, Avery Grace."

She huffs out a breath. "Sorry. I guess I'm too close to my family to understand not keeping them in the loop with what I'm doing."

There's the kicker. Life is easier when there are no expectations for me to fall short of. "That's the difference between you and me."

"Whatever your reasons, you don't come across as the kind of guy who would be this way."

Chuckling, I adjust my position so I'm sitting against the headboard. "I specifically went to Italy for a friend's wedding and spent the whole time with you. This shouldn't come as a shock to you."

"But they're your..." She doesn't finish her sentence, probably because she's remembering what I said earlier. I called Eric my family. My *only* family.

"They wouldn't want to see me," I tell her.

"That's awful."

"And true." I roll my eyes. Unless, of course, I can build my company into something worthy of the West name. Then maybe my dad would stop thinking I'm an impulsive failure. "Do you feel better about your relationship with *your* family now?"

She laughs weakly. "I mean, not really. Now I just feel bad for your family drama."

"I would so much rather talk about your drama. How can I help you feel better about the Poppy situation?"

"You don't have to do that, Benson. I just wanted to complain."

Smiling, I move my phone to the other hand. "Complain all you want."

"I just wish I knew how to talk to Poppy, you know?" she says and sighs heavily.

I wonder what she's doing right now and have to remind myself—again—not to imagine her in bed like I am. These late night conversations are a bad idea.

Avery keeps talking. "She's so much younger than me, so I don't really know her like I should. And I don't know anything about crystals, so that topic's out."

All I know about her cousin is what she told me in the car today, which wasn't much, but talking to people is my whole thing. I've learned to ask the right questions to quickly get to know a person or their company so I can figure out where I need to take my consultation. I doubt I'll come up with the best questions at the moment, given how tired I am after a sleepless night, but I have to try to help. "I'm sure you know more about Poppy than her love of crystals. She works at the airport, right?"

"Yeah."

"Does she enjoy that?"

"I guess so? She seemed happy when I ran into her on my way to Italy."

My eyes jump to the bracelet again, and I grab it, running my fingers over the braided band as my eyes droop with sleepiness. "Is she at the TSA or something, or is she in one of the shops?"

"Shops. I think she's a manager or something, and... Oh! I think she's mentioned wanting to start her own store at some point. I have no idea if she's serious about that or if it was just an idea she had on a whim one day."

I grin and settle a little lower, though now my chin is pressed to my chest because only my head's against the headboard. It's not at all comfortable, but I don't want to lie down and fall asleep while on the phone. Stifling a yawn, I switch to speaker phone and set my phone on my stomach. "Sounds like you should ask her about her goals."

"Oh. Yeah, I guess I could do that, huh? The problem is she'll probably think I'm being condescending."

"Then don't ask in a condescending way."

"Right. But I don't know how to—"

"Avery Baldwin, just be yourself. The woman I met in Italy wasn't at all condescending."

"Even when I was insulting you?"

My face stretches into a wide grin that morphs into another yawn almost instantly. I can't stay in this position, so I scoot down and rest my head on my pillow. "Even then. Snarky Avery is kind of my favorite."

"That says more about you than about me."

She needs to stop being so adorable. "Case in point. Be genuine with Poppy and show interest in her life, and the rest will come."

"I hope you're right."

I chuckle and let my eyes fall closed. "I'm always right." That's so not true, but I say it anyway.

"About most things, maybe." Avery pauses, and her words come out hesitant. "But you're wrong about us, Benson."

Us. It doesn't matter how many times I tell myself that we can't exist as a pair. It's becoming increasingly obvious that I want her. In every way. If we'd met a decade ago, I wouldn't have hesitated to make a move, but now? In my thirty-five years, I've had to learn to check myself. Weigh the consequences. Move forward only when no one will get hurt.

How can I put that into words that Avery will accept? She knows the stakes, but she keeps pushing, and I love the way she's so determined to go for what she wants, no matter the risks.

But can I do the same?

Before I started my company, my life was a series of mess-ups and mistakes, one failure after another, and I'm so close to finally doing something right if I can just stay focused on climbing to the next level. If I can stop letting myself get distracted.

Unsure what to say, I offer up a noncommittal, "Mm."

Maybe I dream what she says next. Maybe it's real. I don't know. But her words settle over me like a thick blanket in the dead of winter.

"You're not willing to admit it yet, but we could be a great us, Benson. You and me, taking on the world together. Trust me."

I don't think I've ever trusted anyone more.

But it's not that easy.

CHAPTER 24
Avery

THURSDAY IS THE BUSIEST day I've had in a long time, and it's simultaneously the best and worst thing to happen right now. Lynda got an influx of submissions and sent over half a dozen that all look promising, though I don't get a chance to look at them because one of our authors calls me in tears because she's stressing about her deadline and needs me to talk her down from the ledge before she gives up on writing entirely.

I spend almost an hour on the phone with her, during which Benson pokes his head into my office to tell me something but my full focus is on the phone call. I mouth an apology to him, but he's busy with his own phone call when I get freed up, so I can't ask him what he was going to say.

When lunchtime rolls around and Benson stops by and offers to order in lunch, I'm in the middle of a video chat with the social media manager I hired yesterday to get her onboarded into the system, so he mutters something about ordering for me and disappears. He's nowhere to be found when the food arrives, and I have to guess which meal he picked for me and leave the other on Eric's desk.

I swear, every second of the day, one of us is busy, and I hardly get to see the man until I'm blearily shutting down my computer at six thirty and thinking about going straight to bed. After such a casual day yesterday, I should have realized today would have to balance things out.

Gathering up my things, I head out and find Benson on the balcony, gazing at the mountains again with his phone in his hand. He's wearing a short-sleeved button-up, along with those dark jeans that looked so good on him yesterday, and I'm liking the way his style is slowly getting more casual, like he's settling in at Rose & Quill.

As I approach his spot at the railing, he turns to look at me and offers a tired smile that seems to be hiding something deeper, but I don't get a chance to ask what's bothering him because my phone vibrates in my purse and pulls my attention. Because of course it does. The universe doesn't want me to talk to Benson today.

The text is from Eric, which only frustrates me more.

Eric:

> You should expect an email in the next day or two from someone named Cathy Stanton. She's a huge literary agent who specializes in fantasy romance and is very interested in building a relationship with us. We got to talking during one of the breakouts, and I told her about how you're the genius behind our catalog and that she should reach out to you specifically.

An agent?

Benson nudges my arm. "Good or bad? I can't tell based on your face."

I can't decide, so I hand him my phone to let him read the text.

His eyebrows pull low as he reads. "Hmm."

"Why would he be talking to an agent?" I ask, though I don't think Benson will have the answer.

He shrugs as he returns my phone. "Because you're a publishing company, and working with agents is pretty standard."

"But if we start working with an agent like this, doesn't that kind of mess with your brand idea of fostering new talent?" The brand idea I love. If an agent is finding all of our books for us, that doesn't leave much room for anyone who would take our workshops.

"You don't have to worry about this yet. Not until she contacts you and you can figure out what her intentions are." Benson bumps his arm into mine again and keeps it there, our arms pressed together. I instantly want to fall against him, take his hand, drop my head on his shoulder like I would have in Italy. He has a spectacularly comfortable shoulder, and this day was exhausting.

And since I feel like I don't have much to lose when it comes to him, I give in, leaning into him and taking his hand in one swift movement.

He groans but doesn't move away. "You make this impossible, Avery Grace."

"You started it."

He's quiet for a moment, and then he says, "What kept you so busy today?"

I smile and breathe in his clean scent. I've missed this, enjoying a stunning view while being pressed up against him. The only thing missing is a cup of gelato or a cornetto. "Normal things. You?"

Again, it takes him a second to respond, during which he looks at his phone as if seeing something on the black screen. "Finding ways to keep you from having days like today. There isn't the budget for more full-time employees, I know, but there will be. Especially with the way Phillip Rogers has been talking today. So I'm making sure all the tools are in place for when the money comes."

I have no idea what those tools might be, but having resources sounds phenomenal. Most of the time, Eric and I can handle things, but days like today are the worst. "You're pretty amazing, you know that?"

Benson chuckles, and I'm pretty sure he rests his cheek against my head as his thumb brushes along mine. "You're saying that to a guy who fell asleep in the middle of a phone call with you last night."

"After you didn't sleep the night before. I wasn't mad." In fact, I kind of loved it. Eric was never a late night conversationalist, which is fine. I value my sleep as much as the next thirty-year-old. But there's something endearing about listening to a man slowly drift off to dreamland. Benson pretends to be allergic to vulnerability, but what's more vulnerable than falling asleep with someone?

"Done for the day?" he asks.

I nod without opening my eyes. "Technically I have a bunch of submissions I want to get through, but I'm too tired."

"You should go home."

"I don't want to go home."

His fingers gently touch the hair at my temple, tucking it behind my ear. That feels nice. "Why not?"

"Because it's full of books."

"Hate to break it to you, Ave, but I think that's kind of your thing."

I snort a laugh and stand up straight again, though I don't let go of his hand. If he's willing to be this close to me without complaint, maybe he'll be willing to help me with my book nook nightmare. "When I was still jet lagged, I decided to update my second bedroom and turn it into a home library, only my shelves are too heavy for me to move, so everything is piled around the house and in my way."

I could so easily ask him for his help, and he would most likely agree. But I don't. I want him to volunteer, to give me some sort of sign that he's willing to cross that professional line and come to my house. I'm making progress, and there's a part of him that wants to give in, but hearing him talk about tools for when he's gone makes it painfully obvious that I only have so much time with the man unless something changes.

He looks at me for a long time, thoughts warring in his mind, before he groans and pulls his hand from mine. "Do you want help moving the shelves?"

A triumphant smile threatens to break free, but I manage to rein it in. "Are you offering?"

He rolls his eyes. "Obviously."

"Then I would love the help. Come over for dinner?"

"After dinner," he counters, narrowing his eyes. "You're a little too good at getting me to talk if there's food between us."

That was the reason I suggested dinner, but I'll take what I can get. "Fine. I'll text you my address."

He hesitates, as if debating if he should rescind his offer, but then he shoves his hands into his pockets and nods. "Great. I'll, uh, see you later." Without saying anything else, he heads back inside, leaving me with excitement and nerves pooling in my belly.

I'm bouncing with new energy when I open the door for Benson a little after seven. A part of me is surprised he showed up, as his texts since leaving the office were full of reluctance, but he's too good of a guy to go back on his word. I may not know everything about him, but I know that much. It's the whole reason he won't date me.

He looks different tonight, more casual than I've ever seen him in a t-shirt and gym shorts, and for some reason seeing him relaxed like this is making my heart pound in my chest.

"Well," I say, leading him inside. "This is home."

His jaw drops open as he takes it all in. "That's...a lot of books."

I moved my books from my bed to the living room after that first night I accidentally slept in the armchair, and the many piles have taken over my living room and kitchen counter. "It takes a thousand books to have a library, and I'd say I'm at least halfway there."

"You've been living like this for almost two weeks?" The abject horror on his face makes me laugh.

"Are you a neat freak, Benson Jay?"

He rolls his eyes and steps over a pile of historical romances to get deeper into my apartment. "Neat freak adjacent. This is simply an un-inhabitable situation for anyone."

"Poppy said the same thing."

"Poppy sounds smarter and smarter the more I learn about her. Where are these monstrous shelves?"

I point toward my bedroom, only realizing the intimacy of inviting him to that room when he pauses outside the door, hands on either side of the frame. He's hesitant now that he's realized which room I'm asking him to enter, but there's no way to get the shelves *out* of the room without going *into* the room.

Maybe I should tell him that I can hire a couple of movers, if he's so uncomfortable about this situation.

"This is nice," he says, breaking through my growing nerves before I can say anything. "The space feels like you."

"Oh, uh, thanks." I press my hands to my cheeks to try to cool them, glad that he's still peering into the bedroom. I just hope I didn't overlook any dirty clothes lying around or something. I may want to date Benson West, but I'm not ready for him to see my underwear. "It's been deco-rated like that pretty much since I moved in."

He glances back at me. "Before you met Eric?"

"Yeah. Why?"

"No reason." He finally enters the room and studies the first shelf, which is taller than him by at least a foot and feels like it's made of the same heavy wood as my chair. I'm generally pretty frugal, but I refused to scrimp on my bookshelves. He looks the shelf up and down, wiggling it a bit and chuckling. "I can see why you might have trouble moving these with your little stick arms."

I snort and hold both arms up, flexing nonexistent muscles. "Book-worm with an office job. I moved the chair on my own, though, so I'm not entirely useless."

He glances around the room. "What chair?"

"It's in the book nook already. You'll see why it's my claim to fame when you haul this baby in there." I wave my hand in a circle, encouraging him to proceed.

Laughing, he grabs either side of the shelf and lifts it, showing off his muscle. I snap a picture and send the photo to Dani with no context.

"Do you want some help?" I ask, stepping out of his way as he heads for the doorway. "I hope not because I'm admiring this view."

He nearly drops the shelf but scrambles to keep his hold. When it's steady, he narrows his eyes at me. "Play fair. I'm doing you a favor."

I slowly let my eyes roam from his head to his toes and back again, which is more fun than I expected. "You sure are."

"I've created a monster." His voice strains as he starts up his hauling again. "Showed her all my tricks, and now I'm questioning everything I've ever said to a woman."

"You like me being flirty," I argue, following him into the spare room.

"Too much," he agrees and sets the bookshelf against the wall. "Here?"

I shake my head and point to a different wall. "Please," I add, giving him a bright smile.

My phone buzzes with a text, and I grin when I see Dani's response.

Dani:

drooling emoji

Don't tell Mason...

Avery:

I was going to say...

Dani:

> I'm in a happily committed relationship and my man is something to be admired, but I'm not blind!

"Next one right beside it?" Benson asks, pulling my eyes back up. I nod as Dani's next text comes in.

Dani:

> I will point out you are not in a committed relationship. Neither is he. And you're both consenting adults.

Avery:

> Tell HIM that. He's the one who's resisting this.

> And by this I mean me.

Dani:

> How rude of him! Doesn't he know self-control is overrated?

Avery:

> I will get through to him. I am determined. *strong arm emoji*

Dani:

> You can do it!! I believe in you!

Only time will tell if Dani and I are right. At some point a girl has to cut her losses, but I'm not ready to give up the fight just yet.

By the time Benson gets the second and third shelves into place, sweat drips from his temples and has collected at the front of his t-shirt. It's a look that shouldn't be attractive but totally is. He takes a water bottle from me when I offer it and drains the whole thing in one breath in a move that is sexier than it has a right to be. Who knew watching a man's throat could be so much fun?

"Do all these books fit?" he asks, looking around at the many piles.

I bite my lip. "I should get another bookshelf."

He groans. "You need to be stopped." But there's a smile playing on his lips and making his eyes twinkle. We stand there for a long time, watching each other, before he drops his eyes and speaks again. "Do you, uh, want help getting the books in place?"

Excitement bubbles up inside me. Moving the shelves was one thing—I couldn't do that on my own. But for Benson to offer to help me with the books, there has to be a part of him that doesn't want to leave. I don't want him to leave either, but I also don't want to push him too hard.

"If you're offering, I'll take the help, but that's the easy part." But I really mean stressful because there are so many ways to organize a bookshelf, but I'm not about to tell him that I'll likely move the books multiple times before I'm satisfied with the setup.

With eyebrows furrowed, he takes in the dozens of piles littered around my apartment again. "Where do we start?"

We. It takes all my self-control to hold back a *squee* and remain composed. "I like to dedicate a shelf to my favorites. Maybe we start there?" I point to a pile only a few feet away from him.

"Favorites, huh?" He lifts the entire pile with ease—what I wouldn't give for bigger hands—and starts reading the spines as he heads into the book nook. "*Pride and Prejudice* makes sense, and so does *Treasure Island*, but I did not expect to see *Dune* make the list. Was this in the wrong pile?"

With my own armful of books, which is much smaller than Benson's load, I nod to the shelf where he should put the books and give him a big smile. "Nope, it's actually a favorite."

"Huh." He deposits the books in his hands and straightens them. "I didn't think people read the book. I thought we all relied on the weirdness of the original movie to understand what the story was about. At least until the new movies came out, though they're lacking in ginger-haired Sting."

"I haven't seen any of the movies," I admit, laughing when Benson gapes at me. "But the book is great. It's bold, you know? Frank Herbert went all in with his world building in a way no one else was doing at the time, and he wasn't afraid to address the problems that come from certain kinds of politics. And all through that he had an unconventional hero in a story about religion, environmentalism, free will and fate..." I should stop myself before I get carried away.

I reach out and stroke the spine of my well-loved copy. "It's not an easy read, but there's so much to learn from it, you know?"

Benson blinks wordlessly, looks at the book, looks at me, back at the book, and then pulls out his phone. I have to rise on my toes to see what he's doing, but my heart warms when I see him order the eBook of *Dune*. "What books are next?" he asks, slipping his phone back into his pocket like ordering one of my favorite books wasn't an adorably sweet thing to do.

I should set him loose and send him home, but I don't want to. Moving furniture and talking about books feels nice. It feels real. And Benson needs more of that. He needs genuine connection with people. Friends to make sure he's never lonely. Someone to care about him enough to ask him to stay.

"I have all the R&Q books, and after that we can tackle romance." I smile, laughing when he turns a deep red. "Books," I clarify, though I'm not opposed to real romance. "There are a lot of them."

He doesn't make a comment, simply following me to the living room to grab another pile of books.

CHAPTER 25
Benson

At some point you'd think I'd learn. Flirting over text is bad. Flirting at the office is bad. Flirting in Avery's house while sorting books is very, very bad.

I've been ignoring the clock on my phone as it keeps creeping toward midnight. I've been ignoring the sting of exhaustion behind my eyes despite desperately needing to get more than one good night's sleep a week. I've been ignoring the phone call I got this afternoon from the company in Australia, who told me the consultant they hired backed out of the job and they will do whatever it takes to get me to work with them starting next week.

My attention has been entirely on Avery. On the way she lights up every time I ask her about a book. She hasn't read everything in her library, and yet even the books she hasn't read bring a sparkle to her eyes as she tells me who recommended them or why the covers convinced her to buy them.

It's clear this is one of Avery's passions and she was meant to work in books, and I can't fault Eric for following her into a career he never would have chosen for himself had he not met her. If I didn't have an established business and the looming potential of turning it into something more, tonight's bookshelf adventure would have convinced me to follow Avery to the ends of the publishing world.

I thought I discovered the "real" Avery in Florence when I coaxed her out of her strict schedule, but I'm starting to think I was wrong. I saw hints of her, of course, when architecture surprised her or she tasted something delicious, but it wasn't until tonight that I finally saw what makes her tick and brings her joy. She is a woman who loves the human experience in all its forms.

"And that's why everyone should read *Peter Pan* as an adult," she says, finishing her explanation of why Disney's movie doesn't do the book justice. She adds another book to a stack on an overflowing shelf and frowns when she needs to find a place for another book. I've already rearranged the books for her three times because I could see in her eyes that she wasn't satisfied with the current setup, but now we're at a point where she's simply out of space.

"You were right," I admit.

"I'm always right." She smirks at me as she sends my words back to me. "But what was I right about this time?"

"You need another shelf."

She sighs and nods. "I really do. But then I'll have to reorganize everything again, so maybe I should shift things now and plan ahead."

When she reaches up, ready to pull a whole stack of books from a shelf above her head, I'm exhausted just thinking about moving these books again. And Avery was already tired to begin with after the day she had today. So before she can get a firm grip on the books, I grab her around the waist and drag her from the shelves.

Unfortunately, I misjudge the size of the room and topple backward onto the massive armchair in the corner, bringing Avery with me. We sink into the cushion, much deeper than I anticipate, and I already know this was a bad move.

"This is comfier than I expected," I murmur, all too aware of my arms holding Avery pressed to my chest when I should be letting go.

She wiggles a little, like she wants to get free, but instead of getting up when I loosen my grip, she adjusts herself to sit at an angle, her head tucked under my chin and her legs over mine. It's a big enough chair that she isn't sitting on me anymore, which makes this spot all the more comfortable. "I've shared this chair a lot over the years," she murmurs, "but never like this."

Ugh, she'd better not tell me this was her make-out chair with Eric.

Giggling, she lifts her hand to stroke my jaw. "You just got all tense. Whatever you're thinking, you're wrong. Sadie, Dani, and I used to sit and read in this chair when we were kids."

"I can live with that." My hand moves to her thigh, tracing circles on the soft skin above her knee. She changed into sleep shorts soon after the great book migration began, and I am very glad she did.

Boundaries, Benson. But boundaries are impossible to remember when I am too exhausted to think about anything but her warm fingers scraping against the scruff on my face. The way the heat of her body keeps my heart at a rhythm I can't sustain if I want to live to see thirty-six. How she smells like vanilla and peaches.

Avery's hand slides from my face to my collar, then down my chest and stomach, resting on my abs and making me flex on instinct. She's bold, like her favorite books, and I don't know how much longer I can resist the pull I feel toward her. It's all too easy to forget my solid reasons for maintaining distance when everything about being near her feels so good.

It's been a while since I felt the same passion she exudes when it comes to books. Her enthusiasm is what drew me to her in Italy too, like I have this underlying desperation to absorb her excitement about the world around her so I can feel that way again.

"Thanks for your help," she says, her voice low. "I never would have gotten those shelves moved on my own, which is why I've been living in limbo."

"You're welcome to my brawn any time." *For the next few days*, I don't add. If I agree to take on the Australian company like I know I should, I can give R&Q three more days at most. That's enough time to make a solid plan of action, and Avery is perfectly capable of implementing the ideas she's had.

But I've barely come to terms with knowing I can only be around Avery for a couple more weeks, and leaving her sooner brings an ache to my chest. *I'm leaving either way,* I remind myself and mentally run through the reasons I can't be with Avery to begin with, hating each one.

Seeing her in her element has made it clear Avery is exactly where she's supposed to be, so I could never ask Avery to leave her life here. Worse than that, I spend so little time in my own home that I can't have plants, let alone a girlfriend. She would never see me if she moved to New York.

And me relocating here? Eighty percent of my clients are East Coast companies, and if I lock in this company in Australia, I can use their influence and connections to build my clientele around the world. I'll finally be able to bring on others to take some of my load and give me new challenges to spice things up. But I can't leave the East Coast if I do that.

If I choose not to scale up, not many companies west of the Mississippi can afford or need a consultant like me, so if I moved back to Utah, most of my time would either be spent in New York or in California and cities like Seattle, defeating the purpose of moving in the first place.

Then there's my family... Good as I am at keeping my whereabouts on the down low, I don't think I could keep it a secret if I moved into the same state as them, and that would be miserable for everyone involved. My mom already guilts me enough, and my brothers wouldn't hesitate to use the opportunity to show me how much better they are than me. Building a whole consulting firm is the only thing that would bring me to an even playing field for the first time in my life.

There's too much standing in my way for me to win. Either I sacrifice the one thing in my life that I'm proud of and risk reverting back to the man who can't stick with anything to save his life, or I sacrifice this growing connection to Avery and lose the only person who truly seems to see me, hurting her in the process.

"I should go," I say, hearing my own reluctance despite everything.

Avery shakes her head against my chest. "Not yet."

"Avery."

"Just sit with me for a minute, okay? I'm not ready for tonight to end."

Neither am I, which is why I don't fight her. I simply tell myself I have five more minutes as I hold her closer, memorizing the feel of her in my arms and wishing I knew a way we both could get what we want.

I wake with a start, blinking against the lights overhead as vague remnants of my dream slip away. Something about drowning in sand while my brothers laugh at me. Taking a breath, I try to remember where I am at the same time I recall who is fast asleep in my arms.

A curse slips from my tongue. I thought falling asleep on the phone with a woman was bad, but falling asleep with Avery pressed to my chest... I curse again, mentally scrambling for a way out of this situation.

"Bad word," Avery mumbles, only half conscious.

"This was your fault."

It wasn't her fault. Not entirely. I could have left at any point, but I chose to fall asleep in a chair that, while surprisingly comfortable, is not meant to be slept in by a grown man and woman. I have no idea what time it is other than later than I'd like it to be. I might not be able to leave this chair, depending on how long I've been sitting in the same position.

I shift my arm to reach for my phone in my pocket, and Avery lets out a little whimper of complaint that makes me snicker. "Okay, you're being ridiculous now. I stayed, didn't I?"

She lifts her head to meet my gaze, eyes so focused on me that I can't look away. "Why did you stay?" she asks, her words so quiet that I barely hear them.

Because I have no self-control. Because watching the way you see the world makes everything brighter. Because the more I learn about you, the more I don't want to go through life without you. "Because you asked me to," I say, deciding to keep things simple. I don't know what to do with the other thoughts that just ran through my head.

She reaches up and brushes my jaw. "I'm glad you did."

Finally reaching my phone, I pull it out and wince. We were asleep for a couple of hours. "It's two in the morning."

Avery groans. "I don't like that."

Me neither, mostly because I don't have any legitimate reasons to stay. She should sleep, and I should put some distance between us before we both get hurt.

So many *shoulds* in my life lately, which is a recipe for disaster. I've never been good about doing what I should.

"What if we stay here forever?" Avery asks through a yawn. She curls up against me, and the way she fits so perfectly makes my chest tight.

Yes. Yes. Yes. The word won't stop repeating in my mind as I try forcing myself to wake up fully. I don't think anything but a slap in the face will work at this point, but I won't manage that until I no longer have a deeply beautiful woman in my arms. "Ave, we can't sleep in a chair."

"I can. I did it last week."

I snicker. "I'm a bit bigger than you."

"I know. You have all these muscles that make even my sister drool over you."

A laugh chokes out of me. "Excuse me?"

"Yeah." She starts trailing her fingers over my arm, leaving a line of heat as she goes. "I sent her a picture when you were moving the shelves, and apparently she finds you wildly attractive despite being very much in love with her womanizer."

Now I really wish I had Dani's number again so I could tease her about this bit of information. Also, I didn't realize her new boyfriend was (is?) a womanizer, and that surprises me based on what I know about Dani. More than ever, I want to meet Avery's sister. Not only does she seem pretty cool, but I'd be curious to get my own impression of Mason to make sure he's good enough for her.

Whoa. That feels like the kind of thing a brother would do, not a guy who has never met Dani in person. *Don't get in too deep, Bens.*

"Taking secret pictures of me?" I ask, wrapping Avery up more securely as if that might stave off the panic that is slowly building in my chest. "That's definitely crossing a professional boundary."

"You don't care about professional boundaries."

I do, but I can't argue her point when I'm currently snuggled up with her in a giant armchair in her house. "I've never been good about following the rules," I say instead, kissing the top of her head. "Drove my mom crazy."

That was the wrong thing to say. Avery tilts her head up, staring at me with wide eyes. "Is that why you don't like talking about your family?" she asks in the gentlest voice, like she finally understands something crucial. "Because you were a problem child?"

I wince, but she isn't wrong. "Not a great way to put that, but...that's some of it. I had a knack for getting into trouble."

"I already knew that about you after all the stories Eric told about your time in college."

"What you don't know is my older brothers are basically perfect."

"Nobody's perfect."

I should drop the subject, but the words spill out of my mouth like Avery cracked the dam and now things are falling apart, letting loose all the things I don't want her to know. "Kimball and McKay are perfect.

Kimball became a lawyer, like my dad, and even works at the same firm, and he always had top grades in school. He married his high school sweetheart, has a house with a literal white picket fence, and sends out Christmas cards every year with his whole family in matching outfits.

"And McKay?" I scoff. "He's a mechanical engineer who builds airplanes and has angels for children because his wife is a perfect stay-at-home mom who has mastered gentle parenting. He does ultra marathons and climbs mountains in his free time, and I don't think he's ever once broken a law. Not even jaywalking. So yeah, they're perfect, and I'm... Nothing like them. I never have been. I was the kid always getting sent to the principal's office and caught causing mayhem around the neighborhood. It was a miracle that I got *accepted* to college because my grades were terrible, no matter how hard I tried, and I'm convinced I graduated by sheer luck."

I finally shut my mouth, hating the taste of the words I just spoke. This is exactly why I need to take on the Australian company. This could be my best chance to finally be...enough.

"Hey." Avery sits up, adjusting herself so she's straddling my legs and using her palm to nudge my face down to meet her eyes. "Do you remember what I said to you that day we met at the office?"

She could be referencing any number of things, but I know what she's talking about because it's been sitting at the back of my mind for a week and a half now. "You called me perfect," I mumble.

"Chocolate preferences aside, I've thought that about you since the moment I met you, Benson." She brushes her fingers through my hair, sending a shiver down my spine.

"Now you know why you were wrong," I say and attempt a smile.

But she shakes her head. "Nope. The more I know, the more I like. Maybe you're not like your brothers, but that doesn't make you any less wonderful."

Does she have any idea what her words are doing to me? Taking hold of the hand pressed to my face, I touch a gentle kiss to her palm. She's incredible, but she doesn't know there's a good chance I'm going to leave in a few days. "I need to tell you about a phone call I had yesterday," I say before fear holds me back.

She smiles, shaking her head and giving me a soft look that warms me to the core. "Tell me later. You should get some real sleep. We still have to work today."

Taking the out like the coward I am, I lift her off my lap, hating the absence of her touch as soon as we're both on our feet. The walk to the door is nearly impossible. It feels like when I left her at her hotel room that last night in Italy, and I wish that goodbye had been the end. That way I wouldn't be losing my heart to her now.

But Avery is working hard to break through my shields, and I'm not sure I have much energy left to fight her.

"Goodnight, Avery Grace," I tell her at her door, aching to kiss her but knowing I'll never leave if I do.

She smiles back at me, looking adorable with her tousled hair and sleepy eyes. "Goodnight, Benson."

When I get to my rental car, I check my phone to see if I missed anything while I was asleep in the chair. There's an email from the Australian company, asking me to give them an answer by Sunday afternoon so they can either arrange my travel or find someone else to take the project on. My logical side is telling me to say yes right now and make a clean break from Avery and R&Q so I can finally make my family proud.

The other side of me thinks that's the dumbest idea I've ever had and won't fix the restlessness I've been feeling.

Ignoring the email for now, I open a text I got from an unknown number, though it's clear who sent it.

Benson! I thought you were a smart guy, but you're proving me wrong, and I'm starting to think your intelligence is on par with Eric's. Get your act together and date my sister!

If only Dani knew how desperately I wish I could.

CHAPTER 26
Avery

I *REALLY* DON'T WANT to go to this family party.

Now that the day is here, dread has pooled in my stomach, leaving me queasy. But I don't have a choice. I told my mom I would go, and after everything she and Grandma Sue did to help me cancel wedding plans after Eric and I broke up, I owe them both some of my focus. And my grandma sent me a text twenty minutes ago telling me how excited she was to see me, complete with her signature text send-off of *Cordially, Grandma Sue*.

She's adorable.

But my head is not in the right space for dealing with my family's judgment, especially with my focus constantly being pulled to the things Benson told me as we sat in my oversized chair this morning. Things I haven't been able to talk to him about because we both had another busy day.

Which is why Benson finds me face-down on the floor in my office and practicing breathing exercises I found on the internet. Supposedly they will give me the motivation to go to the party with my head held high, but so far they're only making me lightheaded.

"Whoa," Benson says, and I lose count of the seconds I've been holding my breath. "Rough day?"

"No," I grumble. Which is true. Busy as it was, today was pretty standard and uneventful. "Not yet."

"Dare I ask?"

I roll over so I'm no longer breathing in the musty smell of carpet that doesn't get cleaned often enough. "Kaden's party is tonight."

"Ah." Benson offers me a sympathetic grimace as he leans against the door frame. "You could always fake an illness. That usually works for me."

I snort. "Teenage Avery did that so often that my mother doesn't believe me when I claim to be sick."

"Oo, adventurous Avery was also rebellious? Color me intrigued." He steps into the office, and then suddenly he's lying next to me and taking my hand. It's dumb, lying on a floor like this, but I love the way he didn't hesitate to join me. "Is it really going to be that bad?"

"Definitely. Maybe. Probably not." I blow my breath out in a huff and sit up, keeping my hand in Benson's. "It's been a while since I went to a family party like this because I've always had the excuse of being too busy with work."

Benson sits up too. "What if I come with you?"

His question is so out of the blue that I can only gape at him as my mind tries to process what he said. "What?"

He nods, eyes still on our hands. "I can go with you. Offer support, be a distraction, cause a ruckus. Anything you need."

Be still my heart. Does he mean that? After all his efforts to keep a boundary between us, it's difficult to think a family party is the sort of thing he'll willingly go to. Then again, this man fell asleep with me last night and very much looked like he didn't want to leave, so maybe...

Maybe something has changed.

Tilting my head to the side, I ask a question that's not even close to what I really want to ask. "How would you cause a ruckus?"

He grins. "Burst into random karaoke, loudly complain about the food, excessively compliment your dad's hairpiece?"

I reach over and smack his chest. "My dad doesn't have a hairpiece!"

"That's exactly why it would cause a ruckus." Benson lifts our clasped hands and rests them on his knee, a thoughtful look on his face. "I can't promise to be a perfect party guest, but I'll go with you, Ave. If you want me to."

Of course I want him to. If he hasn't figured out by now that I am extremely interested in spending as much time with him as I can, then I don't know what else I can do. At this point, the ball is in his court, and I'm ready. Ready and waiting.

"That would be amazing," I tell him. "We don't have to stay for long. You can be my excuse to leave if things get dicey."

He chuckles. "I doubt your family can be any worse than mine. I'll be fine."

I'm glad he's confident, because I'm not. But rather than worry about my relationships with my family, I try to focus on the fact that he offered to come to a family party, which is very much a boyfriend sort of thing to do. Dani's text was risky, but it might have had some influence. Or maybe Benson's decided he's done resisting me at every turn.

"You wore me down" isn't the most romantic way to get into a relationship, but I'll take what I can get.

Grandma Sue is the one to greet us at the door, and she immediately zeros in on Benson, taking him in from head to toe with keen eyes. "Hello there."

This was a bad idea, but it's too late now. "Grandma, this is my friend, Benson. Benson, this is my Grandma Sue."

Benson breaks out his best friendly smile and holds out a hand, and when Grandma Sue takes it, he wraps his other hand around it so he's holding her with both. "I've heard so many good things about you from your granddaughters, and it's an honor to finally meet you."

I narrow my eyes at him, silently warning him that he's laying it on a bit thick.

He simply chuckles and squeezes Grandma Sue's hand before letting her go. Then his gaze moves past her to the gathering of people down the hall, and something lights up behind his eyes, like he has never been more excited for something in his life. I'm glad he's eager to go deeper into the house, because I certainly am not.

"Come in, come in!" Grandma Sue says, ushering us down the hall to the living room. "Look who's here!"

"Great," I grumble under my breath. This would have been so much easier if I had been able to slowly mingle at my own pace. But no, I have the attention of Grandpa Tom and all of my aunts and uncles as Grandma Sue's announcement stops all conversation.

"Avery!" Mom is the first to say anything, rushing forward to pull me into a hug, though it's awkward because I have Poppy's gift for Kaden tucked under my arm. "So glad you're here."

"Thanks, Mom." I smile at my dad behind her; he's a little too focused on Benson to give me a real greeting. Not that I blame him. I didn't tell anyone I was bringing someone with me. "Um, this is Benson. He's my..." My what? Coworker? Friend? Soulmate who refuses to accept the truth?

"I've been helping Avery with scaling her company," Benson says, answering my question for me as he shakes first my mom's hand, then my dad's. "Your daughter has built something incredible."

Mom considers him for a moment before turning her attention back to me, tucking some hair behind my ear. "Avery, sweetie, you look tired. Have you been sleeping well enough?"

This is not the kind of conversation I want to have in front of the whole family, so I smile and shrug. "I'm fine. Uh, I have a present for Kaden from Poppy."

The crowd of aunts and uncles parts like the Red Sea, giving me a view of my cousin as he paces the den while on the phone. He simultaneously looks like the little kid who so annoyed all of us girls and the recent Harvard grad that he is. He seems way too young to be wearing such a fancy suit, and I have no idea what could be so important that he would be on the phone during his own party.

"He looks like a tool," Benson mutters so only I can hear.

I snort a laugh and try to cover it up with a cough. Benson isn't wrong, and Kaden's trendy haircut and extremely sharp jawline don't help his case. He must have fit right in with the other bros at Harvard.

Eager to get this part over with, I work my way down the open space and come to a stop a few steps from Kaden, though he hasn't noticed me yet. I wait for a few seconds, then clear my throat.

He stops, his eyebrows furrowed in a scowl, and looks at me for a long moment before recognition sets in. "I'll call you back later, okay?" he says into the phone, then slips it into his pocket and tilts his head at me. "Hi?" It's almost a question, like he's confused about why I'm here.

I'm confused too, buddy. "Uh, congratulations," I tell him.

He folds his arms. "Thanks?" Again, it comes out as a question. It's like he has no idea why I'm talking to him because I'm too far beneath him to even bother.

Could this get any more awkward? Yes, because I have no idea what Poppy thought to get him, and this could get messy. "Uh, Poppy wanted me to give this to you." I hold out the box and wince in anticipation.

Wrinkling his nose at the crystal attached to the ribbon on top, he seems as wary as I am as he takes the box and runs his finger beneath the tape holding it closed. He slowly lifts the lid, tensing as he reveals...a bag. A really nice leather messenger bag with the initials K.H. engraved in one corner. Kaden's whole expression shifts to surprise, his eyebrows high as he touches the letters. "This is cool," he says after a moment and looks up at me.

I shrug, too surprised by the thoughtfulness of the gift to know what to say. Why was Poppy so secretive about this? I guess I misjudged her, just like she thought her mom would, and now I get why Benson thinks I need to talk to her and get to know her better. I should probably ask her about the random guy she's been texting. See if that's still a thing.

But I'll save that for tomorrow.

Glancing behind me, I can't help but smile when I see Benson deep in conversation with my dad, who is way more animated than he ever was with Eric. A couple of my aunts and an uncle are hovering nearby, like they want to be part of the conversation too as Benson regales the room with all the work I've been doing to build Rose & Quill.

"So your company's doing well?" Kaden asks.

Hopefully my shock isn't written all over my face when I look at him again. I didn't realize he knew about R&Q. "It's going a little crazy, but in a good way. We're growing a lot thanks to Dani's book."

"I read it. It's good." Kaden glances over my shoulder at Benson. "He looks cooler than your last boyfriend."

Chuckling, I nod and feel myself relax a bit. There's still a chance I'll have to deflect questions about Eric and my failed wedding, but based on the way Benson has captured everyone's attention, maybe I'll be okay.

"Avery!" One of my aunts—Chloe's mom—comes over to me, her eyes alight with excitement. "I had no idea your business was doing so well! What kinds of books are you publishing right now?"

I glance at Kaden—tonight is his night, after all—but he's already on his phone again, the leather bag slung over his shoulder as if he's testing out how it feels. Grinning, I turn back to my aunt and tell her all about our next release.

After more conversations than I can count, I'm peopled out and make my way to the back balcony for some air and to soak up the golden sunset. Benson is still inside, talking about who knows what with my grandpa, and there are too many emotions running through me for me to process.

I want this. I want *him*. I don't think I've really let myself think about what might happen if he still rejects me when all this is over. Right now, his job is keeping him in Utah, but when his work with Rose & Quill is finished, what then? Flirting with him has been fun and freeing, but it has also opened me up and left me vulnerable. I didn't want to leave Benson behind in Italy, but I *really* don't want him to leave me behind now.

I lean on the railing of the balcony and take a deep breath. It will officially be autumn in a couple of days. Utah will take its time to cool down, but I can almost smell the coming change in the air. What is it about changing seasons that makes life feel uncertain?

The back door slides open, and I know without turning who comes outside to join me, even before he speaks. It's like I can feel when he's close because there's this invisible thread barely holding us together, tangible but fragile.

"Your family is great, Avery."

I breathe in deeply once more, holding the air in my lungs for a few seconds and letting it out slowly. "I know. I'm surprised by how nice it is to be around them again." I look behind me and take in Benson's expression, so full of emotions I couldn't put a name to if I tried. I can't decide if he's happy or miserable. Maybe he's both. "Thank you. For everything you said in there."

Leaning one hip against the railing, he tucks an arm around my waist and pulls me close. "I meant every word. What you're doing with R&Q? You're incredible. You deserve for them to see that side of you."

I move my hands to his chest and look up at him. He has seen me from the beginning, and I've never had a cheerleader like him. If I had known this was what unconditional support would feel like, I would have broken up with Eric a long time ago.

But then Eric wouldn't have started the company with me, and I wouldn't have met Benson. I wouldn't have learned to be bold and go after what I want. I wouldn't be standing here and wishing I never had to leave this man's arms.

"What are we doing?" I whisper. That question is so broad, so vague, but I'm desperate for an answer. "You and me. What is this?" *And how do I keep it forever?*

He clenches his jaw, glancing at the back door as if hoping someone might join us and rescue him from this conversation. "Avery."

"I know you think you aren't the type of guy to commit to a relationship, and I understand why. Your job, it..."

He nods. "It makes it impossible."

That has to mean he wants it, right? He wants whatever this is between us, but he doesn't know how to have it. "You don't know that," I argue. "We could—"

"Long distance?" He grimaces, shaking his head even as he pulls me closer and slides one hand along my arm toward my hand. He looks down when his fingers reach the star bracelet on my wrist, eyebrows pulling low like he's in pain as he traces the chain of stars. "Avery, you know we can't do that. Those days we were apart after Italy... They nearly killed me."

My heart stutters in my chest, leaving me lightheaded as I process what he's saying. "So you would rather give up entirely?" I shift my hands to his face, the scruff of his beard rough against my fingers. "Benson, you can't spend your whole life alone."

He closes his eyes. "It's better this—"

"It's not. Trust me. There are so many people in the world who love you and want you in their lives. Including…" I falter over my words, but then he opens his eyes to look at me and there is so much hope in his eyes that I can't let my courage fail. "Including me," I finish, rising up to my toes to press my lips to his.

"Avery, do you—oh!" My mom's words break us apart before our lips touch. "I'm so sorry for interrupting."

Benson takes a step back at the same time a mask slips into place, all traces of vulnerability gone.

I let out a deep sigh and turn to face my mom. "No, it's okay. What's up?"

She bites her lip, glancing between us as she says, "Grandma Sue wondered if you two wanted to join a game of Catan."

I'm not exactly in the mood for Settlers of Catan, but who am I to say no to Grandma Sue? I look at Benson with a question in my eyes, and when he shrugs, I smile at my mom. "We'd love to. Give us a sec, okay?"

Mom slips back inside, leaving us alone, but I already know our conversation is over. For now. I'm not going to let Benson end things when he's so desperate for connection. He needs people and he knows it, but it's going to take something bigger than my affection to convince him to at least try to find a way to have his cake and eat it too.

There's only so much I can do unless he decides to change his solitary life. I can't make that choice for him, and I can only fight for a relationship for so long.

"This isn't over," I tell him, hating the way I don't sound as confident as I want to be.

Benson studies me for a moment, and his gaze softens just enough to give me hope. "I know," he mutters, then makes his way inside.

TICKET
PASSPORT
N
E
S
W
HOTEL
Time To Travel

CHAPTER 27
Benson

AND THE AWARD FOR the biggest jerk goes to Benson West, a guy who can't get his crap together and still hasn't learned to deal with the consequences of his actions.

Avery deserves more, but I'm in too deep to walk away like I should. Especially after meeting her family. Her parents are awesome and her aunts and uncles seem cool and I already know her cousins are crazy supportive of each other despite being so different. This is how a family is supposed to be, and I've never wanted anything more.

That's not true. I want Avery more. I want to hold her during every sunset and stand behind her whenever she needs support. I want her to make me believe in possibility and futures and family. I want her to see the parts of me no one else sees.

So why am I the idiot who has hardly said a word to her since we left the back porch? Because I'm a jerk. Plain and simple. We played games with her family until nearly midnight, when her grandparents finally declared they were going to bed and kicked everyone out, and now we're in her car, on our way back to the office so I can pick up my rental and head back to the hotel room that is starting to feel suffocating. Avery is as quiet as I am, even though she probably wants me to continue the conversation she started on the porch.

She used the word *love*. Not directly, but I would be an idiot to miss the intent behind what she said. She thinks she loves me, but she's wrong.

I'm not the guy people love. I'm a good time for a short time, and I've always been okay with that.

That doesn't feel as true as it used to.

The streets are quiet and empty as we slowly make our way toward the freeway, and this silence is starting to kill me. But what can I say? I can't tell her that I've changed my mind on long distance. I can't tell her that everything will be okay if we give this thing between us a chance. I can predict how a market will shift and the best ways to adapt a company to their circumstances, but I can't predict anything about this.

But I need to say *something*. I take a careful breath. "Avery, I—"

The car sputters, making a sort of grinding noise as it jolts and then starts to slow.

"What's happening?" Avery gasps, staying remarkably calm as she slowly pulls over to the side of the road and turns on her hazard lights. "Oh no, the check engine light just turned on."

I lean over to look despite not having any idea what's happening. A burning smell hits my nose, and I quickly try to remember anything I learned when I took an auto mechanics class in high school. It was fun while I was in it, but I'm pretty sure most of the information I learned has since dissipated from my mind.

"Pop the hood?" I ask, though I'm going to look like an idiot as soon as I take a peek at the engine.

Avery groans and drops her head onto the steering wheel. "This is what I get for being too busy to take my car in for maintenance. Eric used to take it in for me, but we've been..." She glances at me and grimaces. "You're perfect, so what are the chances you know how to fix a car?"

I chuckle. "Extremely low. But I can see if there's anything glaringly obvious if you pop the hood."

"Uh, how do I do that?"

Laughing now, I slip out of the car and come around to her door, opening it and crouching down to find the lever. I pull it, then grin up at her. "I take it you don't often look at your engine?"

"Try never."

"There's a first time for everything." Standing, I hold out my hand to her and feel a thrill of excitement when she takes my fingers and joins me. I shouldn't be this happy that she's willing to stand next to me in the dark, but I am. Because I am so far gone for this woman that pretty much everything she does brings light into my life.

Once I get the hood lifted up and secure, I turn on my phone flashlight and try to find anything that might explain the engine failure. It all looks normal, which means this is far beyond my limited skill set. "We should call a tow," I say and start searching for a place that might be open this late.

Avery shivers and ducks under my arm to curl up next to me. It's not that cold out, somewhere in the sixties, but I'm not going to point that out to her. I will happily hold her as long as she wants me to, even if it's going to make things harder going forward. "Sorry I'm taking up your entire night," she says as she wraps her arms around my torso.

I start rubbing my hand up and down her arm as I scroll through my phone. "It's not your fault. Do you have AAA or anything?"

"Probably? That sounds like a thing Eric would have had me sign up for, but I've never needed to use it so I have no idea what my account info would be."

"That's okay. I can…" I pause when a set of headlights bathes us in blinding light and a giant SUV pulls up behind Avery's car. Instinctively, I pull Avery closer to me and praise the heavens I'm with her so she's not standing out here alone at night. While I'm grateful someone is willing to stop and see if we need help, I'm going to be on my guard.

The driver turns their own hazards on and then steps out of the car, a silhouette coming toward us through the lights. "Hey!" he says, lifting a hand. "Do you need some…Benson?"

A curse slips from my tongue as soon as I recognize the voice. Rather than relaxing at the familiar tone, I tense up more. "Kimball?" I didn't notice what street we were on, and now I'm wishing I'd paid better attention.

My brother gets close enough to step out of the path of his headlights and throw his face into sharp relief. His eyebrows are low, eyes taking in the two of us and Avery's car as he tries to understand why I'm here. "You're in Utah?"

Avery lets out a little gasp, her fingers pinching my side as she likely remembers I haven't just avoided talking about my family. I've avoided talking *to* them.

I clear my throat. "Uh, yeah. I'm doing a consultation with a company in Riverton."

Kimball's gaze shifts to the way I'm holding Avery tight against my side, and his eyes narrow. "How long have you been in town?"

"Not long."

"Hey, I'm Kimball West." He holds a hand out to Avery, who takes it with hesitation. "And you are…?"

"Avery," she says with a glance at me. She's likely wondering how much I want her to say, but I have no idea how to proceed. Seeing my brother has left me reeling and dizzy, almost panicking as I desperately search for a way to get out of this situation before it gets worse.

"Avery," Kimball repeats, meeting my eyes. "How do you know my brother?"

Again, she looks at me, but when I give her nothing but a wide-eyed stare, she stands up straighter and turns into the confident woman I admire. "It's my company he's been helping."

"*Been* helping," Kimball parrots and turns a judgmental glare to me. He's too smart to think I've only been here for a day or two.

I clench my jaw. "I've been busy."

"You're always busy."

"Thanks for stopping, but we need to get the car towed and—"

"It's almost midnight." Kimball folds his arms and looks at the open engine. "How about I take you back to Mom and Dad's while you figure this out. You can stay the night there and deal with this in the morning."

Now I'm *definitely* panicking. "No, we're—"

"That's so nice of you!" Avery interrupts with a tired smile. "But we can get an Uber or something. I don't want to make you go out of your way."

Kimball chuckles. "It's only a block that way," he says and gestures with his head.

Avery's jaw drops, and though I feel her eyes on me, I refuse to look at her. Yeah, my parents live only ten minutes from her grandma. Yeah, I made her think they were still in Logan, an hour and a half away. Yeah, I'm turning into more and more of a jerk as the night goes on. If we're about to go to my parents' house, there's no way I'll be able to make myself look good.

"I don't want to wake them," I mumble, knowing it's a terrible reason to make Avery stay outside on a dark road while we wait for a tow truck we might not be able to get. I *could* order a rideshare, but one look at Avery tells me she's more tired than she'll admit. She looks dead on her feet and is probably stressed out by her car breaking down.

My stomach starts twisting in a knot as I run through our options for the night.

"They're still awake," Kimball says, rolling his eyes at me. "You know Mom and Dad are night owls." He looks at Avery and offers a warm smile. "It won't be an imposition at all. I was just there after dropping off my kids for a sleepover earlier."

I swear under my breath, ignoring the sharp glare my brother gives me. His kids are there? It'll be hard enough facing my mom, and I don't need my nieces and nephew gaping at me like some circus sideshow they've only heard stories about. I can only hope they're already asleep.

But I can't keep Avery out later than she needs to be, and my parents will have a guest bed she can use.

Another curse slips off my tongue as I realize I'm not going to be able to avoid my family tonight.

Kimball lifts an eyebrow. "McKay and Emily are there too."

I swallow. This keeps getting worse.

Avery slides her hand into mine, and I'm surprised to see empathy in her expression, as if she knows exactly how hard this is going to be for me. Maybe she does. She just faced the bulk of her family for the first time after calling off her wedding. But Avery's family? They're great. They welcomed her with open arms and have always been supportive of her.

Mine is a whole different story.

"We don't have to go, Bens," she says gently. "I'm fine to wait for a car."

"Don't be an idiot, Sonny," Kimball counters. "You and Avery shouldn't be out here this late, and we both know Mom won't see you for months if you don't come over now."

I can't argue without feeling like a liar. I turn to Avery, silently asking her what she wants to do. If she'd rather wait for a ride, we'll wait. If she wants to stay at my parents', we'll do it. But she might never look at me the same if we do.

"Whatever you want, Benson," she murmurs, pulling her eyebrows together like she can see the fear written all over my face. I can handle seeing my family. What I can't handle is losing her affection if she sees me through their eyes.

Reaching up, I brush my thumb beneath her eye. "You're tired."

She nods. "But I'll be fine if you're not ready to see your mom yet."

I might as well get this over with. "You'd be okay to spend the night?" My mom won't be satisfied by anything less.

Avery's smile grows. "Would *you* be okay?"

If it means I don't have to endure my family alone? Maybe this is a best case scenario for both of us. "I'll be fine. If you—"

"Are you coming or not?" Kimball asks, eyebrows low as he looks between us. "The rest of us don't run on big city time."

Here goes nothing. "Yeah. We're coming."

I cling to Avery's hand as I shut the hood of her car. Cling to her hand as she grabs her purse and locks the doors. Cling to her as we follow Kimball back to his car. I have to let go so she can sit in the front while I squish into the one seat in the back without a car seat or booster, and I feel like this is symbolic of something, being so far from her as we make the short drive to my parents' house.

As he drives, Kimball asks about Avery's business and listens intently as she tells him about her publishing company and how things have been rapidly growing with the popularity of Dani's book. He keeps looking back at me in the rearview mirror, like he has stuff to say to me but won't in front of Avery.

I'm gladder than ever that she's here to soften everything, much as I hate subjecting her to this nightmare.

We pull up in front of the house, and my stomach churns with fear and guilt. I'm suddenly twelve years old again and sitting in the backseat of the sheriff's cruiser after he caught me digging holes in a neighbor's field. I'm outside the principal's office while my teacher complains about my inability to stay in my seat and pay attention to her excruciatingly boring lectures.

It's been years since I came home without an escape route ready to go, and now I have Avery to look after so I can't simply run away.

"Can't stay back there all night," Kimball says, meeting my eyes in the mirror again.

I scowl at him. "Try me."

Avery leans around her seat and smiles at me, the warmth of it melting some of the tension from my shoulders. "Let's go inside, Bens."

This might be the first time I have truly wanted to say no to her, but I can't do it. With a groan, I shove the seat forward and open the door, scrambling out onto the driveway. The instant Avery is close, I grab her hand and pull her to a stop.

"Benson," she says, her brow furrowing. "If you don't want to—"

"Listen," I say, keeping my voice low so Kimball can't hear me. "I didn't tell my family I'm in town because I have never been good enough for them, and I hate the way that makes me feel. You don't know what it's like to be seen as less because your soul has never been able to settle. I can't..." I shake my head and pull her in close, pressing my forehead to hers as if she might give me the strength to go inside and face my perfect family. "I won't be able to bear it if you think less of me because of them. Please."

Avery touches my jaw, and then she leans up and brushes the softest of kisses to my lips. My whole body reacts, blazing with fire and a desperation for more, but she steps away before I can claim another kiss. "I could never think less of you, Benson West," she whispers, and I desperately want to believe her. "We don't have to stay. We can call a car and go inside while we wait, or we can wait out here if that makes you more comfortable."

Growling, I shake my head. If I'm worried about her thinking less of me, I can't hide on the front porch like a coward. "You need sleep. I'm not making you stay up for hours just because I'm scared of my family."

I've endured a lifetime of my family's scrutiny and have spent most of my adult life avoiding it, so I know exactly what to expect inside. I can survive a night.

Whether or not Avery's affection for me will stay intact remains to be seen.

CHAPTER 28
Benson

"I'm back!" Kimball calls when he steps through the front door. I can hear his amusement when he adds, "You'll never guess who I picked up on the side of the road."

He is far too entertained by this situation, and if not for Avery holding tight to my hand, I'd probably do something reckless. Whether that something is punching Kimball in the nose or running away, I'm not sure.

Avery's expression is guarded, which is most likely my fault, and I wish I had time to prepare her better. My mom is endlessly sweet, so I have no worries about her treating Avery poorly. But as soon as she sees me, she's going to cry or tell me I look scruffy and need a haircut. Probably both because I'm never home enough but I never look appropriate when I am.

Kimball rounds a corner to the kitchen and says, "Brace yourself, Mom," before stepping aside and making room for us to enter the dining area and all the sweet smells it comes with.

My eyes find McKay first, sitting at the dining room table with his wife, Emily, under his arm. His hair is longer than the last time I saw him, curling at his ears, but otherwise he's the spitting image of our dad, who sits a few seats over with a scrutinizing stare fixed on me.

Then there's Mom, who stands frozen in the kitchen with a tray of chocolate chip cookies in her hands and her mouth gaping open as she looks from Avery to me. I'm waiting for her to drop the cookies in shock, but she barely seems to breathe. She might pass out before anyone says anything.

"Mom," Kimball says, thankfully breaking the silence.

She blinks and hurriedly sets the tray on the stove, shucking off the oven mitts she's wearing. "Sonny?"

My grip on Avery's hand tightens involuntarily, and she squeezes me right back, giving me the courage to croak out, "Hey, Mom."

She shuffles forward but stops halfway to us, like she's suddenly unsure if she's welcome any closer. Guilt pools in my belly; I haven't given her many reasons to think I want her close. Her eyes finally shift to Avery and down to our hands, and her many questions flash across her face as she tries to figure out how to proceed. "Um, hello," she says to Avery. "I'm Camille West. Benson's mom." She gestures to the table as Kimball takes the seat next to McKay with the look of someone expecting trouble. "This is my husband, Ray, and my older boys, Kimball and McKay. And my daughter-in-law, Emily."

As everyone gives uncertain waves, Avery reaches out and shakes Mom's hand, which to my horror is trembling. I know why I'm nervous, but why is *Mom*? "I'm Avery," Avery says in the gentle voice she uses every time she pries into my past, and it clearly works better on my mom than it does on me because Mom's shoulders relax partway. "My car broke down, and Kimball found us on the side of the road. He offered to bring us here while we get it all figured out."

Mom nods, her eyes darting to me every couple of seconds, though she's mostly focused on Avery. "Yes, of course! It's too late for you to be out there. How... Uh." She looks down at my hand linked with Avery's again, then looks up at me with wary eyes. "Are you..."

Are we what? She's never going to ask. Mom gave up on asking me about dating at least five years ago, after a particularly heated conversation in which I told her I never planned to get married so she shouldn't expect grandkids from me. Dad got after me for that one, telling me that

Mom cried for a week and I should tell her I changed my mind, no matter that it was untrue. I ignored his request.

There's a chance I'm starting to regret that decision.

"We work together," I say, unwilling to give my mom any false hope. I don't need another argument with my dad, even if a part of me wants to pretend I can be like my brothers when it comes to relationships. "Avery and her partner hired me to help their company."

"Ask him how long he's been in town," Kimball says sharply.

Wincing, I shoot him a glare that he ignores, but the damage is already done.

Dad narrows his eyes. "How long have you been in town?"

Is it too late to follow Avery's suggestion and wait outside for a car? Scrambling for a response that doesn't make it sound like I've been avoiding my family, which I have been, I'm just about to tell my dad that I flew in last week—technically not a lie—when Avery jumps in with a much better answer.

"He's been here for a couple of weeks, but I've been keeping him pretty busy. My company needs a lot of help, and he's been a total lifesaver."

"What line of work are you in?" McKay asks with a raised eyebrow. With the judging look in his eyes, it feels like he's asking how she got mixed up with the likes of me.

But Avery smiles, unconcerned by the tension building between my family and me. "Publishing," she says proudly. "One of my authors hit the best-sellers list this year, so we're trying to expand and keep up with her popularity, which is where Benson has come in."

"Since when do you know anything about publishing?" Dad asks gruffly, folding his arms.

I only halfway hold back a groan. "I don't have to be an expert in every field I work in, Dad." I've told him this a million times. "I do my research.

I didn't know anything about jewelry or telemedicine, but I still brought the companies—"

"Oh, it's too late to be talking about work," Mom says, and though her voice is soft, it feels like a slap. She never wants to hear about my job despite it being one of my biggest accomplishments I'm truly proud of. "Avery, you're welcome to take a seat. Would you like some cookies? McKay and Emily were about to leave, but—"

"This is way more interesting than crashing in our hotel room," McKay says with a chuckle. "We can hang a little longer."

"Hotel?" I ask, furrowing my brow.

"Anniversary," McKay explains simply and kisses Emily's cheek. "Which is why the kids are downstairs. We plan to sleep in all morning long. Among other things."

"McKay Alan!" Mom scolds, her cheeks turning pink as I resist the urge to palm my face. "Avery, forgive my son."

"A sleepover with Grandma is the only way we can get another kid on the way," McKay says with a wink, while Emily smiles and rolls her eyes.

As Mom gasps in horror, McKay and Kimball both start laughing and giving me looks that say they're doing their best to drive me away. It's working, and if not for the late hour and lack of transport, I would be taking Avery as far from here as possible.

"Sit," Kimball says, gesturing to the table. "We'll behave."

"Not likely," I grumble, but I pull out a chair for Avery and take the seat next to her, sitting as close as I can without being on her chair. I'm half worried she'll be so horrified by my family that she'll run, but the other half of me desperately wants her to see what I deal with so she'll finally understand why I can't move back.

No matter how much I wish I could.

"I would love a cookie, Mrs. West," Avery says, taking my hand and squeezing in a way that pulls my attention away from my brothers and down to our interlocked fingers, like there might be some kind of message written there. What is she trying to tell me? "They smell amazing."

"So what's wrong with your car?" McKay asks as Mom grabs a plate and starts loading it with fresh cookies.

Avery shrugs. "No idea. It made a funny noise and stopped moving."

"Haven't done any research on cars, Benson?" Kimball asks with a chuckle.

I stiffen, looking up and clenching my jaw so hard that I feel like the muscle might snap. Does he really want to start this now?

"Could be a transmission issue," McKay says, surprising me by continuing the conversation despite Kimball's perfect setup. "Not a fun one. Or you could get lucky and it's a simple fix. I can take a look at it tomorrow if you want to save some money, though you'll have to wait until later in the day because..." He waggles his eyebrows. "Need that baby."

You've got to be kidding me. "I'll pay to get it towed to a shop," I growl and silently tell McKay that he had better shut up unless he wants me to shut him up myself. I grab my phone, ready to find someone who can get us out of here before Avery runs screaming.

But Avery squeezes my hand again. "If you're willing," she says to my brother, completely ignoring his innuendo, "I would love for you to take a look at it. Benson told me you're a mechanical engineer?"

McKay grins, pleased with himself. "Yep. So your car will be in good hands."

"He loves a good engine puzzle," Emily adds with a loving smile toward her husband. In the strangest way, her look settles heavy in my chest and brings my gaze to Avery again. Has she ever looked at me like that?

Have I ever given her a reason to?

"I wish Michaela could be here," Mom says as she places a plate of cookbook-worthy cookies in between Avery and me, complete with a couple glasses of milk. "Then it would be the whole family."

Kimball smiles at Mom, looking every bit the perfect oldest son. "She'd be here if she could. You know how exhausted she gets during the first trimester."

I freeze halfway to grabbing a cookie, gaping at my oldest brother. "She's pregnant again?" That makes five kids for him, and I feel...something. Horrified? No. He and Michaela are good parents. Nor am I surprised. It's more like the tightness in my chest is akin to...

Jealousy.

That can't be right.

Kimball scoffs. "You would have known that if you would get on the family chat once in a while."

"I'm busy," I grumble, prompting the whole table to roll their eyes. I've said that so many times that they probably don't expect anything else, but it's not like it's a lie. I am always busy, and if they knew how little time I spent in my own home, they would think...

I frown, keeping my eyes on the table so I don't have to endure the stares of my dad and brothers as they wait for me to find a stronger excuse. What *would* they think? Instinct tells me they would think my lifestyle is terrible, but I'll be the first to admit how much my transient life has been wearing on me lately. Which means my family wouldn't be wrong.

They've been wrong about me my whole life, but if they're right about settling down...

What else could they be right about?

"This is so good!" Avery says through a bite of cookie, louder than she needs to. She's pulling attention away from me, and I have never liked her more.

Dad and my brothers chuckle, and the tension of the room dissipates. "She makes the best cookies," Dad says, reaching for mom's hand and pulling it to his lips. "One of the many reasons I married her. I always told my boys they needed to listen to their hearts more than their stomachs when choosing a partner, but the stomach can be hard to ignore. Luckily, they all chose well."

With that, all eyes shift to me again, and for the first time I don't feel like they're judging me. They're looking from me to Avery, likely wondering if she'll be the one to tame the wayward soul and save me from myself.

If only they knew.

I clear my throat and stand, uncertain how to handle the worried looks everyone is giving me. They usually look frustrated, not sympathetic. "It's late," I mutter.

Mom instantly deflates. "Oh. Yes, I suppose you'll want to—"

"Can we stay here tonight?"

Her jaw drops so low it's almost painfully comical, and then her lip trembles, and I scramble for something to say that might stave off her tears. Guess Avery's getting a thorough demonstration of how quickly I do everything wrong.

"Oh," Mom whispers, and her voice grows in strength the more she talks. "Of course. Yes! Your bed is always made up, and it's plenty big for the both—"

"Mom!" I croak before she gets the wrong idea and starts jumping to all sorts of conclusions. Yes, I'm willingly spending the night. No, she's not getting another daughter-in-law and a horde of grandkids. "We're not—"

"I'm sure I have some pajamas you can use," she says to Avery and holds out her hand, which Avery takes without hesitation. My chest grows tighter when I see Avery's broad smile matching my mom's, and

I'm not sure I'll be able to breathe again before the night is over. "Come along, sweetie."

Wait. As my mom practically drags Avery from her chair, I hold tight to Avery's hand, not ready to be on my own with the other West men. Avery meets my gaze, and her smile turns sympathetic.

"Sonny, dear," Mom says, her tone chiding, "you have to let her go."

But I don't want to let her go. I want to hang on to this woman for the rest of... My eyes widen when I realize how my brain was about to finish that sentence.

I want to hang on to this woman for the rest of my life.

My grip falters at that thought, giving my mom the slack she needs to pull Avery from my grip and lead her up the stairs to my room. I'm too rattled from my own thoughts to stop them from leaving. I don't mean that I want to keep Avery forever. I *can't* mean that. Trying a relationship is one thing—a thing I can barely let myself consider—but imagining forever is so beyond anything I've ever thought myself capable of.

I stare at the place she disappeared as a rock settles heavy in my gut.

"Benson Jay." Dad's voice is gruff and pulls my attention back to him and the scowl growing on his face.

Kimball's eyebrows jump high, and McKay whispers something to Emily, who makes an excuse about checking on the kids and slips downstairs. I brace myself for the lecture that's coming.

I don't know what my dad is angry about, but maybe I can head this off before it turns into more than it needs to. "Dad."

"What are you thinking?" he growls, dropping a fist onto the table. "Playing with the girl's heart like that?"

I feel like that fist just slammed into my stomach. "I'm not playing with—"

"It's one thing to date around, but bringing her home to your mother? Son, how heartless can you be?"

Anger rising in my chest, I debate the merits of arguing. He's going to think what he wants to think, and nothing I say is going to change that. But I hate the way he immediately thinks I'm being careless, as if I haven't spent the last three weeks constantly torn between staying away from Avery and giving her what we both want.

My own hands curl into fists on my lap. "She knows I can't commit to anything."

"Won't," Kimball mutters.

"Are you sure she knows that?" Dad asks. "Because she doesn't look like she—"

"You don't know anything about her!" I grind out.

He huffs. "And you do? You've known her for, what, a couple of weeks? And you thought it was a good idea to bring her here in the middle of the night and—"

"I wouldn't have come if Kimball didn't force me," I snap, glaring at my oldest brother.

He glares right back, unfazed by my comment. "She's your client, Sonny. Are you really stupid enough to be out late with your—"

"I was *helping* her."

"Sure."

I look at McKay, who has been quiet so far, and search his face for any sign that he might back me up. Not that he ever has before. "I'm not playing with her heart," I tell him directly.

His eyebrows pull low. "So you're going to stick around for once?"

Cursing under my breath, I stretch my palms out and rub them along my thighs as my anger turns to queasiness. "I can't."

"Won't," Kimball corrects again.

This is exactly why I didn't want to come home. I'm never going to do anything right in their eyes.

"*Can't,*" I repeat, stronger this time. "I'm heading to Australia next week to work with a client who's going to push my business to the next level and help me bring on clients from all over the world." As soon as I say that, my body freezes. I didn't plan on saying anything about Australia because I haven't officially made a decision. But... This could be the only thing that convinces them I'm not a complete mess, so I let the declaration hang in the air between us.

Honestly, I don't know how I expect them to react to that announcement, but it isn't with sadness. There's plenty of frustration in all three of their faces, but it's buried beneath mournful expressions I never see. McKay glances at the stairs while Dad's shoulders drop.

It's Kimball who speaks first. "More work?" he asks quietly. "But you already..."

I scoff. "Yeah, I know you think I can't handle—"

"That's not what I meant."

What else can he have possibly meant?

McKay must see my question in my face because he sits up straighter and says, "You already work a ton, Sonny."

Glancing between him and Kimball, I try to understand how that's any different from what Kimball said. Of course I work a lot. It's the nature of my job, and I've always loved how it keeps my attention and requires my focus. But even as I think that, my exhaustion from the last few months reminds me it's there as my eyes start to sting, begging me to sleep. To rest.

"I'm trying to build something worth your notice," I grumble, getting to my feet. "Sorry it's taking longer than—"

"Worth my notice?" Dad frowns, staring at me like I'm talking nonsense. "I don't even know what you do in your job."

That's exactly the problem, and it's not worth trying to explain yet again. Dead on my feet, I head for the stairs to make sure my mom isn't overwhelming Avery, but my dad's voice stops me on the bottom step.

"But you've always been worth my notice, Benson."

I grip the banister, not sure I heard him right. "What?" I ask, too afraid to look at him without knowing what I might see.

"Your life makes no sense to me," Dad says. "Bouncing around from one thing to the next. But that doesn't mean I don't see you and the way you've turned that into a career."

What is he saying?

"If going to Australia next week and taking on more than what you're doing now is going to make you happy, then do it. But there's never been a trophy waiting for you."

I glance over my shoulder, just enough to catch Kimball and McKay exchanging a look that isn't their usual smugness or judgment. It's...something else. Something new. And I have no idea what to do with that, so I focus on my dad and the hard edge to his gaze. "Trophy?" I repeat with a small laugh. "Yeah, I'm well aware you have no plans to give me a trophy when I've only ever been a failure. But thanks for the reminder."

"Benson."

I ignore him and head upstairs, hoping there isn't another argument waiting for me when I find my mom and Avery. My mom doesn't do confrontation, but if ever there was a time for her to cut me down, it would be tonight. My only consolation is that Avery is up there too, and she makes me feel like I can face anything if she's next to me.

TICKET
PASSPORT
HOTEL
Time To Travel

CHAPTER 29
Avery

"So, did you meet Sonny when he came to your company?" Mrs. West asks as she opens a door and steps into a decent-sized room with a king bed and a large dresser. Male voices rise from downstairs, too quiet for me to understand, and I wonder if I shouldn't have left Benson on his own. He was clinging to me pretty tight, but I didn't want to offend his mom by refusing her kind offer of pajamas.

How much would he want me to say? He's not here, so I decide to be honest. "We actually met on a flight to Italy last month," I admit, "and it was a coincidence that my business partner, Eric, had already hired him to help our company. Eric and Benson were college buddies."

"Italy? Wow." She brushes a wrinkle out of the gray comforter on the bed, clearly still nervous like she was downstairs. I'm going to guess Benson has never brought a girl home to meet his mom, which makes me sad. I can only imagine how excited she was when Kimball and McKay found their wives. "You're a traveler, like him?"

I chuckle. "I used to be. This trip was out of the norm for me."

"Not for Benson. I'm sure you know that." Her smile is wistful as she looks around the room.

There aren't many decorations in here, and if she hadn't said something about this being Benson's room, I would have assumed this was an average guest room. Honestly, outside of looking similar to his brothers—they all have the same light brown hair and blue eyes—it would be hard to guess Benson is a part of this family at all.

"That boy…" Mrs. West clucks her tongue. "Never could stay in one place for long."

I'm overstepping, but I ask anyway. "When was the last time he came home?"

"A year ago last April." She doesn't hesitate, and her pain filters into her voice, leaving it shaky. I would hug her if I didn't think her fragile hold over her emotions would snap if I did. "He only stayed for two days." Her eyes widen as she looks at me. "Oh! But I'm sure he'll stay longer when he comes to visit you." She pats my hand as if that might make her words true.

Huffing out a laugh, I sit on the edge of the bed and shake my head. "I doubt that. He's been pretty clear about the fact that he plans to leave as soon as he's done helping my company." Two weeks. I get two more weeks to prepare my heart for him to leave, and just thinking about losing him brings sharp tears to my eyes.

"You haven't known my boy very long," Mrs. West says gently, "but I can tell you I've never seen him look at someone the way he looks at you. You hold the moon and stars in his world."

"He's not going to change just for me." I sniffle and laugh at how ridiculous this conversation is. I just met this woman. "And I can't ask him to change for me. That's not how people work. Benson isn't going to put down roots anytime soon."

"He has never been one for attachments," she agrees, which doesn't make me feel any better. She's looking around the room again, a sadness in her eyes. "I haven't changed a thing in this room since the day he left for college. Sometimes I come in here and wonder if he even lived here."

"Why is he like this?"

She shrugs.. "I don't know. Kimball and McKay, they have always stayed close to home. Sometimes more than they should. But Benson? Even as a child, he was restless, and he never could stick with one thing for longer than a few weeks."

My stomach twists as I think about the fact that *I've* known Benson for a few weeks. Are we at the point where he'll realize I'm not as exciting as he thought and move on to something—someone—new? My heart aches thinking about it, but can I really expect anything more?

He told me in the beginning what he is. It's on me if I let myself get heartbroken over him.

"Well." Mrs. West says, awkwardly patting my shoulder as she stands and heads for the door. "Who knows? Maybe you've given him a reason to change. I'll see about finding you some pajamas."

A reason to change. I don't want to let myself hope, but my feelings for Benson refuse to let go of those words as I sit on the bed in the empty room. Could she be right? I don't know all of his reasons for staying away from me, but some of them we could solve. Eric? Not a real barrier. His family? Maybe this weekend will help Benson realize that his perspective might be wrong when his mom clearly wants him around. Whatever else there is holding him back, we can figure it out together.

The voices downstairs rise, and though I try to ignore them, the sound carries remarkably well now that I'm not talking to Mrs. West. The first thing I hear makes my heart race.

"So you're going to stick around for once?" It's one of Benson's brothers who asks that, and I hold my breath. Waiting. Hoping.

Benson's response hits me hard, like a kick to the chest. "I can't."

"Won't," someone says.

The silence that stretches between that word and Benson's response nearly kills me.

"Can't," Benson says again. He thinks that, but his reasons aren't as solid as he thinks they are, and we can— "I'm heading to Australia next week to work with a client who's going to push my business to the next level and help me bring on clients from all over the world."

Something in me shatters. Australia? *Next week?* But he hasn't said any...

They keep talking about how much Benson works—too much—but I can barely concentrate. He's leaving? I thought his next client was in Alabama, and that job wasn't supposed to start for another couple of weeks. And he said he lost the Australian client. We had a whole conversation about it. So is he just making stuff up to try to sound good in front of his family?

I know Benson better than that. He's not the kind of guy who lies.

Australia. Next week...

"Here you are, dear," Mrs. West says, making me jump as she appears at the door with a bundle of clothes. She pauses, studying me for a moment as her brow furrows. "Is everything okay?"

No. I'm as far from okay as a person can get, but I can't tell her that. "Fine," I whisper. The conversation downstairs has either stopped or gotten too quiet to hear, but I heard enough. "I'm just tired."

She smiles warmly and comes to my side, handing me some silk pajamas and an unopened toothbrush. "If there's anything else you need, please don't hesitate to ask."

I need to know if Benson was serious about leaving next week, but that's not a question she can answer. "Thank you," I say weakly. "You're so sweet to let me stay on such short notice."

"It's nothing. You're welcome any time."

"Hey." Benson appears in the doorway, looking like he's never been as exhausted as he is now. And he's planning on taking on even more work? That can't be good for him. Sparing only a glance at his mom, he watches me for a long moment and frowns, reminding me how good he is at reading me. "Mom, can you give us a minute?"

"Oh! Yes. Of course." She pats my arm again and heads for the door, pausing for a moment when she reaches Benson, like she wants to say something to him. But she stays quiet, shaking her head before she steps into the hall and disappears.

Though a part of me wants to pretend everything is fine and I didn't hear any of the conversation downstairs, I'm tired too. I'll never sleep if I don't know the truth.

Benson takes a breath, forcing a smile. "Do you need—"

"When were you going to tell me about Australia?"

Paling, he gapes at me for a long few seconds before his eyes drop to the floor. "It's not what it—"

"So you lied to your family?" I stand and hug my middle, hating how much I would rather be tucked into his arms than my own. I'm thinking that's not going to be an option anymore.

Benson blinks, then takes a step deeper into the room and closes the door behind him. "I didn't... It's more complicated than that."

I scoff. "*Everything* is complicated with you, Benson. But it shouldn't be. Are you going to Australia or not?"

"Maybe. I haven't signed the deal yet."

"You're *maybe* abandoning my company next week?"

He groans, running a hand through his hair. "I'm not going to abandon you, Avery."

"It sure feels like you are."

"It's not that simple. I'm trying to figure out what I—"

"Do you hear yourself?" Tears prick at my eyes, but I hold them back. I need to get this out, and then I can let myself cry. "Benson, if you're thinking about going to Australia next week, we need to call this what it is."

His eyebrows dip low, and he takes another step toward me. I step back, and his frown deepens as he takes in the movement. "What are you saying?"

Something I probably should have said that first day he showed up at Rose & Quill. "I'm saying you clearly don't want to be with me, so I'm not going to waste any more of my time trying to convince you otherwise. I'm not your priority, and that's okay." It's not okay, but what can I do about it? I've been fighting a losing battle from the start.

Benson swallows hard. "Avery." That's all he says, which is pretty telling on its own. He hasn't fought for me before, so why would he now?

I take a shaky breath and pray I can keep my voice steady. "We should go to bed."

He glances at the bed behind me, and though a spark of desire lights in his eyes, he backs toward the door. "I'll sleep on the couch."

"You can have your bed," I argue, even though the thought of sleeping in a common area of the house when my heart is breaking sounds like the worst.

Already pulling the door open, he shakes his head, pausing halfway into the hall. "I'm sorry," he whispers. I think he means it.

I'm sorry too, but I can't bring myself to say the words out loud. I think I could have spent my life with this man, but he clearly has no room in his life for me.

"Goodnight, Avery Grace," he adds, waiting a few seconds as if expecting me to reply.

I don't.

The door clicks shut. I don't move. Not until my knees give out and I collapse onto the bed while my few remaining hopes crumble around me.

CHAPTER 30
Benson

I DON'T KNOW HOW long I've been staring at the ceiling, but the soft strip of light peeking through the curtains tells me the night is finally over. Not that I slept. How could I have possibly slept last night after everything?

Sighing, I roll over to my side and take in the way the line of light rests in the middle of the family portraits mounted on the wall in the den. Naturally, the light divides my picture from the rest of the family's, highlighting the way my picture hasn't been changed since high school. McKay and Kimball have their whole families with them, Mom and Dad have each other, and then there's me.

Alone.

Always alone because I mess everything up.

My body aches, not so much from the couch but from the exhaustion that runs so much deeper than my bones. It's in my *soul*. Every time I closed my eyes last night to try to get some sleep, all I could see was Avery's face. The pain in her eyes when she made my choice for me.

I never wanted to hurt her.

But I think hurting people I care about is all I've ever been good at.

Sighing, I dig my phone out of the couch cushions and blearily look at the million notifications waiting for me. I half expect one of them to be from Eric, like he would have sensed how thoroughly I did exactly what he didn't want me to do and hurt Avery, but he's been radio silent since Thursday. Strange, with how intent he was on reminding me to stay away from her.

There's another email from the Australian company, presumably offering me more perks based on the first few lines, but that's the last thing I want to look at right now. Same with the string of texts from Phillip Rogers with more ideas for R&Q's marketing plan, as if I'm part of the company instead of a temporary blip in their story. And email after email from potential clients and past clients and upcoming jobs leave me feeling like I have nothing left of myself to give.

I hate how badly I want one of these texts to be from Avery, telling me she's changed her mind and isn't ready to give up on me. But she's not going to do that because she's grown too much over the last few weeks to set aside self-respect. She made the right choice by cutting me loose, even if her choice leaves me feeling like I'm never going to breathe again.

My hand shifts to my pocket, where the bracelet Poppy gave her seems to burn through the fabric and into my skin like it knows things are over between me and its owner. Whether Avery knows I have it, I can never give it back now. Not when it might be the only thing I have left. I pull it out, slipping it onto my wrist even though it makes my chest ache to see the little pink stone and the love it supposedly represents.

Sitting up with a groan, I run a hand down my face, trying to decide what to do next. I don't want to abandon Avery to deal with her car on her own, but neither do I want to force my presence on her now that she's done with me. Now that it's not the middle of the night, I can find her a tow truck and pay for everything in advance to alleviate some of that stress, but she's still going to have to get home. Get a rental. Figure out insurance. Things she shouldn't have to face alone.

My phone buzzes in my hand, and my eyes slide to the text that drops down from the top. I read the short message, then blink, not sure I saw it right. But after three more read-throughs, the words stay the same.

> For the record, you've always been a pain in the butt, Benson. But never a failure.

I don't... What does... I stare at the text with my breath held in my lungs and my body tense, like I'm waiting for the knockout punch that's coming now that he's caught me off guard. But it doesn't come.

This isn't the kind of text someone sends at six in the morning just for fun.

Never a failure. He can't really mean that. Can he?

I sit frozen, staring at my phone until my dad's words from last night repeat in my head, echoing Kimball's text. *You've always been worth my notice.*

Neither of these things make any sense. They don't fit with the life and family I've known, but my dad has never been a liar. Neither has Kimball. If they didn't want me around, they wouldn't bother saying things that make me want to stay.

Oh.

I press a hand to my chest, feeling like my heart is going to give out on me as that realization hits me hard. *I want to stay.* I'm so tired of running. Hiding. Pretending I haven't been slowly falling to pieces with every year I've remained unsettled. All that time I've spent staring at the mountains over the last couple of weeks, and I've been too stupid to realize that I've been *homesick.* Desperate for a safe place to land.

And when I finally found it—found *her*—I went and messed everything up.

"Who are you?"

Startled by the sound of a small voice, I look up to find a little girl in the doorway of the den. She must have come up from the basement, the first of the kids to wake up, and she's staring at me with narrowed eyes as she hugs a stuffed cow.

I swallow. "I'm Benson. Your...your uncle." I've met her before. I know I have, but I struggle to remember who she is. One of McKay's, I think? "What's your name?" I hate that I have to ask.

She tilts her head to the side. "Marilee. I have a Uncle Benson?"

Cursing under my breath, I run a hand through my hair and look around the dim room as if I might find someone to save me from this conversation. Of course she doesn't know me. "Apparently," I mutter.

"I just know about Uncle Kimball and Uncle Sonny," she says, a bit of pride in her voice. "I see Uncle Kimball lots, but Dad says Uncle Sonny lives far away and is always helping people. So he's kinda like a superhero, and that's why we don't see him."

The air slides from my lungs, leaving me dizzy. McKay said that? About *me*?

"Are you going to live with Grandma and Grandpa?" Marilee asks, inching closer now that I'm no longer a stranger. She's studying me with unveiled interest, like discovering another uncle is the best thing to happen to her all week.

"No." The word tastes bitter, especially when Marilee's shoulders fall, and I scramble to amend my answer. "But I can come visit."

She smiles and flops onto the couch next to me, talking to her stuffed cow on her lap. "I like when we visit Grandma. She makes us waffles and lets us put chocolate on them."

I can't stop the laugh that eases out of me. "Chocolate, huh?"

"Chocolate's my favorite. Is it your favorite too?"

My mind drifts to Florence and tiramisu and kisses under the Tuscan moon as my eyes slide to the bracelet I'm wearing. "My most favorite," I breathe as something settles inside me, simultaneously easing the ache and making it sharper. I think I've made the worst mistake of my life.

But it might not be too late to fix it.

"Hey, uh, I need to..." I frown down at my niece, unsure about the proper way to end this conversation. "Do you need any help?"

She looks up at me, her head cocked again. "Do you know how to make waffles?"

"No."

"Oh."

"Sorry." Clearly I have no idea how to be an uncle, but now's not the time to learn. Groaning internally, I content myself with patting her on the head before jumping up and rushing for the stairs. "It's nice to meet you, Marilee!" I call back.

By the time I reach the top floor, I'm moving so fast that I barely see my mom before I nearly collide with her. I skid to a halt, crashing into the wall, and grimace as she stares at me with wide eyes. "Sorry," I say again. I have a feeling I'm going to be saying that a lot. "Uh, good morning."

Mom looks like she just woke up, her hair in a messy bun and a robe tucked around her pajamas, and she squints at me in the dim hallway. "Is everything okay, Sonny?" she asks eventually. "You look...tired."

I exhale in something like a laugh. She has no idea. "Didn't sleep," I croak.

Her gaze turns even more scrutinizing as she studies me. "You look different," she says next. Then her eyes move to the closed door of my bedroom like she knows exactly *why* I look different. My parents' room is right next to mine—an effort to catch me when I inevitably snuck out—and suddenly I wonder if she heard my conversation with Avery last night. "Are you sure you know what you're doing, Benson?"

Smiling despite the tension building inside me, I shake my head. "Not even a little bit." I just know I have to make things right if I can.

To my shock, my response brings a smile to my mom's face, and she puts her hand on my chest, the gesture warm if not familiar. "Sounds like you're doing something right, then," she mutters and continues down the stairs, leaving me alone in the hall.

I hope she's right. Now that I'm here, I'm terrified, and a part of me wants to run back down the stairs and beg my mom to tell me how to fix this. I've never confided in her in my life, but I wish I had. I wish I'd had the courage to trust that my family would accept me, flaws and all.

Like Avery did.

Moving to the door, I press my forehead against the wood and take a deep breath. There's always the chance that Avery won't listen to me and won't change her mind, and I have to accept that. But I also have to show her that I'm willing to fight for her. Lay my heart on the line like she did.

Before I can talk myself out of it, I knock on the door and wait, holding my breath.

What if she's still asleep? What if she left hours ago without telling anyone? What if she heard me talking to my mom and is purposefully ignoring me?

"Come in," a soft voice says.

Exhaling in relief, I slowly push the door open, just enough to see Avery sitting on the bed with her arms around one of her knees. Soft sunlight from the open blinds makes her seem to glow, but it also puts into sharp relief how tired she looks. She looks like she slept as poorly as I did, and guilt settles heavy in my chest. "Sorry," I breathe. "I shouldn't have—"

"Do you need something?"

I swallow. "I was hoping we could talk."

She comes as close to rolling her eyes as she can without actually doing it. "Is there anything more for us to talk about?"

Everything. I want to talk to her about everything for the rest of forever, but how do I tell her that in a way she'll believe?

She drops her head on her shoulder and sighs. "I'm going to text my dad. He can help me get my car to a shop, so you don't have to—"

"Don't give up on me." I wince at the desperation in my words, no matter how accurate it is. I am *desperate* to have Avery in my life. "Please."

Her eyebrows pull low. "Benson."

"I know." I slip into the room, closing the door behind me but keeping my back against it so she doesn't feel like I'm pushing her. Standing in the same place I was last night, I can barely breathe in enough air to say what I need to say. If I can't change her mind this morning, I won't have any chances left. "I don't deserve another chance," I croak. "I've been an idiot in every way, and you are so much better off without me."

She blinks. "Okay."

This is not going how I wanted this to go. Clenching my jaw, I dig deep for the strength to get this out. "You scare the hell out of me, Avery Grace. From the moment I met you, you took hold of something inside me and refused to let go, and I was so convinced that giving in and letting you have it would make me less of a person when I already struggle with feeling like I'm enough. But you don't..."

I groan and run a hand through my hair. She's looking at me blankly, and I'm clearly not making any sense. "I've always thought that if I kept moving, I wouldn't be in one place long enough to screw anything up. I've felt like a disappointment my entire life, and I've been searching for that magical thing that will fill in the missing pieces and make me complete."

She slowly lifts her head, brow furrowed. "Are you trying to tell me that I complete you?"

"Yes." I shake my head. "No. No, I'm..." What am I saying? I growl and start to pace. Will there ever be a time when I have the right words when it comes to this woman? "I'm saying you never saw me as anything less than whole. You always just saw *me*." Coming to a halt, with my heart racing and my lungs burning, I meet her uncertain gaze. "No one has ever done that the way you do."

She's still for a long time, simply watching me, but after a moment she unfolds herself and sits up straight, her gaze not leaving mine. "You hurt me."

Those three words are a knife in my chest. "I know. And I'll regret it for the rest of my life."

"What about Australia? Your business?"

Hope springs to life in my belly, but I rein it in. I can't jump to conclusions and assume I know what's going to happen here. All of this is up to her. "I'm turning down the client. I'm stretched thin as it is, and I've already committed my time to Rose & Quill. To...to you."

Avery looks down at her hands as they gather up fistfuls of fabric from the t-shirt she's wearing. *My* t-shirt. The pajamas my mom brought her are sitting in a neat pile on the chair in the corner, which means Avery chose to raid my sparse closet even after everything.

The spark of hope burns brighter, leaving me lightheaded, like it's burning up all the oxygen in the room.

"Avery," I say, my voice cracking, "you stole my heart in Florence, and I don't want it back. It's always going to belong to you. If you tell me I'm too late and need to walk away, I'll do it, but I'll never stop hoping there's a place for me in your life. I don't want to keep running. I don't want to keep fighting. I...I want to *come home*." And I don't mean my parents' house that hasn't felt like home in years, so I swallow the emotion rising in my throat and add, "Wherever you are, that's where I want to be."

Because she *is* home.

A sound escapes from Avery, halfway between a laugh and a sob as she finally looks up at me, tears shining in her eyes. "You're going to leave in two weeks."

"I'll come back." I take a step closer, then another when she doesn't react. "I'll always come back."

She shakes her head. "And when you get tired of all the traveling back and forth? When you get tired of...of me?"

I drop to my knees in front of her, blinking my own tears out of my eyes as I take her hands. "That's never going to happen." Can I actually promise that? I'm already tired of traveling. But when it comes to her...

I will spend my whole life trying to get back to her, no matter how far life takes me. "Avery, you are the most interesting person I've ever met. I could spend a lifetime getting to know you and never get bored. I knew it the moment I met you."

Her breath hitches, but she seems to have run out of words.

I lift one of her hands to my lips and close my eyes, leaving her knuckles pressed to my mouth.

As she slips her other hand free of my hold, my stomach dips in fear, but then she touches the bracelet sitting on my wrist. "I wondered where it went."

I open my eyes, meeting her tearful gaze as a knot forms in my chest. "I didn't mean to take it. But I think it worked even better than Poppy thought it would."

Her eyebrows pull low. "Worked?"

"I don't have all the answers, and I don't know what's going to happen. But I'm..." Swallowing, I tell myself that I can't hold back. *Lay it all on the line.* "I'm in love with you, Avery Grace." I've never said that out loud before, but no words have ever felt more right. "I'm choosing you. Now and forever."

Sniffling, she squeezes my fingers, though she still looks terrified by the uncertain future. But the words that come out of her mouth are not the ones I expect. "What about Eric?"

The blood rushes from my head, and I gape at her. Eric? The man who has steamrolled her and stifled her and stuck his nose into places it doesn't belong? After everything, is she telling me she's still not over her ex when he has the personality of a slug dipped in—

"Oh my gosh," Avery says with a roll of her eyes, and she presses her palms to my cheeks. "Are you seriously jealous of *Eric Greer*?"

I scowl. "I'm not jealous."

"You are!" She laughs, and then her mouth is on mine.

I'm so caught off guard by this sudden shift that it takes me half a second to realize she's kissing me. But when my brain catches up, my body takes over, bringing me up to my feet and pressing my hand into the mattress behind her as I lean into her. I wrap my other arm around her back and pull her close, and her arms go around my neck as she opens her mouth to me and the kiss turns molten.

I love you. The words are on repeat in my head as I lose myself in her. *I love you.*

"Bens," she gasps a moment later, tilting her head back with a laugh as I trail kisses down her neck. "I need to... Will you stop for a second?"

Groaning, I stand up straight, reeling from that kiss and the way she cut it far too short. I have to peel my hands from her waist before I convince myself to ignore anything she might want to say and kiss her again. "Need to what?"

"Explain," she finishes breathlessly, then stands with me and brushes her thumb along my cheek. "You're the one who was using Eric as an excuse. Not me. I just wondered..."

Forcing a breath, I run a hand through my hair. "Right." That reason for keeping my distance hasn't magically gone away overnight. "I don't want to break my promise, but..." But I thought I lost Avery last night. I'm not willing to go through that again if I can help it.

Avery sighs and places her other hand on my cheek, once again holding my face beneath her soft palms. "He and I broke up. You're not stealing anything from him." She tilts her head and smiles, a bit of mischief in her eyes. "Especially because I'm choosing you right back."

A curse slips from my tongue along with the last of my resolve, and I grab her, pulling her mouth back to mine so I can resume what she started.

Kissing her here is so much better than it was in Italy, when in the back of my mind I knew it wouldn't last. But now? Now I can't get enough of her, and I tug her against my body, determined to keep her as close as

I can. Her hands roam my chest, my shoulders, my jaw, and I tangle my fingers up in her auburn hair and kiss her like my life depends on it.

I still don't know how we're going to make this work, but I don't care.

For the first time in my life, I refuse to give up just because something is hard.

I'm not going anywhere.

TICKET
PASSPORT
HOTEL
Time To Travel

CHAPTER 31
Avery

"I learned so much that my head is still swimming. Oh, and the people I met! I wish you could have been there, Avie."

I should be annoyed by Eric's non-stop chatter when he talks as though I was the one who chose not to go to the conference, but I'm not annoyed. In fact, it's nice to see him excited about something. I hadn't noticed until he showed up to the office this morning with a giant grin on his face, but Eric was as lost and miserable as I was after the breakup.

"I can't wait to go through your notes," I say, expecting him to go back to his office because he's not one for dilly-dallying. I need to tell him about the social media manager I hired—she's showing up here soon—but I'm finding it difficult to dim his good mood and was hoping for the excuse of him being too busy to warn him.

But Eric remains in my doorway, his eyes darting to the empty desk next to mine. "Where's Sonny this morning?"

I bite the inside of my lips to keep from smiling. "He had something to take care of this morning, but he'll be in soon. He didn't give me details."

While that may be true, I know exactly why Benson isn't here yet. After McKay declared my transmission toast and we took my car to a mechanic Saturday afternoon, Benson spent the rest of the day with me at my apartment. Then he spent all day with me on Sunday. And after sleeping on my couch last night because he stayed too late, he dropped me off at the office before heading to his hotel to shower and change.

We didn't come to the office together because we agreed we need to ease Eric into our tentative relationship, as much for our own sakes as for his. Benson is still dealing with the guilt of betraying a friend, and I need to make sure my personal relationship with Benson won't hurt my working relationship with Eric. Neither of us knows how this is going to work, so we figured we should keep things on the down low until we're a little more...sure.

I'm choosing to be cautiously optimistic, but I haven't asked Benson about what's going to happen when his time at R&Q is up. I'm worried he's not going to have an answer, so instead of dwelling on the uncertain future, I'm living in the moment.

Taking things one minute at a time.

Eric is still standing in my doorway, a thoughtful look on his face, so I search for some topic of conversation before things turn awkward. "I never did get an email from that agent, by the way." Not that I care, since an agent would only get in the way of the workshop idea that Benson and I came up with, but it's an innocent enough topic.

For some reason, Eric blushes a deep shade of red. "Right. Well, it turns out she had some free time, so she decided to take a trip here to Utah to check out our office and meet you in person."

My eyebrows jump up as I take a sip of my coffee. "Oh. Cool, I guess? Though, I don't know how many more books we can take on until we stabilize, so I don't know if we can—"

"She doesn't care if it takes a bit before we can collaborate," Eric said, waving his hand. "Publishing is a long game, right?"

"Right." But I feel like I'm missing something.

"She's, uh..." He coughs. "She's coming today."

Choking, I nearly dump my coffee on my keyboard and scramble to set the cup down on the desk. "Today?" I gasp. "But—"

"Oh Benson, you shouldn't have!" Lynda's voice carries from the lobby, sending my heart skittering even more as my full focus shifts in that direction. Toward Benson.

It's only been two hours since I saw the guy, and I shouldn't be this excited. Still, I follow a curious Eric out to the lobby, where Lynda is smelling a vibrant wildflower bouquet and Benson is looking entirely scrumptious in a white button-up and khakis.

"I'm glad you're feeling better," Benson tells Lynda and kisses her cheek. Then his smile turns to me, heating me from the inside out as my mind gets lost in memories of the weekend. "Good morning, R&Q! Eric, good to have you back."

"You were sick?" Eric asks his mom, still red in the face. "You should have told me."

"You were out of town, and it was only a little head cold. Avery and Benson had things handled here." She winks at me, and I have to hold back a giggle. I don't know how she knows that something happened between Benson and me, but she knows. I wouldn't be surprised if the ghosts of Benson's kisses are tattooed on my skin.

Benson plucks a deep scarlet cosmos from the bouquet and hands it to me. "Morning," he says, his voice so gentle that it makes me shiver.

I have no idea if I ever mentioned my favorite flower to him over the weeks I've known him, but I love how well he knows me. After this weekend, it feels like we've known each other forever. Benson the flirt was fun, but Benson the man who's all in? Hoo boy, I was not prepared for the way he makes me feel.

"You're in a good mood this morning," I say, unable to hold back my smile as I breathe in the chocolate-like scent of the flower.

Benson shrugs. "Good weekend," he says like it was a perfectly average couple of days. His gaze lingers on me for a few seconds, heating the whole room this time, before he turns to Eric again. "Do you need me to walk you through some of the plans we started putting into place last week?"

Eric blinks, glancing from Benson to me and back again, then shakes his head. "No, uh, I'm sure you two have everything handled. Unless there's something you need from me?"

"At some point we'll need to walk through the budget together. I..." Benson pauses when the main office door opens behind him and the new social media manager steps inside, giving all of us a nervous smile.

"Melissa!" I say, and my own nerves spike higher. I haven't had a chance to warn Eric about my unilateral hiring decision. "I'm so glad you made it. Um, Benson, would you mind showing Melissa to the desk in my office and get her set up in the system while I...uh..." I jerk my head toward Eric, who furrows his brow and glances from me to Melissa.

"Of course," Benson says, though his hesitant steps make it clear he doesn't want to leave me on my own with Eric.

"Oh, I can get her settled!" Lynda says brightly. Blessed woman doesn't know about Melissa either, but she gives me a wink as she takes Melissa down the hall. *I love her.*

As soon as they're gone, my office door shutting with a click, Eric folds his arms and gives me a stern look that used to be enough to get me to back down on whatever differing opinion I had. Now it just makes him look petulant. "Avery, who's Melissa?"

I stand tall despite a tremble in my hands. "Our new social media manager."

"But I said we didn't need—"

"You were wrong," I argue. Based on the way Benson's eyebrows fly up, I must sound stronger than I feel, and I take that to heart, folding my arms to match Eric. "Social media has always been under my purview, but it's time to give the responsibility to someone better suited to marketing so I can focus on acquisitions and production."

Eric's jaw slips open partway as he stares at me. I wonder if I've ever talked to him like that. Chances are high that this is the first time I've really shown him any backbone.

It feels good.

"I thought her reasoning was solid," Benson says with a poorly masked grin. "So I agreed with the idea."

Eric glares at him. "That's not your—" He cuts himself off as the door opens and a woman who looks to be in her thirties steps in, a polite smile on her face as she takes in the lobby. All of Eric's anger dissipates in an instant. "Cathy!" It's more of a squeak than an actual word. I've never heard him sound like that, and he's redder than he was in my office as he hurries forward. "I mean Ms. Stanton. You made it."

She smiles sweetly, adjusting wire-frame glasses on her nose. "Hi, Eric."

This is the agent? I wasn't sure why she would go to the trouble of coming all the way out here with no promise that Rose & Quill would work with an agent right now, but with the way Eric is staring at her with a dorky grin...

The puzzle pieces start falling into place. No wonder Eric hasn't sent any messages over the last couple of days. Benson and I were trying to figure out why he would spend so much energy keeping us apart and then drop the subject without a word. But if the cartoon hearts in Cathy's eyes are any indication, I don't think she came here just to meet me and see the Rose & Quill office. Based on Benson's smothered laughter, he's thinking the same thing.

I clear my throat, breaking the intense eye contact between Eric and Cathy and pulling their gazes my way. "Hi," I say, holding my hand out to the agent. "I'm Avery Baldwin. CEO."

"Yes! Hi!" Cathy takes my hand with enthusiasm. "Oh, I've been so excited to come here and meet you, Ms. Baldwin."

"Unfortunately, I don't have a lot of time to talk to you today," I reply, since I can't honestly say I'm happy to meet her.

Cathy's smile doesn't falter. "Oh, that's okay. I plan to be around for a few days." She sends a smile to Eric, who seems to have swallowed his tongue.

I'm honestly impressed he learned anything at the conference if his attention was so otherwise occupied.

"Well," I say, fighting the urge to roll my eyes, "I should get back to bringing our new employee up to speed. Nice to meet you, Cathy."

She barely spares me a glance because her focus has returned to Eric, and I look at Benson, matching his amused smile before I head back to my office to hug Lynda and get to work.

"Hey, sorry to interrupt." According to the twinkle in Benson's eye, he's not sorry at all, and I playfully narrow my eyes at him while Melissa keeps exploring the scheduling software I use for our socials.

"What's up?" I ask.

"Phillip Rogers is out on the balcony."

My stomach does a little flip. "Is he? Why?" *Don't tell me he's changed his mind about investing.*

Benson's smile softens, like he can read my thoughts. "He wanted to talk marketing plans with me while I'm still in town."

I hate those words. *Still in town.* My misery leaks into my voice as I say, "Oh. That's good."

Benson's expression softens even more, and I can feel Melissa's attention shifting from me to him and back again. I don't blame her, since we're giving each other all sorts of heavy looks. "He wants to talk to you now," he says. "I can hang with Melissa and walk her through some of the plans of action I'm putting together."

"What about Eric?" Heat splashes across my face when that question evokes instant memories of Saturday morning, the last time I said those words. Memories of the way Benson kissed me senseless when I told him that I was choosing him too.

Benson chuckles and looks at Eric's closed door behind him. "I think he's busy. But Rogers specifically wants to talk to you, so I don't think he'll mind."

Taking a steadying breath, I stand to swap places with Benson. As we pass, his hand brushes against mine, giving me some much-needed reassurance. I've lost track of the number of times he's told me that he'll find a way for us to be together, but without any solutions, it isn't easy to believe it. Either one of us loses something we love, or we never see each other.

But I trust Benson, and that will have to be enough for now. We have a couple of weeks to figure things out.

I find Rogers at the same table we sat at the first time we were here, his gaze on the mountains and looking far too relaxed given the waves of heat rolling off the building. Summer temperatures are still holding strong. "Mr. Rogers," I say when I reach him. "I'm so sorry we don't have more space. You must be melting out here."

"I like the heat." Grinning, he gives me a firm handshake before gesturing to the chair next to him. "I spend half my time in Arizona and the other half here."

"A bit different from England."

"Indeed."

When we sit in silence for a moment, I figure I should nudge our conversation forward so I can get back to Melissa. Back to *Benson*. "You wanted to talk to me?"

"I did." He stretches his legs out, looking like he's never been more comfortable. "After talking to Benson, I wanted to get your opinion on something, as the two of you seem to work rather well together."

We more than *work* well together, but Rogers doesn't need to know that. "Okay?"

"Do you think there's any chance Benson might consider selling his business?"

My jaw slips open. "You want to...buy Benson's consulting business?"

"Heavens no." Rogers laughs, the sound deep and hearty. "I'm simply curious if you think he would ever sell and come work with me."

I have no idea why this is the topic he wanted to discuss with me, and I wish I had a way to get out of it. The last thing I want to talk about right now is the biggest thing standing in the way of Benson and me being together. "Benson loves his business," I say quietly. It's the very reason I haven't suggested exactly what Rogers asked about. Everything about our relationship still feels tenuous, and I'm terrified to push Benson more than he's already been pushed.

"He loves what he *does* with his business," Rogers counters. "There's a difference."

"Maybe." I shrug. "But I've only just managed to convince him to give a long-distance relationship a try, and I don't know if he would be ready to uproot the life he's built in New York."

"Ah, I wondered if there was something brewing between the two of you." He sits forward, his eyes dancing with interest. "I saw it the last time I was here, but it has certainly evolved."

"Yeah," I breathe, too mournful to hide it. I run my finger along the edge of the table and consider Rogers's question again. Would Benson ever sell his business? "I can't ask him to do something that big, though. He's worked so hard to build his company, and I just want him to be happy."

"That's very selfless of you, Miss Baldwin." Rogers offers a softer smile this time, a thoughtful look in his eyes as he studies me. "It would be a lot to ask of someone, I agree, and my line of work can be incredibly difficult, which makes it an even harder decision. Not many people want to dive into something so unpredictable—most prefer something more consistent—but Benson..."

I can't help but laugh a little despite everything. "Benson loves a good challenge."

"I've noticed that about him. It's probably why he asked if I would be interested in taking him on as a partner."

"He's really..." I stop. Blink. Look at the man next to me with my eyebrows drawn. "Wait, he did what?"

Rogers chuckles, taking in my shock with a new light in his eyes. "He called me early this morning and asked for a chat, and he was quite determined to convince me of the idea."

Benson is thinking about selling his company? "And..." I shake my head to try to clear my thoughts. They're all buzzy, like my head is full of static electricity. "And what did you say to him?"

His smile grows. "I told him I would only consider taking on a partner when I found the right person."

"Oh." There goes my hope.

"And I don't think there would be anyone more perfect to join me than him."

My breath catches in my throat, and I stare at this man with his beard and bird shirt and apparently the answers to all my problems. But I have to be sure I'm not misunderstanding. "He's going to sell his company?"

Rogers nods once.

"And he's going to work with you?"

Another nod.

Dare I ask? "Here in...in Utah?"

"He'll have to spend some time in Arizona until he's up to speed, but I imagine we can make a decent split of things and save us both from too much time on the road."

If this man wasn't our biggest investor, I would throw my arms around him and give him the tightest hug imaginable. But since I can't do that, I content myself with a teary smile that hopefully conveys everything I'm feeling. "You have no idea what... Thank you." But then I frown. "Why are you the one telling me this? Why didn't Benson...?"

With another warm smile, Rogers gets to his feet and pats my shoulder. "I think he wanted you to be certain it was real and not just words. So did I, to be frank, after some of the conversations we had last week. This is quite a shift from his plans before. But seeing your reaction, I understand why he would choose this. A man who's willing to do anything for the woman he loves is a man worth investing in. I can't wait to see what all of us do together." He winks, and then he's gone, leaving me in a puddle in my seat.

Benson said he would find a way to make this work. And he did.

Something loosens in my chest, like a long-tied knot that I didn't notice until it unravels and falls away, letting me breathe. Hope doesn't feel dangerous like it did a few minutes ago. It feels *possible*.

When my limbs gain enough strength to work again, I stumble back inside right as Benson appears in the lobby, his eyes full of questions.

"Eric's with Melissa," he says, pointing a thumb behind him. "I guess Cathy had a conference call, and he wanted to—"

Grabbing his hand, I tug him past a snickering Lynda and her "I'll pretend I didn't see you" and into the storage closet behind her desk. I pull the door shut, and then I throw my arms around Benson's neck and pull myself in tight. "I love you," I say into his neck.

His arms wrap around me in a strong embrace that feels like it's the only thing holding me together as I process the conversation I just had. "I told you," he whispers. "I'm not going anywhere."

Sinking my weight back onto my feet, I tilt my head back to meet his gaze. "But how did you...?" Actually, I don't care. Locking my hands around his neck, I pull him down until our mouths collide.

Benson rises to the occasion splendidly, coaxing the kiss deeper and guiding me back until my shoulders rest against the nearest shelf. "I couldn't sleep last night," he says when he breaks away to give me a chance to breathe. His kisses move to my jaw and down my neck as he talks, leaving a trail of heat behind. "I've been so desperate for a way to make this work, and then it hit me."

"But your business," I say, though the words come out breathless when his lips press against my throat. "You love what you do."

He chuckles and comes back up to brush a kiss against my lips. "I also love facing something new. It won't be that different, anyway."

"But you won't get to see as many cool places."

"I've already seen them."

"And you won't have as many—

"Avery." Placing his hands on the shelf on either side of my head, bracketing me in like the heroes do in the books around us, he levels me with a firm stare that quiets all my thoughts. "Like I said, I couldn't sleep last night, so I had a lot of time to think about this. My job means nothing if it means I can't have you. I *want* fewer companies to work with." He kisses my forehead. "I *want* to try something more stable. Something where I have actual stakes in the game." He kisses the corner of my mouth, lingering there in a way that makes my legs turn to jelly. "And I don't want to go anywhere if you're not going with me."

He snakes his hand behind my neck as his lips find mine again, and he kisses me long and slow and deep, so languid that I feel like I might combust here in this closet. *At work.*

As if remembering where we are at the same time I do, Benson groans and drops his head to my shoulder. "Whose idea was it to keep this a secret?"

I laugh and tangle my fingers into his hair despite knowing I'll have to fix it. I have come to learn that I *love* his hair and running my hands through it while he kisses me. "Yours."

"I'm an idiot." The look he gives me when he lifts his head is so full of attraction and desire that I'm kissing him again when Lynda's voice cuts through the moment.

"Oh, I'm sure they're around here somewhere, Eric."

Cursing, Benson leaps back and stumbles over a box of books, crashing into the shelf on the opposite side of the closet. I barely have time to grab the nearest thing before the door opens and Eric appears, his eyes jumping from one of us to the other.

"Found it," Benson chokes out, holding up a copy of Dani's book.

I grimace. That book is literally all over this closet. "And here is the..." I hold up my offering, wincing when I see the box of staples I grabbed. I don't even know if I have a stapler on my desk.

Eric's eyebrows pull low as he continues to look from Benson to me. He's not an idiot, and we covered our tracks about as well as a toddler with a handful of broken crackers. "Did you two—"

"Yes," I blurt out. Benson groans, but I move to his side of the closet and take his hand, smiling when he laces our fingers together like he can't help it. We were going to get found out anyway because we clearly can't stay away from each other, and at this point I don't want to pretend I'm anything but who I am.

And I'm a woman madly in love with the man next to me. Eric has obviously moved on, so I can too, and he has no say in who I love.

I lift my head high to meet Eric's incredulous stare. "In Florence, actually."

Eric's confusion shifts to surprise. "Florence? But how did...?"

Benson turns to me, those beautiful blue eyes of his taking in my features the same way he did that day we first ran into each other on the street. "It's a long story," he says, squeezing my hand as a smile blossoms across his face. "But it's a good one."

TICKET
PASSPORT
HOTEL
Time To Travel

EPILOGUE
Avery

One year later

"Wʜᴀᴛ ɪs ɪᴛ ᴡɪᴛʜ this city not having enough taxis?" I lean around the line of people queued up to get an elusive ride.

The woman in front of me glances back, her eyes trailing from my hair that badly needs a wash to my shoes that are more like slippers. She huffs and mutters something in Italian before turning back around to face forward. Apparently she did not like what she saw, and she is content to wait for a taxi in silence.

Pity. I've been starved for conversation for the last eighteen hours, and from the looks of this line, I'll be here for a while longer. I could try to pull the guy behind me into a chat, but he looks a bit too much like he could be Italian mafia with the way his eyes have been shifty since we got off the train from Rome. He might be a perfectly nice man who is eager to get home, but I don't know if I should take my chances.

Grabbing my phone, I refresh all my messaging apps in the hope that something might come through. I've paid to have better mobile data on this trip, but I haven't heard a word from anyone since my flight left Salt Lake. Granted, my cousins all have their own lives, but not a peep from any of them? I haven't even gotten a message on my work app despite Dani's second book coming out in less than a month. I guess Eric meant it when he said he would handle things while I was gone.

It helps that we're no longer a team of three. There are six of us full-time Rose & Quill employees now, and it's really starting to feel like we're building something that will last.

"*Mi scusi, signorina,*" a male voice says nearby. "*Hai bisogno di un passaggio?*"

Still focused on my phone, I curse my lack of Italian, though I've been trying to learn over the last few months. Maybe the woman in front of me would be more open to chat if I spoke her language. Most Italians know English, but crossing the language barrier shouldn't be all on them.

"*Sei eccezionalmente bella,*" the same voice says.

A nap is starting to sound extra nice despite being the worst possible thing I could do today. It's only ten in the morning, and I should force myself to stay awake to beat the jet lag quickly. But *sleep*. The flight was brutal, and I was stuck next to a stressed-out woman with a fussy baby. I spent a lot of the flight trying to entertain her child and save the rest of the passengers from a long, loud night.

"*Com'è possibile che il tuo telefono sia più interessante di me,* Avery Grace?"

My heart stumbles over a beat or two at the sound of my name, and I finally look up to see the owner of the voice. I break into a grin. "Benson."

He wasn't supposed to get here until later tonight, but there he is, leaning out the window of a taxi with a smile that leaves me breathless. With his scruffy chin on his arm and his blue eyes bright in the Tuscan sun, he is the most beautiful thing I've seen in weeks. "Need a ride?" he asks, and his lips twist into a smirk.

A few people nearby start muttering in complaint, and the déjà vu of this moment nearly makes me laugh. "I wouldn't want you to go out of your way," I tell him.

Slipping from the car, he looks at the line of people with an exaggerated grimace. "You're welcome to get your own car, but I don't think it'll be very easy."

I raise an eyebrow and slowly step out of the line, feeling the eyes of my fellow taxi-wanters on my back as I roll my suitcase along the cobblestone. "Where did you get yours?"

Benson leans in close and speaks in my ear. "Trade secret."

Ignoring the shiver that runs through me at his nearness, I lean back to look at him and tilt my head to the side. "No woman in her right mind would agree to a ride after a line like that."

Benson snakes his arm around me, pulling me against his body and breathing me in. "*You* did."

"I clearly wasn't in my right mind."

"I'm so glad about that."

His kiss is warm and familiar, everything I've fallen in love with. I melt into him, hardly caring about our rather large audience. "I missed you," I say when I eventually break away.

Chuckling, he tucks my hair behind my ear, then grabs my suitcase to load it into the trunk. "I was only in Arizona for three weeks."

"It was way too long." I shouldn't complain. Benson started working with Phillip Rogers six months ago and has been able to spend most of his time in Utah since switching careers. I got used to him being away while he finished up with his contracted consultant jobs before the switch, but I was spoiled these last few months, having him around.

Benson kisses me again, then opens the cab door, sliding in after me and telling the driver he can head to our hotel. "How was your flight?" He laces our hands together, lifting them to his lips and looking at me like his world is complete now that we're next to each other again. I will never get tired of that look.

I drop my head on his shoulder. "Terrible. How are you here? I thought your flight was coming in tonight."

"Phillip got sick of my moping and put me on an earlier flight so I could make sure you got to the hotel safely."

"Really?" I can't tell if he's being serious or teasing me, but I don't care. He's here, we're together, and Florence awaits. "Do you really think I'm not capable of traveling by myself?"

He bursts into hearty laughter and then kisses me like a man starved. "I know you're fully capable of anything you want to do," he says against my mouth. "But I know how these Italian men can be, and you are far too much of a temptation for them to resist."

He settles back in his seat then, closing his eyes and leaning his head on the back of the seat. He looks so content, like everything in his life is perfect now that we're together again.

I know how he feels. This last year has been hard in a lot of ways, and the first time I had to say goodbye to him before he flew out of Utah for his next consulting job left me a complete mess. Dani, Lucy, and Poppy had to spend the whole weekend with me to keep me distracted so I wouldn't cry non-stop. But Benson called me every day and sent me constant texts to tell me he was thinking about me, and he flew back the following Friday to spend the weekend with me.

That's one of the things I've come to love most about Benson. No matter how many times he leaves, he always comes back.

I lift his hand and kiss his knuckles, drawing a smile out of him.

"I missed you," he whispers, brushing my cheek with his other hand. He's about to kiss me when the Duomo comes into view, and I shove him away, leaning into the window to get the best view as he laughs. "I see how it is," he mutters and squeezes my hand.

"You're pretty," I say, "but not as pretty as this cathedral."

"What every man wants to hear."

Waiting until the Duomo is out of sight, I kiss Benson's cheek and run my fingers through his hair. "You know I love you, right?"

He takes a deep breath, as if trying to inhale my words and hold them in his lungs. "I know. I love you too." He kisses me gently, and a thoughtful look crosses his face when he pulls away. He doesn't explain, instead tucking me under his arm and spending the rest of the drive to the hotel holding me in silence.

We barely make it into the lobby when an excited male voice shouts, "Bens! You made it!" Riccardo looks much the same as he did last year, except today he has a tiny baby strapped to his chest. He pulls Benson into an enthusiastic (and thankfully careful) hug, doing the same with me even though we've only spoken once or twice over the phone since his wedding. "I thought for sure you were going to be too busy to come."

"And miss you christening your daughter?" Benson chuckles and gently touches the sleeping baby's head. "Never."

"Do you want to hold her?"

When I watched Benson hold Kimball's newest baby for the first time several months ago, I almost fell apart. He was so unsure of himself, afraid of hurting him or doing something wrong. But as he takes Riccardo's baby in his arms and smiles down at her, there's a new confidence in him. And he has never been more attractive. I snap a picture, grinning when Benson gives me a knowing look.

I haven't been subtle about wanting to move our relationship forward, and he hasn't been subtle about letting me know that things will change when the timing is right. As it turns out, I'm not nearly as patient as I would like to be and am eager to get to the white dress and domesticity and babies he keeps hinting at, but Benson is the one who has been slowly adapting his life to fit mine. If I can be in a relationship with a guy for six years without it going anywhere, I can wait however long it takes for the true love of my life to be ready for a major commitment.

Having Benson in my life for the last year has been the best thing to ever happen to me, and we have both come out stronger from navigating all of this.

The baby starts crying, and Riccardo takes her back, smiling down at his tiny daughter. "I'm glad you're here," he tells Benson as he tucks the baby against his chest. "But I should get this little lady back to her mama." He narrows his eyes. "You booked a room this time, right?"

Benson laughs and brushes the baby's head once more. "Don't worry. I've been planning this trip for a while." The smile he gives me makes me melt into the floor.

We may be here for the christening, but I'm pretty sure Benson has other plans as well.

"Is there anything better than Florence at sunset?" I ask and lean into Benson's chest behind me.

He tucks his arms around me, chin resting on my head. "I can think of a few things, but this is pretty great."

After taking a power nap and showering, we've been wandering the streets of Florence mostly in silence. I think we're both glad to have a break, and I've been enjoying my time with Benson. We have a whole week with no work to distract us, and I plan to take advantage of this time. Even if that means simply standing in front of the Duomo as it's bathed in golden sunlight. The cathedral is as beautiful as it was the last time I was here. Maybe even more so.

The last time I stood in this spot, Benson ran away from me.

Hooking my hands on his arms, I tilt my head up to try to see his face, though I mostly just see his scruffy jaw. "You're not going to run away from me as soon as the bells start ringing, are you?"

He chuckles, and the sound reverberates through me. "You're never going to let me live that down."

"Considering how hard I had to work to get you to admit you're in love with me, no. Never."

He sighs heavily. "You never should have given me a chance."

Spinning to face him, I reach up and brush my fingers along his jaw. "I'm glad I did."

"Me too." He smiles right as the bells fill the air with their music. The people around us stop walking to admire the moment, and Benson sinks down to one knee.

The air slides out of my lungs.

"Avery Grace," he says, though I can barely hear him over the tolling bells. "My entire life, I never knew what I wanted. I was chasing something I couldn't see, this intangible something that seemed to be just out of reach. And I was tired. I was ready to give up. Then I met you, and you saw right through all the pretense. You saw *me*. You saved me from myself, and everything I have in my life now I owe to you."

I furiously blink away tears as the bells continue to ring around us. I might have been able to keep it together if Benson wasn't teary-eyed too. He *never* cries. "Benson," I whisper.

He takes a shaky breath and pulls a ring from his pocket. The simple diamond reflects the golden sun, but it's the stars in the band that hit me hard. He picked this out himself, and it's perfect. "I love you, Avery Grace. I love your passion, your dedication, your complete inability to proofread a book without getting sucked into the story."

The bell tower falls silent, but I'm pretty sure my heart is beating just as loudly as the bells rang.

"I love your family," Benson continues, his voice dropping lower. People have started to notice us, their whispers and murmurs growing louder, but Benson's eyes never leave mine. "And I love that you helped me become a part of mine. But I want to build a home and a family with you, Avery. Our very own. Marry me?"

It has taken everything in me to hold my tongue, so his question is hardly out of his mouth before I shout, "Yes! Of course! Yes!" Then I tackle him.

He grunts when he hits the ground, arms wrapping around me protectively as our spectators laugh and clap. "Not the reaction I was ex—"

I press my lips to his, trying to show him exactly how happy he just made me, and he meets my kiss with equal enthusiasm. "Sorry," I say in between kisses. "Are you okay?"

"Great. I wasn't sure if you would say yes."

"Are you kidding?" I push myself up on my hands so I can smirk at him. He's still crying, but his smile is wide. "Did you think all those times I brought up our future wedding was me being facetious?"

He leans up and kisses the tip of my nose, then gently pushes me off him so he can sit up. "You? Facetious? *Never.*" He takes my left hand and slips the ring onto my finger, smiling so wide that he looks like he might start crying again. "You said yes," he whispers, like he still can't believe it.

We might be sitting in the middle of the street, but I am too overwhelmed and happy to move. "We're getting married. When?"

He opens his mouth but stops himself before he says anything, his eyebrows dropping low. "That's a good question. You have three major releases before the end of the year, including Dani's."

We would need more time than that to plan the wedding anyway. I would know. "You're going to be too busy in the spring with all the plans Rogers has set you up with," I mutter, frowning to match Benson's expression.

"Summer weddings in Utah are a nightmare," Benson says with a shake of his head.

"Everything is probably booked," I agree. "And with the workshops starting up in May, and my fall lineup next year already looking pretty crazy..."

The idea hits us both at once, and we look at the cathedral in front of us in tandem.

"Any idea how hard it is to get a marriage license in Italy?" I ask slowly.

Benson already has his phone out, a wild grin on his face as he types. "We'll need our birth certificates," he mutters. "And we'll probably have to get some paperwork from the embassy."

That doesn't sound too difficult outside the fact that my birth certificate is back in Utah. Oh... "My cousins are going to kill me if I get married without them," I say as some of my excitement fades.

"I'll fly them out here," Benson replies without hesitation, then leans over and kisses me. "It'll take a couple of days to get everything sorted anyway. Or we have a second ceremony after we get back so both our families can be there." He thinks for a moment, wrinkling his nose. "Maybe not my brothers, unless they decide to stop being pains in the neck... But we can also wait."

Sighing, I brush my hand through his hair and smile when he closes his eyes. It was hard enough to get us both here for Riccardo's baby. And honestly, his brothers kind of drive me nuts; the idea of avoiding whatever dumb joke they would decide to play at our wedding if we had one is a little too tempting. "I don't want to wait."

"Neither do I." He opens his eyes and brushes his thumb along my cheek, wiping a lingering tear. "What do you want to do?"

I want to do whatever it takes to know this man is going to be in my life forever. I've waited long enough. "I'll have Dani bring me my birth certificate."

Benson grins. "I'll handle everything else." He hops up and helps me to my feet, smiling down at the ring sparkling on my finger. "Then we'll get married."

Grabbing my phone, I consider what I'm about to do as I pull up my text thread with my sister. Benson and I have been dating for a year now, so this isn't completely crazy. Is it? Even if it is, the thought of marrying Benson in the city where we first started to fall in love just feels *right*. And it's not just me. Benson thought the same thing, and so far our ideas together have never steered us wrong.

I take a deep breath, then send out a text I won't be able to take back. Dani responds immediately.

Avery:

> If I fly you out to Italy in a couple of days, will you be my maid of honor?

Dani:

> Maid of...

> Days?!

> What??

> Avery!!

I look at Benson, who returns my gaze with the kind of look that melts me from the inside out. Yeah, this might be the best idea we've ever had.

Not ready to say goodbye to Benson and Avery? Get a free bonus epilogue at **https://BookHip.com/FVBRSHT**, or scan the code below!

NEXT UP

AND DON'T MISS THE REST OF THE SERIES!

The Risks of Reuniting by Aspen Hadley
The Dangers of Daydreaming by Karen Thornell
The Perils of Pretending by Amanda P. Jones
The Ruse of Romancing by Hillary Slaughter
The Fear of Falling by Dana LeCheminant
The Disasters of Dating by Mindy Burbidge Strunk

ALSO BY DANA LECHEMINANT

Starstruck Love Stories

Moonstruck

Lovestruck

Dumbstruck

Thunderstruck

Awestruck

Wonderstruck

Love in Sun City

Kiss Me if You Can

She Likes It, Hey Micah

The Chad Next Door

Crossing the Brooklyn Briggs

Houston, We Have a Problem

Standalone Romances

For Butter or For Worse

The Fear of Falling

The Wonder Boys

Love on Camera

Love in Writing

Love on Display

Love in Disguise

Historical Romances

The Thief and the Noble

A Twist of Christmas (part of The Holly and the Ivy anthology)

What Dreams May Come

This above All

Never Doubt I Love

Terms of Inheritance (Sweet Romance)

Forever You and Me

Holding On to Everything

A World without You

Love, Strictly Speaking

Simple Love Stories (Sweet Love Stories)

Simplicity

Growing Young

Bittersweet Brews

In Front of Me

As Long as You Love Me

Dear Dalia

Let Go

ABOUT THE AUTHOR

Dana LeCheminant writes sweet romantic comedies, heartwarming contemporary love stories, and swoony historical romances—with a twist. Known for putting a fresh spin on beloved tropes, she lets her characters lead the way, believing they always know their stories best. Her books are full of banter, emotion, and connection—all of the swoon without any spice. When she's not dreaming up her next twisty trope or emotional arc, she's hiking the remote Utah backcountry or cruising down rivers in search of new inspiration. Dana has been telling stories since before she could spell and has no plans to stop anytime soon.

Dana loves connecting with her readers!
You can find her on social media (**@authordanalecheminant**) and on her website, **lecheminantbooks.com**.